AQUA II

WAVES OF SAGE

Nona Schrader

Aqua II Waves of Sage
Copyright © 2025 by Nona Schrader

This is a work of fiction. While actual places and geographic features are real, all of the characters and events are the product of the author's imagination; any resemblance to actual persons, living or deceased, is purely coincidental.

ISBN: 979-8-9915372-3-0
Library of Congress Control Number: 2025931691

Artwork by: Kami Deromedi

For my siblings, Susan, Linda, Sylvia,
and the twins, Sally and Steve.

Acknowledgments

With gratitude to Amy Anderson, Wyoming Game and Fish Habitat Biologist, for her valuable assistance with my research on beavers, and to Cory Klecker, Jefferson High School Latin teacher, for his expert advice on Latin terms.

FROM THE LATIN

Aqua Antiqua	Ancient Water
Granita Antiqua	Ancient Granite
Arbor Antiqua	Ancient Tree
Rupes Antiqua	Ancient Cliff
Glaciarium Antiquum	Ancient Glacier
Lacus Antiquus	Ancient Lake
Flumen Antiquum	Ancient River
Nympha Antiqua	Ancient Nymph
Avia Antiqua	Ancient Ancestor
Cerva Antiqua	Ancient Cow Elk
Cervus Antiquus	Ancient Bull Elk

THE ANCIENTS AWAKEN

Wyoming, once covered by an ancient sea, now harbors hills, valleys, and plateaus of sagebrush, holding the memory of water. Each spring, high in the Wind River Mountains, glaciers feed alpine lakes while soaring birds inhale the scent of damp granite, a pattern that has continued for one hundred thousand years. But now the glaciers are diminishing, the winters bring less snow, and the rivers no longer supply enough water throughout the West for humans, animals, and the land.

The birth of Diana of the Wind Rivers was foretold, and she has awakened the Ancients from their long slumber. They sense she is coming into her powers. Diana will call upon them to save Earth's most precious natural resource: *Aqua Antiqua,* ancient water.

CHAPTER ONE
CINNAMON SURPRISE

I am Diana of the Wind Rivers, destined to work with the Greek gods and goddesses to protect pure water on the planet. How can I tell Dad I'm not just an ordinary college sophomore?

Dad is a practical person. Convincing him of my new reality, a blend of fantasy and rugged mountain peaks, is going to be no easy task. I need the help of my grandmother on my mom's side, Helen, and her new husband, Willy, our Eastern Shoshone and Crow family friend. They know the truth about me.

Last June, I met Persephone, queen of the underworld. With her emerald-green eyes and the hope of spring in her smile, she is the daughter of Demeter, goddess of agriculture. Along with our companion, a Mountain Bluebird named Indigo, Persephone and I set off on a quest to preserve clean water.

I returned to the ranch during spring break at the end of March, determined to tell Dad the truth about my adventures. I am just about to join the Greek gods on a rescue mission to prevent an iceberg chunk from crashing into South Georgia Island in the Antarctic.

I know the gods need my help, but I can't stop tendrils of resentment twining through my brain, threatening to overwhelm my sense of duty. Last summer, I learned to accept my role as Diana of the Wind Rivers, but that doesn't mean I am automatically delighted to do everything the gods demand. Throughout my second year of college, I looked forward to spring break and returning to the ranch to spend time cross-country skiing with Dad, an activity we have enjoyed since I was old enough for my first pair of skis. Events seemed to be moving ahead without my permission.

Today, Dad and I are sitting at our oak kitchen table, enjoying morning coffee. Outside, snowflakes swirl above the deck, while inside, the rich aroma of coffee and cinnamon rolls permeates the air. Grams and Willy sit with us while I serve up the delicious rolls Grams made on special occasions. I need them not only for moral support, but also to convince Dad that my unbelievable tale is true.

I tried to tell him about it last fall, but just couldn't find a way. But I had no choice. Instead of following ski trails with him on the ranch and up Sinks Canyon, I will leave tomorrow. I also promised Indigo I would tell Dad about her.

"Dad, remember last fall when I asked how you felt about flying horses?" I said.

"Vaguely," he said. "I thought you just wanted to talk about Greek mythology. Man, these rolls are outstanding, as usual, Helen." He took another large bite of the yeasty feast and nodded at Grams.

"I'd like to talk about flying horses some more," I said.

"Great. Can you hand me another roll?" He eagerly reached toward the pan.

"Dad, you need to focus. Here's a roll. Now please listen."

"Right," he said. "Can I have some more coffee?"

Willy chuckled. "Evan, we want to tell you something."

Dad knows Willy is my biological grandfather. "Do you and Helen have more secrets from the past?" Wiggling his eyebrows in a leering manner at Grams, he finished his roll with a groan of satisfaction. "Okay. I can focus now."

"Good," I said. Glancing at Grams, I continue after her encouraging smile. "While you worked in the oil fields of North Dakota last summer, I helped the Greek goddess Persephone prevent a disaster in the Gulf of Mexico."

"Right," Dad said. His eyebrows drew together in a scowl, and then formed an arch. "Maybe you should lighten up on the rolls. I hear cinnamon is powerful." He leaned back and chuckled, clearly pleased with his comment.

"Seriously, Dad. I can prove it," I said.

"This, I gotta hear," he said, picking up his coffee cup.

I looked at Grams, who nodded slightly. I proceeded to tell Dad the truth from the beginning. "Last summer, I went to Sinks Cave on the morning you left for North Dakota. I was upset that we couldn't take our summer pack trip. As I stood on a boulder, thinking about Mom, the cliff above the river opened like an elevator door, and out came a huge chariot pulled by two winged black horses."

Dad laughed and shook his head. "You're kidding me. Did you tell your grandmother about this? Did you have her checked out by a doctor?" He looked at Grams.

"Just listen, Evan," Grams said. "She knows what she's talking about."

"Seriously, Dad. This is the truth," I said. "Stop teasing." Tired of his silly jokes, I glared at him. Most of the time, I appreciate his corny sense of humor, but today, I had no patience for that.

"Okay," he said. "I'll listen, but it sounds like you've been reading a little too much mythology."

Relieved I had his attention at last, I filled my dad in, telling him of my summer of immortal flying horses, of gods and goddesses who shimmered with iridescent colors, who lived in amazing caves or deep forests or even on top of a garbage heap in the Pacific Ocean. I spoke of meeting elk, grizzlies, beavers, and a certain Mountain Bluebird who saved my life.

"Artemis gave me this moonstone ring and the ability to understand Indigo," I said.

"Remind me again about Indigo," Dad said, clearly focused now, even if he didn't believe it yet.

How could I convince Dad that my new little friend saved my life and dedicated herself to saving pure water on our planet? Indigo longed to be as blue as her cerulean father, but she learned that her inner blue was more important than her outer blue, and that courage comes from within.

"She's the little Mountain Bluebird who came to the ranch last summer," I said. "Remember when you wondered why she was hanging around?"

"Did she have anything to do with the bluebirds at the wedding?" he said.

"Yes," I said. "She organized the birds who flew around Grams and Willy when they kissed during the ceremony. And she saved my life on our quest. What do you think of that?"

Dad leaned back in his chair. "Are you taking a creative writing class at school right now? Because that's a pretty good story." He looked at Grams and Willy. "So, you guys believe this? Is it a joke on me?"

"It's no joke, Dad. Here's the ring." I pulled my elk tooth necklace from under my shirt. "The elk is my animal, Dad. Willy told me that."

Willy nodded. "It's true, Evan. This is a powerful ring."

"Diana told me about the power of the ring," Grams added. "I believe her."

Grateful for their support, I held up the ring, but kept it on the necklace, nestled next to the two elk teeth. Handed down through generations of Willy's family, the necklace was destined to reach me. Last July, when I returned with Artemis to the source of the Yellowstone River, I met the spirit of my great-great-great-grandmother, Running Elk Moon. She told me I was the child of a prophecy, born in the Wind River Mountains, destined to help save pure water on our planet in a time of great need. Running Elk Moon was the first in a line of women in our family who passed on the necklace until it reached Willy, who gave it to me.

"I can't let you wear the ring, Dad, but it gives me the power to understand animals," I said. "By talking with animals, I can help humans learn how to keep ecosystems intact, saving pure water. Did you know the ponds beavers create benefit all wildlife and preserve water?"

"Yes, I know about beaver dams. But this ring thing is nonsense. I know you like this story you've created, but, Diana, it can't be true," Dad said. "It's not April first, so what are you guys up to by telling me this?"

"Evan, Diana is telling the truth," Grams said.

"I can prove it," I said. I looked at the old-fashioned wall clock next to the doorway. "Let's go outside. I've arranged for an appointment with my evidence."

"Okay," Dad said. "I don't know what you mean, but I'll go along for now." I'd already arranged for Hades to send his horses and chariot to the ranch this morning. I not only needed them for my journey to the Antarctic tomorrow, but also to show Dad my new reality. Hades and I had planned to have the horses arrive about now.

We put on our boots and coats, and the others followed me outside. The sky was still overcast, but it had stopped snowing. I whistled loudly. "Here they come, Dad," I said, pointing to the sky. "The proof that I'm working with the Greek gods and goddesses."

As I spoke, two black horses pulling a chariot flew over the rim of the canyon, gliding to a smooth landing at the edge of our snow-covered yard. The magnificent stallions looked our way and whinnied a greeting as I turned to watch Dad's incredulous face.

"How did they get here by themselves?" he said. "There's no driver in that chariot."

"Hades sent the horses even though he couldn't be here right now. Now do you believe me?" I smiled as he shook his head.

"I'll be darned," he said. "Is this for real? Did you put whiskey in that coffee?" He turned to Grams. "Do you guys see this?"

"Yes, Evan, it's real," Grams said. "I've known since she was young that Diana was destined to work with the gods and goddesses."

"And I knew that one day, I would pass the necklace on to the child of the prophecy," Willy said.

"I must be dreaming," Dad said, shaking his head. "Why didn't you tell me?"

"We had to allow the prophecy to reach fulfillment before we could tell you," Willy said.

"Come on." Grabbing Dad's hand, I pulled him off the deck and into the yard. We approached the horses, who softly nickered. "These are Hades' horses, Alastor and Aethon. It's okay to pet them." I knew these horses well from my adventures with Persephone and Indigo last summer.

All our lives, Dad was in control. Our roles reversed when he reached out to stroke the neck of the nearest horse, Alastor. "This seems real," he said. "They're beautiful animals. So big."

On the ranch, in the mountains, and in most aspects of my life, Dad was my guide. This time, I was in charge, and it was glorious. "Let's take a spin." I pulled him toward the chariot.

I stepped in, picked up the reins, and looked back to see Dad climbing on board. "Hang on."

Dad sat down on the padded bench and gripped the side of the chariot. "Are we really going to fly?"

"Yes! You'll be fine. It's pretty smooth," I said. "Take to the sky!" At my command, the horses trotted forward, moving us through the snow at the edge of the yard. Gaining speed, they became airborne.

As they lifted the chariot, I sang a high pure note. Immediately, a flock of Dark-eyed Juncos flew up from the trees, filling in the space below and to the sides.

"What's with those birds?" Dad yelled, his voice revealing his panic. A tall man, he seemed vulnerable as he sat on the bench behind me.

"Come on up here with me," I said. "You can see better." The horses flew side by side at first, each one spreading his outer wing. As we flew higher in the sky, they moved apart, extending both wings in a magnificent expression of their flying power. From behind, their brilliant black coats glimmered, their broad wings making flight seem effortless.

I glanced back to see that he gripped one side of the chariot with both hands, looking around in shock. "It's okay. Stand up and come to the front."

"Right," he said. His pale face emphasized his wide eyes.

I turned to the front again, hoping he'd join me. After a short wait, he grabbed my shoulder and then stood next to me, gripping the front edge. Looking to the side, I flashed him a smile. "See? It's okay."

"If you say so," he said, his eyes forward.

"When I sing out to the birds, a flock rises up to provide cover for us. Nobody on the ground can see us. They just think we're a flock of birds," I said. "Pretty nifty, right?"

Dad was able to turn and look at me now, but he still clutched the front of the chariot. "It's ingenious." His smile was more like a grimace.

"I'm going to turn the chariot around so we can fly over Sinks Canyon," I said, using the reins to direct the horses. "You'll like seeing the river from above." Turning in a wide arc, the stallions led us back over the ranch and toward the canyon. As if on cue, the birds separated a bit underneath. "Look down," I yelled. "There's Grams and Willy!"

He looked over the edge just in time to see them waving from below. Releasing one hand, he waved back, and then the birds closed ranks again. We flew above the narrow entrance to the canyon. On the left, lodgepole pines covered the steep hillside, while a broad rock face formed the right wall of the canyon.

In a short while, we were over the cave where the Middle Fork of the Popo Agie River disappeared into the ground. "That's where Hades and Persephone stay," I said. "Deep inside the cliff is an underground lake, just like the scientists thought. Look ahead and you can see the river coming down the canyon."

Sure enough, in spite of the snow piled on its banks, the river still flowed. Ice and snow narrowed the river channel, but underneath that, I knew the water made its way swiftly over and around boulders, now piled with mini snowcaps. The fresh mountain water was dark against the white snow on this cloudy day.

Ahead, the paved road mirrored the path of the river as we headed up the narrow canyon to the point where the pavement ended in a large dirt parking lot. At that point, the highway was buried under a white blanket. Even though the highway climbed up the mountain into the forest in a switch-back pattern on its way to Louis Lake, the snowplows didn't clear any of the road beyond this in winter.

The brisk wind chilled my cheeks and brought tears to my eyes. I glanced at Dad, who seemed mesmerized by the horses. They were spread apart, giving their wings ample room to keep us aloft.

"I'm going to turn around and head back to the ranch," I said when the canyon began to narrow again in the path forged by the river.

Dad nodded. "Okay. Let me sit down first."

"Good idea. It will be easier when we land." When I glanced back to make sure he was secure, he seemed relieved to return to the bench.

We quickly arrived at the ranch, and I warned Dad before we landed in the pasture. As the horses slowed to a trot, Grams and Willy walked from the warmth of the barn.

"Now it's our turn for a ride," Grams said, smiling broadly.

"Are you ready to get out?" I asked Dad when the horses stopped.

"Sure," he said. "Let me get my land legs back first." He stood up and inhaled. "What just happened?"

I laughed. "We flew in a chariot pulled by winged horses," I said, moving back to hug him. "Hold on while you step down. I felt shaky after my first ride also." I held out my hand for him to grab as he jumped to the ground.

Pausing in place for a moment, he grinned. "I never expected something like that to happen. These guys are magnificent." He walked forward, patting Aethon's smooth rump on his way past. "Your turn," he said to Grams and Willy. "I'll feed the other horses while you're gone."

Grams climbed in first, and Willy followed, placing a plaid blanket over her lap. I smiled as I watched, happy to see their open affection for one another. For decades, Grams and Willy hid their love from the world because they were married to other people who had since passed away. After their wedding last summer, they openly revealed their feelings while including me in their circle of love.

"Ready?" I asked, turning around.

"Yes," Grams said. "You're in charge."

Willy smiled and nodded.

Clicking my tongue at Alastor and Aethon, I signaled they should move forward by lightly moving the reins. As they trotted, we gained speed and the chariot rose into the sky again. I heard Grams' delight from behind, her musical laugh making her sound like a teenage girl.

"Follow the highway," I directed the horses, and Alastor whinnied in response. The flock of juncos immediately rose up from the pasture, shielding our progress from anyone who might be in the canyon. "You guys okay?" I turned to assess Grams and Willy.

"We're fine," Willy said, reaching out to enclose Grams' mittened hand in his.

Smiling, I faced the front again, remembering the countless times he'd held my hand when I was a child. Both Grams and Willy were my teachers as I grew up on the ranch. Willy taught me the ways of the forest while Grams became my surrogate mother, holding me close when I cried. Dad, Grams, and Willy comforted me as I tried to understand the loss of my mother, who died when I was five. It was only last summer during my adventures with Persephone and Indigo that I finally reached a point of peace with Mom's death.

Willy and Grams were fine on their first chariot ride, so I didn't look back for a bit. Instead, I focused my gaze ahead on the canyon I loved so dearly, the canyon I felt belonged to me, even though it was a state park that everyone owned. Below, the cave where the river disappeared underground flashed by quickly, and we followed the snow-covered boulders obscuring the full force of the river. Beneath the chariot, the canyon floor broadened. On the right, the sagebrush formed lumps under the winter snow cover as the ground gradually climbed to meet steep cliffs where peregrine falcons nested in the summer.

The highway snaked a path parallel to the river, and to the left, snow-flocked lodgepole pines stood straight and tall, forming a dense cover on the steep canyon walls. When we reached the parking lot at the base of the road leading to Louis Lake, the canyon narrowed again, winding in a path carved by centuries of pure water, *Aqua Pura*, flowing from the heights of the Wind River Mountains. I didn't yet understand my full power as Diana of the Wind Rivers, but I knew it came from the headwaters of the Yellowstone River in the Absaroka Mountains of Wyoming.

And how am I supposed to save pure water on our planet if I don't even know my own powers? I don't have a way to stop the drought in the West, I can't prevent people from using too much water, and I don't know how on Earth to deal with the issue of microplastics in water and air on the planet. What would be the impact of that? Be patient, I counselled myself. *Start with learning how to fly with these magnificent creatures. Then deal with the iceberg chunk in the Antarctic.*

By the time we returned to the ranch and landed at the edge of the yard, I was confident in my ability to control Alastor and Aethon. I would need them on my journey tomorrow.

"I'll help Diana put the horses away and you guys go inside," Dad said to Willy and Grams as their booted feet landed on the ground.

"Will you open the barn door? I'm leaving early tomorrow, and I want to keep the horses hidden inside for tonight," I said as Grams and Willy walked toward the house.

I led the horses into the barn behind Dad. We worked together to unhitch the animals. Once their bridles were off, they looked around with interest and followed me toward a large stall located at the side of the barn. "You guys stay in here together tonight. I already put some hay and water in there for you."

Dad efficiently pulled the chariot to the side of the barn. All our horses were out in the pasture eating hay. Being tough mountain horses, they didn't come into the barn unless a vicious storm hit the ranch. They were used to winged horses by now, having seen them plenty of times last summer when Dad was gone.

Dad joined me in the stall as I patted Alastor's muscular neck. "You know how the muzzle is the softest part of a horse?" I asked.

"Yeah," Dad said.

"Well, with these guys, their wing sprouts are softer. Feel it." He touched the downy feathers near the horse's shoulder.

"You're right," Dad said, looking over at me with a smile. "This is so soft."

Leaving Alastor and Aethon happily eating hay, we headed back to the house. "So, what do you think, Dad?"

He looped one arm over my shoulder, pulling me close as we walked. "I think you're an amazing daughter. I'm glad you're mine."

"Thanks, Dad," I said. His words warmed my insides like hot chocolate on a winter day.

CHAPTER TWO
PENGUINS ON ICE

The obsidian chariot raced across the sky as Alastor and Aethon flew over the ocean, carrying me toward my rendezvous with Eos, goddess of the dawn. While most college kids were celebrating spring break in the sun on the white sandy beaches of Florida, I sped toward the River Oceanus at the far edge of the world. Even though I'm not a bikini kind of girl—cowboy boots and jeans are more my style—my friends had invited me to join them on the sunny beaches. But that's not why I'm not in Florida.

Poseidon, god of the ocean, needed my help stopping an immense iceberg chunk from crashing into South Georgia Island in the cold seas of the southern hemisphere. The berg couldn't move the island, but when it passed close by, it would destroy the habitat of millions of penguins, seals, and nesting seabirds. We had to prevent that.

Was it just yesterday that I told Dad the truth about last summer, taking him for a ride in the chariot as proof I am Diana of the Wind Rivers?

The alert about an iceberg on the loose came from a little bird, sent with a message from Poseidon. Last week, on the Wednesday before spring break, I sat in my dorm room, studying for an exam. The late-afternoon sun filled my room with light. Turning the page in my biology textbook, I looked up at the sound of tapping. A small Black-capped Chickadee sat on the cement ledge just outside my window on the tenth floor.

I stood to get a better look at the little guy. Winter still had its grip on Laramie, Wyoming, and a few flakes drifted down on the bird, who insistently tapped against the window. I opened it, expecting him to fly away. Instead, he looked up at me from his perch on the ledge, chirping. Even though I lived alone in my single dorm room, I reflexively looked back to make sure no one saw us.

"Come on in," I said, as if birds visited me every day.

He cheeped once and flew in, landing on my desk next to my biology book. Lowering his head, he reached down to peck the pages.

"Hey, no eating the book," I said. Sitting down, I reached under my shirt to pull out my elk tooth necklace. I unclasped the silver chain and removed the moonstone ring, placing it on my finger. Closing my eyes,

I focused on the bird, ignoring all the other animal voices that flooded my brain. Did the university maintenance crew know we had mice in the basement? I could hear them, even up here on the tenth floor. Their little voices carried through the spaces for pipes in the walls. I didn't have time to listen to them talk about crumbs in the cafeteria, so I shoved their cute vocalizations aside.

Right now, Persephone was about to give birth to twins, the first gods born since the time of the ancient Greeks. Her mother, Demeter, goddess of agriculture, attended Persephone in Sinks Canyon Cave, along with Eileithyia, goddess of childbirth.

"What's going on?" I asked the chickadee. "What's your name? I'm Diana."

"My name is Chester," the bird replied. "Poseidon sent me with an important message."

"Is everything okay?" I asked, stroking the little guy's black head. Because I wore the ring, I understood his speech and he understood mine.

Pushing up against my finger, he briefly closed his eyes as I ran my hand down his back and then up his tail, gently gripping his tail feathers. Indigo loved this stroking, and apparently, the chickadee also did.

"Poseidon said he needs your help preventing a giant iceberg chunk from crashing into South Georgia Island in the southern Atlantic Ocean. If it hits the island, the berg will destroy the coastal feeding ground," Chester said, opening his eyes. "Do that some more. I've never felt anything like it."

I stroked his back and tail feathers again. "How can I help?"

"Poseidon said he'll send Hades' chariot when you return to the ranch next week. You're going to fly to the southern Atlantic to meet with him. Eos, Artemis, and you will use your chariots to move the iceberg," Chester said. "Is that food I can eat?" He nodded toward the half-eaten granola bar on my desk. "It smells very good."

As I crumbled small pieces of granola bar for Chester, he hopped over to the pile and began munching. "Demeter is helping Persephone in Sinks Canyon Cave, so you must help Poseidon," the chickadee said between bites. "He'll give you more directions when you meet him, but he wants you to rendezvous with Eos in five days."

"Did you see Poseidon?" I asked.

"No, he sent word with a seabird who passed the message along the bird chain until it came to one of the sea gulls who hangs out here at the dump outside of town," he said. "The gull found me and told me where to find you."

After thanking the chickadee with more crumbs from my granola bar, I opened the window so he could fly away. Could I do all this, saving pure water on the planet and finish studying for exams? Resentment took hold in my head. I was irritated that Poseidon expected me to drop my spring break skiing plans and fly to the Antarctic to stop the berg chunk. With a resigned sigh, I turned back to my biology notes.

Now, the day after telling my dad the truth about my identity, I drove the sleek black flying horses across the sky toward the Antarctic at breakneck speed. My face was protected by the ski mask and goggles I used to cross-country ski on our ranch, my hands were encased in layers of gloves and huge leather mittens, and my feet were toasty warm in my bamboo boots made by Demeter.

What really protected me was my special bamboo long underwear, also made by Demeter. Covering me from neck to wrists and ankles, the long underwear was reinforced with goose down, voluntarily surrendered to Demeter by Canadian geese. A commercial for these could honestly claim, "No animals were injured in the making of this product."

Even though I knew I had to arrive at the island ahead of the ice chunk to help the others avert disaster, I still wrestled with my resentment over not spending more time with Dad. In early May, before I came home from school, he planned to return to the Bakken Oil Fields of North Dakota, where he worked last summer. The weather wouldn't be ideal up there in May, but he had no choice; that's when the oil company had openings, and the money was too good to pass up. To top off my frustration, he worked there because we needed the money to help pay for school. I had some scholarships, but not enough to cover all my tuition and living costs.

The ultimate irony is that he was an oil worker, pulling the black ooze out of the ground with the fracturing method that polluted the underground water I vowed to protect. This spring break was my only chance to spend time with him. Did I totally lose control over my life when I vowed to help the gods save pure water on the planet?

Normally, when I flew in a chariot with the gods, we used a protective flock of birds to hide our progress through the sky, but not today. Alastor and Aethon traveled so fast that any ships on the ocean below wouldn't recognize a chariot pulled by horses. We looked more like a passing dark cloud.

Slowing the horses, I looked down to see if there was any evidence of plastic in the water below. I saw a pod of over a hundred dolphins swimming through the water and leaping into the air in columns of four, looking like a ready-for-battle synchronized swimming team. No sign of plastic. But after reading an article at the end of the semester in biology class, I know there were many times more tons of plastic particles than had been in the ocean five years ago. None of it appeared in the waters below as we sped across the ocean. Microplastics are almost too small to see, so that didn't mean the ocean here was safe and clean. Sometimes this burden seems too much for one person to fix.

Rosy fingers of light stretching across the horizon in the distance told me Eos was bringing up the dawn with her chariot pulled by the immortal horses Lampos and Phaeton. Aided by the light, I spotted a dot on the horizon that must be South Georgia Island.

"Faster," I yelled. The horses responded with renewed speed. Ahead, on the other side of the island, I saw a towering block of ice, which I knew had calved from an ice sheet in the Antarctic. "We just might beat this thing."

The red tones of dawn turned orange, peach, and then yellow, revealing the extent of the towering chunk of ice. Certain it was much larger below the surface of the cold Atlantic waters, I literally looked at the tip of the iceberg.

As I flew over the island toward the berg, I saw Eos, hovering in the sky as if she alone could stop the mass of ice. I couldn't bear to tell her how vulnerable she looked with the recently calved ice chunk as a massive backdrop. Even though it already became smaller by splitting apart, it nonetheless towered over her in the sky. But I knew better than to underestimate Eos.

Standing tall and strong in her pearlescent chariot, she was a slender figure with magnificent white wings. Moving closer, I saw her hair, the color of new spring grass, streaming behind in the wind. Her violet skin contrasted vividly with her white wings and green hair. Eos stood still as I approached, her blue eyes challenging and honest. She folded her wings, and the feathers shimmered in the morning sun as my eyes were drawn away from the goddess of the dawn toward her bay horses.

Lampos and Phaeton reared, pawing the air while enthusiastically whinnying at me. I knew these two well from our adventures last summer when I borrowed them from Eos for our fight against the oil monster in the Gulf of Mexico.

"Lampos and Phaeton," I shouted, "thank you for this wonderful greeting." They bobbed their heads in reply.

"Artemis will be here soon," Eos said, only a few feet from me in the air. "I've already talked to Poseidon about his plan."

"I have the rope from Demeter," I said. I know from experience that this bamboo and spider silk rope is amazingly strong.

"I'm going to tie the rope to anchors," Eos said. "I have them right here. The merfolk found them at the bottom of the ocean because, after all, they know where all the shipwrecks are."

I gasped as she reached behind to grab a tall, rusted anchor. She was ten feet tall, but the anchor rose above her head at least another ten feet. She held it aloft with apparent ease. A vicious-looking split hook curled up on either side at the bottom, and a long iron handle rose above her head. At the top was an iron loop where she could attach the rope.

I wondered how her chariot could remain aloft, and then reminded myself of the powerful nature of her immortal horses. I'd learned last summer that very little could faze these two, not even the weight of ancient ship anchors.

"Wow!" I said. "Where did the merfolk find those?"

"Ironically, these are from whaling ships sunk long ago in the days when humans killed whales almost to extinction," she said. "I think it's fitting that we use these anchors from those death ships to save the habitat of other sea creatures. Don't you?"

"Yes," I said. "That's a perfect use for that rusted iron."

"Now throw me that rope and I'll tie it to the anchors," she said, leaning down to place the anchor back in her chariot. "I also have these grappling hooks." She held up another rusted piece of iron with a shorter tail and four curved hooks at the top. "I'll tell you the plan while I work."

One at a time, I tossed the five ropes that Hades had placed in the chariot before his horses brought it to the ranch yesterday.

"Artemis will be here soon, and Poseidon, too," Eos said while she kneeled and efficiently started securing the ropes to the anchors and hooks. "We'll wrap the two anchors around the iceberg, and Poseidon will pull at the base with his hippocamps and chariot. You, Artemis, and I will secure the grappling hooks at the top and pull with our chariots."

"Will that do the trick?" I said, eying the massive chunk. Already it seemed closer to us where we hovered between the iceberg and island.

"No, that's not enough. Poseidon is bringing merfolk and whales to push from under the water," she said. "What we now see is just the tip, as you know."

"Why do they need us, then?" I asked. "It seems a bunch of whales and merfolk could do the job without us."

"Poseidon couldn't get as many whales as he wanted," she said. "Right now, many whales are giving birth around the globe, and he could only find a few males close enough to get here in time."

"Why didn't we move this berg before it floated this close to the island?" I asked, watching her strong hands work with the creamy rope, her violet skin vivid against the rust-red iron anchor.

"When it first calved from the Antarctic ice sheet, the berg seemed to be headed east. Then it broke apart, and this portion drifted north with the changing current. Even though it's not as big as the original, it can still do serious damage if it hits the island."

"You mean it could break off part of the island?"

"No, it could destroy the excellent feeding grounds on the southern coast. Millions of penguins, seals, and birds feed in these rich, unspoiled waters," Eos said, attaching the last rope to a grappling hook.

Hades' horses whinnied and I turned to see Artemis speeding above the island in her chariot drawn by deer. She stopped near us, suspended in the air even though her deer had no wings. I'd ridden across the Wind River Mountains with Artemis, and I knew the swift, silent flight of those deer. Last summer, she'd taken me into the mountains to learn how to communicate with animals while wearing my moonstone ring.

Artemis was slim, but tall, with kind eyes. When she looked at me, compassion poured into my soul from the goddess of the moon and protector of animals. I was her namesake. Diana was the Roman version of the Greek Artemis.

She gave me many gifts last year, including a bow and arrow with homing pigeon feathers so that my arrows always returned to the quiver, my moonstone ring, and the gift of communication with Indigo. On Squaretop Mountain in Wyoming, she gave me my official name, Diana of the Wind Rivers. I smiled my joy at seeing her again.

A high, watery whinny announced the coming of Poseidon. The last time I saw him, he ruled from a shell throne atop the Giant Pacific Garbage Patch, which he corralled with the force of his ocean currents. I knew whales swam around the patch to contain it while Poseidon was gone.

Whipping up the water so that it looked like the egg whites Grams blended when she made lemon meringue pie, two hippocamps swiftly pulled Poseidon's golden chariot through the cold water. Completely covering their bodies in foam, the waves caressed their horse heads, almost obscuring their finny manes. All around his chariot, dolphins jumped and returned to the water, keeping up with the incredible speed of the hippocamps. I'd read about these creatures in Greek mythology, but never imagined the dynamic energy of their presence. Screeching overhead, giant sea birds accompanied the chariot.

"Greetings, fellow travelers," Poseidon shouted as he pulled up below us. "Diana of the Wind Rivers, in June, I will send a pair of foals to the ranch. Don't forget about that."

While devouring Greek mythology as a child, I'd learned about hippocamps, Poseidon's sea creatures with the upper body of a horse, front legs and hooves, and long fish tails that propelled them through the water. They eat seaweed. Their huge upper bodies rose above the waves, which calmed as they paused in the water. One was brilliant blue, the color of an autumn sky, his bright green mane and forelock perfectly matching the color of the second hippocamp. This second creature was the vivid green of aloe vera plants, while his mane mirrored the blue of his partner. Shiny fish scales covered their muscular bodies. Strong wings, the same color as their manes, were folded against their sides now that they'd stopped. Beneath the waves, I could see their long fish tails weaving back and forth, much as my arms did when I tread water to keep myself afloat in a swimming pool. Their eyes were brilliant sapphire blue, sparkling like water in the sun.

Alastor and Aethon whinnied loudly at their water cousins, making me realize that Hades and his brother Poseidon had certainly met like this before. The hippocamps reared, revealing the smooth skin of their underbellies. There, they had no fish scales, just green or blue skin, depending on the color of each water horse. They tossed their heads, causing their fin manes to flow back and forth in the air. The morning sun beamed into their manes, creating a translucent quality.

A booming laugh drew my attention to Poseidon, who mastered these magnificent water horses with ease. I was struck again by the sight of his massive blue body, the color of the sky. The sky at dawn, the sky at sunset, the sky when it's turquoise near the horizon and clear blue above. I wondered, did Poseidon reflect the sky or did the sky reflect him? Did Poseidon infuse clear water, turning it blue when viewed from above, or did he gain his color from water?

Nothing compared to the majestic blue of Poseidon. A shifting blue, his skin was at one moment, deep blue like the summer sky, and the next, an aquamarine that I saw only in photographs of the Caribbean. When he stood to greet us, he changed to the vibrant blue of early evening.

"Is everyone ready?" He didn't wait for an answer as his voice boomed across the water. "You all know the plan? Let's get going. We can talk when it's over."

One by one, Eos tossed him the anchors and grappling hooks.

I knew Poseidon was strong, but I marveled when he threw the giant anchor over the mass of ice, Demeter's rope snaking silently behind with a soft hissing noise.

"I heard it enter the water on the other side," Poseidon said after a short while.

"I didn't hear anything," I said.

"I know and hear all things that happen in the ocean," he said.

"Well done," Artemis said.

Poseidon smiled at his niece and looked down. I followed his gaze to the base of the iceberg where it disappeared into the ocean. After a several minutes, a merman surfaced, triumphantly holding up the anchor, which was still attached to the spider web and bamboo rope.

We'll test the strength of that spider silk soon, I thought.

The merman swam to Poseidon's chariot and tossed the anchor up to Poseidon, who threw it over the berg again. The merman dove under the water, and after many moments, he again appeared, taking the anchor to Poseidon.

"Now, I'll attach the grappling hooks at the top," Poseidon said. "When I toss the hook, each of you will grab the rope so you can pull it tight and keep the tension going until we start pulling together."

I watched as he threw the first hook over the top of the white ice. Eos quickly steered her chariot to grab the rope before it fell. Her horses pulled against the rope, securing the grappling hook on the other side while she looped it around the back edge of her chariot, over and under a small railing on the top.

Poseidon threw the second grappling hook, sending it aloft. Artemis' deer raced after the rope so she could catch the end, and she pulled back to create tension and hold it in place.

Finally, Poseidon looked at me. "Are you ready?"

"Yes," I said, bracing my legs and bending my knees slightly. I could tell this was just like roping a horse at home on the ranch. I know how to circle the rope above my head and send it flying over the neck of a horse, and then loop the end around my saddle horn, while my horse pulled back, creating enough tension to hold the other animal in place. This seemed similar, except that now, I'd tie the rope to the back of my chariot.

At my nod, Poseidon threw the grappling hook over the top. A soft hissing accompanied the rope as it sailed past my chariot. I reached out to grab it, grateful for my leather mittens. Hanging on to the rope, I secured it around the brass knob at the back of Hades' chariot. His horses knew just what to do, pulling back to create tension and hold the hook in place.

"What we'll do is turn our chariots the other way," Eos shouted. "We have to spread out so our animals can fly, and then we'll pull at Poseidon's command."

My stomach was queasy. Eos was to my left, and Artemis to my right. Below, the hippocamps started churning up water. This seemed dangerous. Would it work?

"I have some merfolk, dolphins, and a few whales on the other side," Poseidon said. "When I give the order, we will pull, and the others will push." He looked up one more time. "Ready?"

I nodded. Already the power of the current pulled me back a bit as the giant berg floated toward the island, but Alastor and Aethon resisted.

"Forward," Poseidon yelled.

At first, nothing happened. We all remained in place. This isn't working, I thought. Then, I felt movement and glanced to my left and right. Lampos and Phaeton strained forward, their immortal bodies inching Eos' chariot through the sky.

Even without wings, the deer pulling Artemis leaned forward in the air.

Hades' horses whinnied as they worked their wings in the cold air. Suddenly, just like a big truck stuck in the snow breaks free when pulled by a come-a-long winch, the iceberg followed us.

"We're doing it," I yelled, laughing into the wind.

All around, seabirds dove and screeched, seeming to cheer us on. The water around the hippocamps in the waves below rose to their heads, so great was the force created by their churning fish tails. Ahead of Poseidon's chariot, stingrays leapt from the waves, flying as if to herald the way.

Slowly, slowly, slowly, we pulled the berg out of the current that carried it toward the rich, fertile water on the south shore of the island. Glancing that way, it seemed to me that penguins deliberately lined up on the shore, watching as if this were some tractor pull at a county fair.

Giant Wandering Albatrosses flew up and down all around us, their twelve-foot wingspans dwarfed by the size of our cargo. Indigo would love this, I thought, wishing she were here to marvel at the power of sea birds.

Just when it seemed the ropes stretched too thin, when it seemed even spider silk, stronger than steel, could not hold against the weight of the berg we pulled, the load became lighter, and the tension in my rope evaporated.

"We did it," Poseidon exclaimed. "The berg is far enough away that the current is now taking it out to sea."

Hundreds of dolphins emerged from the other side of the iceberg, jumping above the waves. Three whales surfaced, sending water into the sky from their blow holes, and a group of mermen emerged next to them, waving before disappearing under the waves.

Artemis, Eos, and I looked at each other and cheered, our voices overpowered by the screeching celebration of the birds.

"Thank you," Poseidon yelled as all of the sea creatures swam away and the birds flew toward the island. "Let's regroup on the north shore of the island. We'll let the ropes and anchors sink to the bottom. When the ice eventually melts, the merfolk will return them to me."

Eos, Artemis, and I navigated lower, hovering around Poseidon's chariot. As I looked down, a merman swam over to where my chariot waited in the air, treading water right next to me.

"Come for a swim," he said. "I'll show you the beauty of the ocean."

"Don't listen, Diana," Eos said.

Her voice interrupted my perusal of the merman's magnificent physique. His chest rippled smoothly as he gracefully moved his arms back and forth in the waves. For some reason, his green skin made me want to feel those arms around me. His dark hair, shiny and wet, gleamed in the sun.

"Diana," Artemis said sharply. "Stay out of the water."

How did she know I was ready to jump in? His seductive voice and warm sea-green eyes were something I'd never experienced. Hearing Artemis knocked some sense into my head, and I looked away from the merman's gaze. As if sensing my need for distance, Hades' horses pulled the chariot higher. The lure of the merman dissipated, releasing its hold on me.

"That was powerful," I said to Eos and Artemis.

Eos laughed. "Diana of the Wind Rivers has passed another test. She repelled the lure of the merfolk. Humans must watch out for them. They entice you into the sea where you will then remain."

"I wouldn't hurt her," the merman said. "I know who she is, and I knew she could resist my charms." He flashed me a quick grin.

"Well, I don't usually have men trying to lure me anywhere," I said. "I'm flattered."

"I'll be here, waiting," he said in a teasing tone.

"Say hello to my mom," I said. "She's a mermaid now." My mom drowned in a river when I was five, but last summer, I met her on our adventures in the Gulf of Mexico, where I learned she was now a mermaid.

"I know," he replied. "She's helping grey whales give birth near the Baja Peninsula, so she couldn't be here today. She said to give you her love, which I am glad to do."

"Thank you," I said.

He flashed another grin and dove under the water, his green dolphin tail surfacing when he entered the waves without a splash.

"I can't stay. I already told Poseidon I have to check on new foals in my stable. They were only born yesterday," Eos said. "Diana, I will see you again, I am sure. You must bring Indigo back so she can fly in the spray of the River Oceanus, just as she did last summer."

"I'll try," I said. "I want to see the river as well." The River Oceanus was the source of all rivers, lakes, streams, and aquifers, which I'd vowed to protect.

Eos waved goodbye, darting southward through the sky toward her island.

Artemis and I followed Poseidon across the ocean, the hippocamps swiftly carrying his chariot through the waves. Poseidon followed the coast, slowing down when he reached the northern shore. He stopped at a narrow beach at the base of towering cliffs. Snow-covered mountains rose above the cliffs. Artemis and I landed on the beach while Poseidon stopped in the shallows, jumped out of his chariot, unhitched his hippocamps, and waded through the waves to the shore.

Artemis and Poseidon joined me in Hades' chariot. "He has such a luxurious ride," Artemis said, stroking the soft cushion in the back.

"That was amazing," I said.

We sat in companionable silence, watching the hippocamps dive in the water.

"What are they eating?" I said.

"This shore has especially delicious seaweed," Poseidon said. "They love it here."

"I hate to bring it up, but I've been thinking about the problem of microplastics," I said. "We have to stop it at the source. It's wrong — and unreasonable — to expect consumers to recycle everything. I read an article in biology class that said it ends up in landfills anyhow."

"Right," Poseidon said, absently stroking the seabird that had landed on his thigh. "We also have to clean up the existing trash. The gods can't change human behavior, but you can. We have to educate humans about what they can do. Many people are already working on this problem, but we need your help."

"We're going to need a two-pronged approach," Artemis said. "We have to clean up the current trash in the ocean *and* tackle it at the source."

"Humans should stop making single-use plastic," I said. "American corporations produce more of this stuff than most other countries in the world. I'll find a way to get at this problem."

We fell silent again, the splashing of the hippocamps filling the silence. They dove like ducks, putting their heads and shoulders under, sending their blue and green tails in the air.

"They're changing colors," I said. As one hippocamp dove under, his tail turned from blue to green, shining in the sun.

"They do that when they're happy," Poseidon said. "They like the seaweed growing in these cold waters."

Alastor and Aethon whinnied and pawed the ground, vibrating the chariot.

"They want some," Artemis said. "Poseidon, tell your water steeds to pull up seaweed for the horses and my deer."

"Hippocamps," yelled Poseidon. Two heads popped out of the water.

I laughed at the comical scene. Water dripped from their mouths as seaweed dangled over their chests.

"Pull up some food for your cousins over here! Bring some for the deer also," Poseidon said.

With a watery whinny, the hippocamps nodded and dove again, quickly coming up with mouthfuls of seaweed. Racing toward the shore, they tossed it on the pebbles covering the beach. I grabbed the reins as Hades' horses pulled the chariot along in their rush toward the seaweed.

"Whoa," I said with a laugh. "There's plenty for everyone!"

Hades' horses whinnied and delicately picked up seaweed with their lips, quickly chewing after the first bite. Artemis' deer pulled her chariot along as they raced to the seaweed buffet.

"Get some more," yelled Poseidon, and the hippocamps dove again, returning to the shore with more food for the sky horses and deer.

In the comfortable silence, as we watched the animals eat their treat, my elation at our victory subsided to fatigue. I was bone weary, just as I felt when plopping into a chair on the deck at the end of the day during haying season after we worked long hours. My joy gave way to depressing thoughts.

"I read an article about manatees dying in the waters of Florida," I said, looking down at my hands and then over at Poseidon. "Did you know about that?"

"Yes," he said, his brilliant blue eyes dimming. "Humans use fertilizer in farming and also dump sewage into the surrounding water. That's killing the seagrass, and my creatures starve. I've tried to grow new grass, but the water is too polluted."

"And tons of plastic still float in the ocean. Sometimes it seems like too much to do. How can we save everything?" I looked for an answer in Poseidon's eyes.

"We need Indigo to cheer us up, don't we?" he said.

I remembered the time last summer when we first discovered microplastics were in glaciers, which meant they were in the River Oceanus. When we told Poseidon, he'd turned white. Indigo encouraged him to find his blue, which helped Poseidon recover.

I felt overwhelmed. "I know we're forming a plan, but sometimes, it seems like too much to accomplish. Humans have taken the planet to a dark place by putting clean water in jeopardy." Suddenly, I had to vent. "It's too much. Manatees are dying because my species is killing sea grass. Microplastics are at the bottom of the ocean and maybe in the River Oceanus. We found them in glaciers."

"We'll take it one step at a time," Artemis said. "Today was a victory. We didn't win the war, but we can take heart from the fact that we won this battle and prevented the ice chunk from destroying the feeding grounds in the water along the coast."

"Why doesn't Zeus help us?" I asked, looking toward the sky.

"Right now, he's dealing with his own issues just above the ozone layer," Artemis said.

"Air pollution?" I said.

"No. Space debris. Not only have humans trashed the planet, but your race has also littered outer space. Tons of debris orbit the Earth," Artemis said. "Did you hear about that?"

"Yes. I just saw a news report about all the junk floating around the planet. Billionaires are putting satellites in space. Nobody is trying to control how much junk we send up there. What's Zeus doing?"

"He is shoring up the ozone layer because it's damaged by the debris falling from outer space to Earth," Artemis said. "All the rockets leaving the atmosphere do damage as well."

"It's hard to remain optimistic," I said.

"He knows about you," Poseidon said. "Someday, you'll meet him. We can't lose hope."

"Hope is the thing with feathers," I said, thinking out loud.

"Do you mean Indigo?" Poseidon asked.

"No," I said. "That's the first line of my favorite poem by Emily Dickinson. The first stanza goes like this." I recited:

> *Hope is the thing with feathers*
> *That perches in the soul*
> *And sings the tune without the words*
> *And never stops at all*

"That's beautiful," Artemis said. "It makes me think of Indigo."

"Yes," I said. "We studied Emily Dickinson last year in sophomore English. It reminds me that I still have hope in my heart." The memory of Indigo's courage helped me.

"The best weapon against despair is action," Poseidon said. "Now that we have you, Diana of the Wind Rivers, Artemis and I have hope as well."

"And you two give me hope," I said. "I'll keep the poem in my heart also."

As we said goodbye and I flew away, I couldn't resist soaring over the iceberg chunk just to see it up close. Peering over the edge of the chariot, I saw a small group of penguins standing on top, looking around as if they sailed by on a cruise ship.

"You guys go back into the water," I shouted. They looked up. To my surprise, one by one, they demonstrated their cliff-diving skills by jumping in, disappearing into the ocean, where their food source was now secure.

CHAPTER THREE
THE BONDING BEGINS

My gift from Poseidon arrived on the ranch in the middle of June. Demeter flew from the Platte River in a specially designed chariot pulled by Golden and Glenda, the palomino mares I knew from my adventures with Persephone last summer. On board were twin fillies, secured with harnesses in the front section next to Demeter. Concealed by a flock of meadowlarks, the chariot landed far from prying eyes in the pasture behind the barn. Grams and Willy were in town, so I was the only one to greet the new horses as the meadowlarks flew away.

I wish Dad could be here to see Glenda and Golden land the chariot with their precious cargo on board, but he had already left to work the oil fields in North Dakota.

Persephone is also taking care of youngsters this summer, after giving birth to a boy and girl in March. Her twins are the first immortal deities born since the time when ancient Greeks worshipped the gods, so everyone on Mount Olympus was thrilled, according to reports from Demeter. I hadn't met the twins yet.

The fact that my horses are twins was a surprise. Poseidon also directed Hephaestus, the smith god, to build a special chariot for me. Hephaestus had plenty of time because the fillies were too young to fly on their own, anyhow. In fact, their little wings were not even developed.

"Flying horses don't grow their wings until they're six months old," Poseidon said last summer when he told me of his intention to find mates for Golden and Glenda.

In August of last year, Demeter flew with the mares to the River Oceanus near the island of Eos, goddess of the dawn. Far and wide, the Greek gods admired her stables. Only Zeus owned horses comparable to those of Eos. Demeter took the mares there so each one could choose a mate.

Demeter told me that Golden chose Metamorphosis, a magnificent chestnut-colored stallion with kind eyes, to be the father of her child. Golden's child, along with that of her sister, Glenda, would be the beginning of Wind River Stables, the new name Poseidon assigned to our ranch.

Once they arrived at the island, Glenda had surprised everyone by refusing a mate. She told Demeter that she didn't want to be a mother because she wanted a flying career. Instead of bearing a foal, she would offer support while her sister became a mother to twins. Glenda said she would provide guidance as their loving aunt, and Demeter agreed to this arrangement. I admired Glenda's stance. Not every female has to become a mother, Demeter told me.

Walking toward the chariot, I thought about the unique reason I owned flying horses. Last summer, I'd traveled with Persephone using Demeter's mares, but in the future, Poseidon wanted me to have my own horses and chariot so I could continue the fight to save pure water on our planet. The new winged horses would fly on their own by the time they were age one. Deep inside, I am excited to see the fillies, who are only two weeks old.

Turning their heads to look my way, the little ones whinnied.

"We've told them all about you, Diana," Demeter said. "We haven't mentioned any specific plans for the future because they're too young to understand, and we wanted to make sure you all bonded completely. That happens at around four months, so we'll know before you return to school at the end of August whether it was successful. Sometimes, if the bonding is strong, it happens in the third month."

"I can't keep them when I'm living in the dorm at school," I said.

"Once you bond, you can be separated for a while because they will have their mother. We'll make sure they periodically see you when you're back in school next year," Demeter said. "We could meet in the Snowy Range Mountains near Laramie."

Fifty miles west of Laramie, the Snowy Range is home to small glacial lakes. I drove to the mountains and hiked around the area last fall when I returned to school, searching for a glacial nymph so I could tell her I knew *Tixi Pagos*, the guardian on Younts Peak in Wyoming's Teton National Park, headwaters of the Yellowstone River, the longest river without a dam in the continental United States. The Crow people in Montana called it the Elk River because for thousands of years, vast herds of elk migrated through their native land on the banks of the river. Even though I looked and called out, I couldn't find a nymph in the Snowy Range.

"That would be a good place for us to meet in early fall," I said. "But you know they close the mountain pass during the winter."

"Right," said Demeter. By now, we stood next to the chariot. Glenda and Golden whinnied softly as the tiny fillies turned to look at me.

Short wispy tails matched their fluffy white manes and scruffy forelocks jutting between their perfectly formed ears.

Demeter spoke as if they could understand her every word. "Little ones, this is Diana of the Wind Rivers. Diana, this is Galene and

Daphne."

"Hello, Galene and Daphne," I said, extending my hand.

Short whiskers on identical noses tickled my palm as they sniffed my outstretched hand. Great stomping followed. They were clearly excited to be here. I laughed, causing them to neigh in unison. Captivated by their energy and charm, I looked into their golden-brown eyes. Time paused, noise ceased, and I was in a vacuum, but a very safe and loving vacuum, as I gazed into the eyes of my very own matched pair of flying horses.

"They're quite a handful," Demeter said.

"What just happened?" I turned to Demeter. "I was totally lost in their eyes just now."

"That's good," she said. "The bonding begins."

The horses stomped their feet, anxious to get out of the chariot. "Help me take off the harnesses," Demeter said. "You're going to have to be firm when you give directions." She removed the harness from one of the horses, handing me the lead rope. "You're leading Galene."

"Come," I said firmly, tugging on the lead rope. Luckily, the little horse followed, moving out with a hop.

Demeter pulled the harness from Daphne and led her out of the chariot. "For the next two weeks, you are the only human they can be with. After that, Willy and Grams can be around because the horses will have established their initial connection with you."

"We're all set up for that," I said. "Willy and Grams will stay in the main house, and I'll live in the bunkhouse this summer."

The word bunkhouse, traditionally a large room with space for ranch hands to sleep, did not do justice to the cabin where Willy had lived for many years. Located on the other side of the barn near the cottonwoods nestled against the base of Table Mountain, the bunkhouse was extremely comfortable, with beautiful leather furniture and hardwood floors peppered with area rugs. A rock fireplace, built by my great-grandfather, adorned one wall, directly across from a large picture window that looked over the small pasture encased in a log fence.

This pasture was tucked nicely out of sight from the house and provided perfect cover for keeping the foals. They would sleep in the barn at night and roam in the pasture during the day. Nobody would notice their wing buds, positioned just behind their shoulders and right below the withers, the ridge above the shoulders.

"Perfect," Demeter said. "By the end of August, you'll be completely bonded."

"What happens then?" I said.

"They'll be yours for life. Winged horses live at least a hundred and fifty years, so they'll belong to your descendants as well, as long as you introduce them to your children as soon as possible after they are born, so the horses know their scent."

"One hundred and fifty years?" I said, looking up from where my hand caressed Daphne's neck. At least I think it was Daphne. Galene pushed her nose under my hand, wanting some love as well. "How old are Glenda and Golden?"

"Seventy-five," Demeter said. "This is the prime of their lives."

"Wow," I said slowly. "They'll outlive me."

"They're not immortal, but they do live longer than humans," Demeter said.

I looked at the matched foals. "They're absolutely adorable."

"And they know it," Demeter said. "They're going to be a challenge."

I loved them already, but I knew she was right as I watched one filly stomp her foot.

"She wants to run around, doesn't she?"

"Good. You're sensing their needs," Demeter said. "Now, help me unhitch Glenda and Golden."

When we entered the barn with its smell of fresh hay, Glenda and Golden immediately walked into one large stall, and the twins followed, pushing their noses under Golden's belly, latching on to nurse, one on either side of the mare.

"I don't know if I can train two horses at once," I said.

"You trained Daisy," Demeter said.

"Willy helped me with that."

"You helped and he's still here," Demeter said. "After being alone with them for two weeks, you can let Willy and Grams help you. The twins are young, but by the end of the summer, they'll fully understand you."

The foals were demanding little beasts, and I know I would need help from their mother and aunt. After nursing, they began stomping their feet and bucking. They were so little that it was adorable, but I know it wouldn't be as cute when they were three years old and seventeen hands high.

I had to begin socializing them now. I sharply clapped my hands twice. They stopped frolicking and looked up in surprise, ears perked forward. I forced myself to ignore the cuteness overload.

"No bucking in the stall," I said. "Someone might get hurt. We have horse blankets to cover your mom and aunt, so nobody sees their wings. Let's put those on and we can go out into the pasture. Then you can run and buck and stomp as much as you want." I wasn't sure they understood me, but I thought it was worth a try.

Glenda neighed at the twins, and they immediately calmed down, watching as Demeter and I secured lightweight blankets on the mares.

"When we leave the barn, you must always walk. No running in the barn. Somebody might get hurt," I said. "Follow me."

Demeter nodded and smiled.

Once outside, the foals looked at me expectantly. This might work out, I thought.

"You can run around," I said, gesturing toward the grassy area. As soon as I finished talking, the twins raced into the pasture. I couldn't tell which was the faster, Galene or Daphne.

"Very nice job of taking control," Demeter said. "If you don't start now, it will become more difficult as they grow." We watched Glenda and Golden walk side by side, following the little ones.

"How can I tell them apart?" I asked.

"You'll figure out a way," Demeter said.

"Who chose their names?"

"I talked with Golden, and we named Galene after a nymph who was also goddess of the calm seas. Daphne is named after a Naiad, a nymph of freshwater lakes and streams," Demeter said. "We figured since their father lived near Oceanus, the source of all fresh water on the planet, they should have water names."

"I like that." I called out to them. "Daphne, Galene."

From across the pasture, the little ones stopped their frolicking and raced our way, stopping directly in front of me. "Whoa," I said with a laugh as they nuzzled my stomach. "You two are fast. You can go play again." They turned and ran, their short tails high in the air.

"They know their names pretty well," I said, turning to Demeter.

She laughed. "I think you'll be impressed with their ability to learn quickly," she said. "Now, show me your cabin. Glenda and Golden will keep an eye on them, and we can see them from the window."

"Can you stay for a while?" I said.

"Yes," Demeter said. "Just for a bit. Then I'm off to monitor spring crops in Nebraska."

"Thanks," I said. "I made some fresh lemonade."

"Soon, you'll meet the other new twins." Demeter smiled happily, a proud grandmother. "Persephone told me she'll come here at the end of two weeks. She knows I'm here today."

"I can't wait," I said. Internally, I began to hyperventilate at the thought of more twins.

As we walked toward the bunkhouse, Indigo flew to the small porch. "I'm here," she shouted. "I couldn't get away from the hatchlings until just now!" She was breathing heavily, and her head feathers were unevenly ruffled, spiking up in odd places.

"What's wrong?" I asked. I walked up to the porch and smoothed her head in the way she loved, following the contour of her back, all the way to the end of her tail feathers.

"Maybe I'm not a good mother. I couldn't wait to get away from the nest," she said. Even though her nesting box was on the ranch, I didn't see much of Indigo because she was constantly feeding her current batch of hatchlings.

"All parents are challenged," Demeter said with a laugh. "Welcome to family life."

I thought about that. Would I have kids someday? I hoped I would, but it sounded like a lot of work, and I wasn't sure I was ready for a commitment to children yet. Besides, I am still trying to understand myself. Then it occurred to me. Who would take care of my flying horses if I never had children?

My flock returned from our winter migration in early spring. Snow still covered the meadow above Sinks Canyon where I was born. Throughout the three-day flight, I thought of nothing but love, because this year, I would become a mother. I was supposed to raise hatchlings last summer, but I'd postponed that joy to help Diana and Persephone on their quest to preserve clean water on the planet.

Last year, I met my new friends, The Birds of Dawn, who lived near the River Oceanus at the far end of the world. I hoped to see them again sometime and fly in the spray of the River Oceanus.

But this spring, I would choose a mate and have two batches of hatchlings, just like my mother. In fact, last summer, I helped Mother and Father feed their second brood, so I already knew what to do.

When we landed in late afternoon in our snow-covered meadow above Sinks Canyon, I thought about the many attractive, unattached males I'd seen on the flight home. Cerulean like my father, the male of my species is outstanding in color. A blue like none other on the planet, the cerulean of males doesn't extend to females like me. I had to settle for blue wingtips and tailfeathers. But last summer, I learned my inner blue was my real strength, and my outer blue didn't matter.

As the sunset colored the sky with red and orange streaks, I sat on a branch near the nesting cavity where I was born, watching my mother and father update the old nest. "The meadow seems very crowded," I said as Mother plucked a few of her own downy feathers to line the inside of the nest.

"I know," she said, pausing in her work. "I think birds from another flock joined us here. Finding a nesting site at the edge of the meadow might be difficult."

"What should we do?" I asked. I knew I'd compete with other females to choose the best mate, but I never thought nesting space would be a problem.

"I don't want you to leave, but you might have to find another meadow with your mate," Mother said.

"I want to be here with you and Father," I said. "That's been my daydream all winter, nesting here in our meadow with you."

"Well, you might have to move on," Mother said. "I don't want to upset you, but sometimes we have to separate to find good nesting sites." She arranged dried meadow grass in the nest with her beak.

"I know what to do," I said. "Diana told me that Willy and Grams planned to build birdhouses all last winter. I wonder if they installed them. Should I fly to the ranch and check it out?"

"Yes," Mother said. "Go there tomorrow and report back right away. In the meantime, you can sleep in the nest with us tonight."

The next morning, as the first rays of dawn crept across the meadow, I flew down the canyon to the ranch. It was still cold, and a fresh coating of snow covered the hay fields. I saw Diana's dad standing on the deck outside the ranch house, so I perched on the railing and peeped a greeting. He said something, but the only human I could understand was Diana, who'd promised she would tell her father about me over the winter. She must have, because he kept looking at me.

I remained on the railing as he walked closer. Standing in front of me, he reached out his large hand, extending a finger. Accepting his invitation, I hopped on board, gripping with my feet. He laughed and brought me up to his eye level.

Turning at the sound of the patio door opening, Diana's dad kept talking as he held up the finger where I perched. Grams and Willy came out, smiling when they saw me. They talked with Evan, Diana's dad, and then Willy left the deck, gesturing for us to follow.

"Did you set up the nesting boxes?" I twittered. Last summer, Artemis gave me the gift of communication so that Diana and I could easily talk. This didn't extend to other humans, but I chattered on nonetheless as I flew from Evan's finger to follow Willy. Glancing back, I saw that Evan and Grams were close behind. I wished Diana were here with us, but I knew she was far away in Laramie, finishing the school year.

In the hay field beyond the barn, I saw wooden boxes mounted high off the ground on top of the fenceposts, spaced far enough apart for nesting birds to have privacy. I darted ahead of the others and decided this was a perfect location. The fence ran along the base of Table Mountain, and the bird boxes faced the hay fields. It was a good thing they weren't on the horse pasture fence because those creatures might chew the boxes or scare our babies if they peeked inside. Once the snow melted and the hay grew higher, this would be ideal for teaching young bluebirds how to hover above the ground like a helicopter, scaring up bugs.

I chirruped my joy and landed on the closest bird box, peeking inside to check it out. Hopping in, I laughed out loud with pleasure.

This would be perfect. Now all I had to do was find a mate. Moving out of the box, I flew to Willy's shoulder, rubbing my head against his cheek. Then I did the same with Grams, who patted my head gently with one finger. Evan said something, so I jumped to his shoulder and cheeped my thanks before hurrying back to the meadow.

Mother was inside the nesting cavity when I returned. I sat on a branch, waiting for her to come out. "Mom, Willy and Grams made ten nesting boxes. Lots of us can go live on the ranch. And the good thing is I can come back to visit you often because it's so close."

"That's wonderful news, Indigo," she said. Sitting beside me, she placed a wing over my back. "You must find a mate and convince others to join you on the ranch. It's time to start laying eggs. After showing your leadership last summer, you can have any male in our flock. Your fame has spread."

"I don't think I'm famous yet, Mom," I said. "But I did enjoy encouraging the others to join me at the wedding." Last summer, I convinced a large portion of our flock to help me with a grand surprise. On the morning of Grams' wedding, almost thirty birds joined me as we flew to the ranch just in time to complete a bluebird buzz of Grams and Willy as they kissed during the ceremony. First, we lined up on the fence, causing quite a bit of excitement on the part of wedding guests. On my command, we flew off the rail in a line, smoothly circling the kissing couple. The excited chatter of the guests told me that our efforts were successful. In a dramatic flair, we ringed the kissing couple a second time, beginning at the ground and spiraling past their heads before flying above the crowd, back to our meadow above Sinks Canyon. Maybe some handsome male in our flock would remember that event, I thought.

As my mother squeezed me close with her wing, I inhaled the familiar scent of her warm feathers. "I love you, Mom. I'll let you know when I take off."

Suddenly, a blue streak landed on the branch next to us. "Indigo. Hello. My name is Jasper. We haven't met, but I've heard about you. You know my sister, Betty," the handsome blue male said. I remembered meeting his sister last summer, but thoughts of Betty evaporated as I realized this guy was large and incredibly blue.

Drawn to his sky-bright color, I chittered, sniffing the vibrant air around him. He puffed up in pride, expanding his chest.

"I know where we can find some nesting boxes," I blurted, eager to show my willingness to mate.

He pulled back.

I've blown it now, I thought. Because I mentioned the nesting boxes, he was offended. I know it was because male bluebirds traditionally choose the nesting site. He can't handle that break with tradition, I thought.

"Leave the meadow?" he said. "Why would we leave this beautiful place?"

"Because it's too crowded," I said, trying to ignore the laughter of the other birds. Somehow, this had become a public event. Several other males and females perched nearby, Betty among them.

"I'll go with you," a firm voice announced over the laughter of the other birds.

I turned to see a brilliant blue male, somewhat smaller than the others.

"I'm Rock," he said, hopping next to me on the branch. "I'll go with you to see these nesting boxes."

Mother spoke up. "Hello, Rock. It's nice to see you. I know your mother, Jenny," she said. "Indigo, I'm going back to work, but let me know when you leave."

"Okay," I said absently, my gaze fixed on Rock. Maybe he'll accept me as I am, I thought. If he's willing to let me find a nesting site, maybe he'll even understand when I tell him about my adventures with Diana. The noise of the others faded away as I considered my new suitor.

The beauty of my father dimmed in comparison to this young male named Rock. I fluttered closer to him on the branch, soaking in the splendor of his feathers. He reached out one wing, gently touching the blue tip of mine, and I was overcome by blue fever. The sky opened with joy, and we took flight, swooping and diving above the pines. He's the one, I thought.

As he followed me over the meadow, I described the nesting boxes on the ranch. "Want to go see them?" I asked.

"Yes. Let's go."

When we arrived at the ranch, Willy came out of the barn. As if he knew Rock might not like humans, Willy remained a safe distance away and watched as I showed off the boxes.

"There are enough boxes for ten nesting pairs," Rock said, perching on the second box from the end. "Let's look at this one." Without waiting for me, he hopped inside the box.

I perched at the opening, watching as he inspected the interior. "What do you think?" I asked.

"Come closer so I can tell you." His black eyes contrasted vividly with his azure head, and I gave in to the lure of blue, joining him in the box. "We will raise beautiful and kind babies," he said, wrapping a sky-colored wing around me.

Comforted by the warmth and weight of his wing, I realized that even though I suggested we come to the ranch to see the cozy boxes, he chose the exact location of our nest. This is more like a partnership, I thought. I think we'll cooperate in our parenting, I told myself. Nestling closer to his body, I inhaled the clean blue scent of his wing.

Things happened quickly after that. We flew back to the meadow and called high and low for others to join us. Not everyone wanted to leave, but the overcrowded meadow convinced several young pairs of birds to make the move. In the end, eight other couples flew with us to the ranch, choosing boxes after we showed them the perfect set-up.

Ten days later, I was exhausted from sitting on the eggs for that long. Rock was indeed as solid as a rock, bringing me food many times throughout the day while I kept our eggs warm. When the first baby hatched with riotous tufts of feathers on its head, joy replaced my fatigue. Then the real work started as Rock and I tirelessly took turns scaring up bugs to feed our young ones.

By the time Diana returned from college at the end of May, the babies had taken wing for the first time, joining the other youngsters soaring over the hay field. The cottonwoods at the edge of the lawn provided a terrific landing point for the fledgling flyers. At first, they couldn't travel that far, but after several days, they made it safely from the boxes to the trees. After resting, we returned to the nest.

I flew to the deck and checked in with Diana when she came home, but Rock and I were so busy, I didn't even have time to stay for a visit. When Demeter came with the new horses, I realized I needed a break. Seeing Diana with the little ones sparked a pang of jealousy in my heart. Would she have time for me now?

My instinct to find a mate and hatch babies had eclipsed my desire to help Diana, but I felt that old urge for adventure coming back. "How can I help you this summer when I have babies to take care of?" I asked Demeter and Diana as we met on the bunkhouse porch.

Demeter sat in one of the green shell-shaped metal deck chairs. Because she was a goddess, she understood my birdspeak. "You have to make tough choices as a working mother," she said. "I am lucky in that I could take Persephone with me during spring planting."

"My fledglings aren't old enough to come along," I said. "And Mountain Bluebirds usually have a second brood, so Rock and I will be busy all summer."

"Come here," Demeter said, extending her hand.

I flew to her finger, and then her shoulder. "Does this mean I can't help Diana this summer?"

"We could find a way," Demeter said. "Remember how you helped your mother and father feed the second batch of babies last summer? You could ask someone in your batch to do that when they are old enough."

"That's true," I said. "But how can I leave them?"

"Maybe Rock could take charge while you're gone," Diana said. "One of the projects Artemis wants us to work on is transporting a family of beavers to a new location so they can create ponds to conserve water. We're going to be an unofficial arm of the federal government programs."

"Really?" I said. "How are you going to do that?"

"Zosime, the beaver we met in the mountains last summer, has been rounding up young beavers in her area. It's getting kind of crowded in her meadow," Diana said.

"I remember her," I said, hopping from Demeter's shoulder to the arm of her chair. "How are you going to move them to a new place?"

"Artemis is working on that," Demeter said. "Basically, we're going to carry them in a chariot from the eastern side of the Wind River Mountains to the other side of the Continental Divide near Green River Basin."

"The beaver transport will be only a one-day trip, so you wouldn't be gone overnight if you want to help," Diana said.

I know the critical role beavers play in any ecosystem. When they built dams to create a pond, many creatures benefited, especially birds. We caught more insects around ponds, and that's where I'd tasted my first mountain dragonfly. Delicious with crunchy wings. Double wings. Double the crunch.

"You could talk to Rock and see what he thinks of you taking day trips," Demeter said. "It's hard to be a working mom, and sometimes it takes extra effort from your partner."

"That's a good idea," I said, dragging my thoughts away from crunchy double wings. "I'll talk to him tonight when the fledglings are asleep."

"We're not leaving until August," Diana said. "So, you have time to work it out. Now come here so I can pet you."

I flew to her shoulder and rubbed my head against her cheek. I missed talking with Diana. We spent all of last summer together and being with her again reminded me of that. While Diana continued talking with Demeter, I relished the gentle stroke of her fingers on my back. After she sat in the chair next to Demeter, I hopped to her leg. Her fingers traveled from my back all the way to the end of my tail, gently separating my feathers in the way I loved. I forgot about my babies and Rock as I relished the moment.

"Let's take you to meet those fillies," Demeter said.

"Right," Diana said, interrupting her caress of my back.

"Okay," I said, opening my eyes. "I've never been around baby horses before."

"Well, they are cute," Diana said. "But they're going to be a challenge, I can tell."

"Hey, you're almost like a new mom," I said, following her to the pasture.

Diana laughed. "Maybe you can give me some parenting advice. Being their trainer is kind of like being a parent."

The small horses seemed large to me after Diana called them toward us. Glenda and Golden whinnied a greeting, and I flew to the safety of Glenda's back.

"This is Galene and Daphne," Diana said. They looked curiously at me. "This is Indigo. She is a mother also, so she knows how to take care of little ones."

"Will they fly one day?" I asked.

"Their wing buds don't sprout until they're six months old," Diana said. "Until then, no one who comes to the ranch will know they are flying horses."

We admired them until they started nursing again, one on each side of Golden. Watching them eagerly push against the mare's belly, I remembered my own duties.

"Well, I've got to get home," I said. "I'll talk to Rock and get back to you."

After saying goodbye, I flew back to the hay field, stopping to scare up some grasshoppers on the way. They were still small but would make a good meal for the youngsters. As I held one in my beak on the way back to our nest, I thought about the quandary facing every working mom and dad. I loved my babies but wanted to help Diana.

Would Rock cooperate? Would one of our daughters help feed the second brood the way I'd helped my parents? Am I a terrible mother for wanting adventure? I was counting on Rock to help me do the right thing, and tonight I would bring it up when we watched the sunset together while the kids fell asleep. I'd already told Rock about my adventures last summer, and I know he is interested. In fact, his calm acceptance of my experiences further illuminated his personality. He is as solid as a rock, and I am fairly certain I could count on him to support my efforts to become a working mom.

CHAPTER FIVE
TITANIUM AND COPPER

During the first week after Demeter left, I settled into a routine. Every day at dawn, I woke up and joined the horses in the barn, watching the little ones nurse while Golden and Glenda ate hay in the stall. Then I covered the mares with blankets to hide their wings and released all four horses into the pasture. Throughout the day, I completed ranch chores but frequently stopped to brush Daphne and Galene, talking to them and getting to know their every feature. I relished the pattern of our days, taking comfort in physical work and time with the animals. Each evening, I joined Grams and Willy in the house for dinner before returning to the pasture to put the horses in the barn for the night.

Early one morning at the end of the second week, noises from the barn woke me from a sound sleep. Jumping out of bed, I threw on a shirt, jeans, and my bamboo boots, and ran out the bunkhouse door as the sun crested the horizon, touching the barnyard with golden rays.

Who or what was in the barn with the horses? A mountain lion? We'd never had one come to the ranch, even though Sinks Canyon trails led from the mountains into the canyon. From there, any animal could walk onto our property. Was it a wolf? A bear? Those animals didn't need to come here in search of food when plenty of their favorite meals lived in the mountains.

I slid open the barn door and ran to the stalls. Empty. Was someone in the process of stealing the horses? Excited neighing drew me to the back door. I grabbed a pitchfork on the way out, my weapon raised high. Ready to kill, I ran outside, opening my mouth to issue my battle cry.

The scene in the corral on the back side of the barn stopped me in my tracks with the pitchfork raised over my head.

"Diana," a deep, resonant voice exclaimed, followed by happy greetings from Daphne and Galene, who rubbed their heads against the giant creature sitting on the ground in the middle of the corral.

Glenda and Golden were eating hay off to the side, looking up in surprise as I rushed out. Golden whinnied, ending on a high note as if asking why I was alarmed and armed. Glenda bobbed her head and resumed eating. In the background, birds twittered their morning songs. The fillies ran toward me, their tails raised high as they left their colorful visitor behind.

I stopped to pet them, and lowered my pitchfork, keeping a wary eye on the figure who stood up, brushing off corral dust. The horses were excited, but not afraid. Glancing beyond the towering figure, I spotted a black winged horse attached to a chariot, his nose buried in hay. Bright metal glinted in the sun.

"Who are you?" I asked, my voice more aggressive than I expected. "How did you get here?" I realized that was a silly question when he extended a hand toward the chariot. "Right," I said.

"You can put down your weapon." He smiled, coming toward me with a curious limp, made more obvious by his size.

"Hephaestus," I said as my brain registered his limp and enormous physique.

"I made your chariot, just as Poseidon ordered," he said, walking closer.

I instinctively backed up, reaching out to protect the fillies. They eluded my grasp and ran toward the god, obviously not in need of my help. They turned to face me, one on each side of him, leaning against his legs as he rubbed their backs. The little traitors, I thought. They were my horses, but I could see that they liked him.

His skin was the color of Grams' beautiful silver tea service which she displayed on a hutch in the dining room. Every few months, we polished the surface of all the items and the tray until the tarnish was replaced with a gleaming shine. Grams' grandmother brought it when they immigrated from Greece years ago.

"Keep this in the family," she said each time we polished the silver, reliving our history. "It's been with us for generations."

Hephaestus' silver skin was vibrant in the morning sun. Instead of a hard surface like the tea service, his skin rippled as it covered his strong arms. Brilliant blue eyes glimmered when he smiled.

"It's okay," he said, pausing a few feet away.

I realized I still held the pitchfork and put it outside the corral.

"Hephaestus?" I repeated, turning to face him again.

"Yes," he said. "I'm happy you recognized me."

I didn't tell him the limp was my first clue. I knew the story that Hera, his mother and queen of the gods, threw him from Mount Olympus when she saw that he was shriveled and sickly at birth. She later brought him back after learning of his skill at creating beautiful items like jewelry and fine silver flasks.

He became the smith god, crafting thunderbolts for Zeus, his father, and weapons for the other gods. Last summer, Poseidon told me Hephaestus would make a new chariot for me; apparently, he was here now to deliver the goods.

"This chariot is my gift to you," he said. Despite his size and strength, he looked vulnerable as he gestured toward it, seeming to realize I knew the sad story behind his limp. How could his mother reject her child? I shoved those thoughts aside, not wanting to embarrass him.

"It's beautiful," I said, surprised to see his silver skin turning copper, gleaming like the pots and pans hanging from racks in fancy kitchens in magazines. Shiny, warm, liquid copper. "Your skin changed."

"That happens when I'm happy," he said. "I'm honored to meet you, Diana of the Wind Rivers. I'm pleased you like my gift." He approached as I admired the smooth, silver metal rimming the top. "It's titanium and bamboo," he said.

The chariot looked like the old-time sleigh we stored covered in a tarp in the back of the barn, except this had four burnished silver wheels. Grams loved sleigh rides in winter, so Willy and Dad hitched the horses to the sleigh and we zipped around the pasture. Grams' laugh accompanied the sound of bells jingling on the harness, and she looked like a young girl with her red scarf and bright cheeks. I loved this winter ritual as much as she did.

Now, as I touched the titanium rim, a tingle of recognition shot through my arm, right to my heart. "What was that?" I pulled my arm back in surprise.

"Look at the front."

I did and gasped at the copper plate with an elk etched in darker lines on the left side. "That matches my flask," I said. Last summer, Demeter gave me a flask to hold *Aqua Pura*, water from the source of the Yellowstone River. Etched on the front was a grazing elk who looked up at me whenever I held the flask.

This elk on the chariot faced forward, but turned as I reached out my hand. "She knows me."

"I put some of your hair in there."

"My baby hair?"

"Yes. I saved some."

Demeter had also told me that Grams had given her some of my baby hair so that Hephaestus could use it when he created my bronze flask. I was horrified when I first learned about it, but now I was used to the idea that he used my hair to create magical things.

Hephaestus remained silent as I smoothed my hand over the copper plate, and we both watched the elk turn her etched head to sniff my hand. Then she faced the front again, a silent sentinel.

"There's another one like her on the other side," he said.

Glancing at the beautiful black winged horse who was still hitched to the chariot, I looked over at Hephaestus.

"That's Zephyrus," he said. "He's actually the god of the West Wind, but sometimes he takes the shape of a horse to pull Zeus' chariot. He agreed to bring me here. I'll fly home on his back and leave the chariot with you."

Zephyrus whinnied, and a strong breeze blew across the pasture. Farther out, the ranch horses began to run, while Glenda and Golden neighed. Daphne and Galene bucked and kicked up their heels. After ruffling my hair, the breeze dissipated, and everyone calmed down.

I looked inside the chariot. An olive green cushioned seat provided a convenient place for passengers, while the front section contained a step-up platform that would give me a clear view while I flew through the sky. Zephyus stood quietly while I got in. First, I sat in the passenger seat, running my hand across the velvety-soft bench. Although the chariot was small, the bench seat was wide enough for a passenger to lie down if they curled their knees a bit. Next, I stepped onto the raised platform at the front and picked up the reins. Zephyus turned to gaze at me with a questioning look, clearly ready to take me for a spin.

"Not now," I said to him, remembering that he was a god in horse form, and probably understood human speech. "This is beautiful." I looked at Hephaestus. "Thank you."

"The pleasure is mine," he said, extending his silver hand in an invitation for me to step out. "I enjoy creating beautiful things for you, Diana." His skin turned copper again.

"These elk on the front are wonderful," I said to cover up his shyness.

"You'll find they are as responsive as the elk on your flask," he said, his skin once again completely silver. "The elk is your animal and will help you in many ways."

"What do you mean?" I asked, removing my hand from the chariot to pat Zephyrus' rump. When he looked back at me, I stopped, again remembering he was a god in horse form, and deserved more respect than a rump pat.

"You'll see," Hephaestus said mysteriously. "It wouldn't be any fun if I told you everything now."

"Okay," I said, willing to let that slide. "Should I take this for a test flight?"

"No," he replied. "I'm headed back to Mount Olympus and Zephyrus has some wind things to do. I'll be back another time to find out how things are going."

"Thank you again, Hephaestus." I automatically helped as he began to unharness the flying steed. After we stored the chariot in a stall in the barn, I watched as he jumped on Zephyrus' back. The horse quickly trotted and then galloped before becoming airborne. Before I finished waving goodbye, he was a small speck in the sky. I walked back to the house to share the news of my new gift with Grams and Willy.

Later that afternoon, I asked Indigo if she wanted to join me for a test flight. She eagerly agreed because her partner, Rock, was teaching the fledglings how to catch bugs. Today, Indigo could escape.

We had a little trouble after we harnessed Glenda to the chariot because Indigo's babies wanted to go along, and she heard them crying to her. I put on my ring so I could understand what they were saying.

"They'll be fine," Rock said when Indigo landed in the chariot. "You go ahead with Diana. I'm going to teach them how to hover like a hawk and catch grasshoppers."

I could tell he was as kind as Indigo described, so I took off the ring, and we left her hatchlings behind.

I had a dual purpose for this trip: try out the new chariot and to see if I could spot elk on the Wind River Reservation. I hoped my necklace would help me find them.

I sang out as the chariot rose into the sky, and a number of meadowlarks flew up from the pasture to surround us on the sides and below. The flock blocked us from view, providing cover from any eyes. We were hidden in plain sight because the chariot looked like a flock of birds. Even though meadowlarks didn't travel in large flocks at this time of year, I figured anyone on the ground would see it as a curiosity, not something alarming. Indigo chirped at the other birds after flying to join me in the front, gripping the rim with her little feet.

We left the ranch behind. Skirting the western edge of Lander, we banked northwest to fly over the Wind River Reservation. I knew the elk migrated to the Gros Ventre Range, and we sailed that way. Flying over reservation land, I looked down to see we were already above Bull Lake, a familiar landmark.

Last night, I'd told Willy about the Wyoming Migration Initiative, a partnership between government agencies and the University of Wyoming. This spring at school, I'd learned researchers and biologists tracked the migration of elk, deer, and antelope to better understand the routes the animals traversed and to help educate the public.

"I think using GPS collars on the elk will help follow them," I said after explaining the initiative to Willy.

"The Shoshone people know that every spring, elk move from their winter range in the foothills of the Owl Creek Mountains on the reservation to their summer feeding grounds in the Bridger-Teton National Forest. The elk spend the summer eating sweet mountain meadow grass in the Gros Ventre Mountains. Others from different areas travel to the Absaroka Mountains," Willy said.

"I was in the Absarokas last summer with Persephone, and, later, Artemis," I said. "I filled my flask at the source of the Yellowstone River on Younts Peak."

"Yes. The Crow people call it the Elk River."

"The water from the source of that river brings great strength to me," I said, even though he already knew that.

"The elk is your animal," he said, nodding.

When I described the Elk Migration Initiative to him, he said,. "I've heard about this program. Even though our people know the migratory path of the elk that leave our reservation, it's a good thing they will use science to study it more. White people like to confirm what the Shoshone already know."

We shared a smile at his subtle humor.

***

As we travelled toward the Gros Ventre Range, I absorbed the new chariot smell, a combination of rich cotton fabric and warm wood stain in the sun. Travelling through the sky in my new gift, a delicious scent of fresh rain merged with the warm air, making me feel like I was racing along the road in a convertible on a summer afternoon.

A whinny from Glenda brought me back to the present. At the same time, the flock of meadowlarks flew away, revealing a broad meadow in the forest below. At the edge of the pines, a small group of elk grazed, looking up as we flew over. Glenda turned a wide arc in the sky and landed in the meadow. It was a smooth landing indeed. She is an experienced horse, and my new chariot proved to be an excellent ride as its wheels glided smoothly over the meadow grass.

We slowed to a stop, and the elk looked at us. Six females. And now that I was up close, I could see six spotted calves moving closer to their mothers. Even before I could finish sliding on my ring, one female walked forward.

"I am Diana of the Wind Rivers," I said after stepping onto the meadow grass.

"The elk have passed on word of your coming," she said.

Her little one hid, peeking around the side of her mother's tall leg.

"I'm pleased to meet you," I said. "Will you stay in this meadow all summer?"

"We have several meadows where we feed," she said.

By now, the others had returned to grazing and the calves began to nurse. As I watched, her calf began to nurse as well, pushing eagerly against her mother's underbelly.

"May I pet you?"

"Yes." She lowered her head and sniffed my cheek.

Stroking her soft, warm forehead, I admired her deep brown eyes. As she gazed calmly back at me, I was transported to another time and place, running along a riverbank. Hearing the soft beat of my moccasin-clad feet on the trail, I looked across the river to see a small herd of female elk keeping pace as I ran. Or was I keeping pace with them? It didn't matter. The wind blew back my braids and I laughed with joy at the strength in my legs. Suddenly, I returned to the present to find myself stroking the elk's head again.

The same experience had happened to me last summer when I met an elk in the mountains. This flashback to another time, this transport to another place was familiar. I inhaled and let the moment pass. "When was your calf born?" I asked.

"Some time ago," she said. "But we did reach this meadow before I gave birth."

"Do you always come to this place?"

"We follow the trails our ancestors have always used. We pass this knowledge on to our young, and in this way, we have survived in spite of humans."

"I know you are hunted," I said, uncertain about what else to say because my father and Willy hunted elk.

Across the meadow, the other elk walked toward the trees. "We're moving up the mountain," she said. "I want to keep up with them."

"Thank you for talking with me," I said, slipping off my ring when she turned and followed the others. I boarded the chariot, and Indigo joined me, sitting on the bench in the back.

As the chariot rose from the meadow, I again called for birds. A flock of Black-billed Magpies rose from the pines on the southern edge of the meadow, filling the sky with their raucous calls. We had plenty of these guys on the ranch, and many people didn't like them because of their obnoxious call. They appeared to be black and white, but, in sunlight, their wings and tails turned iridescent green and blue.

I had seen a flock of magpies one time before, years ago when Willy and I were walking through the forest on a pack trip. As we'd left the cover of trees and entered a meadow, loud bird squawks interrupted the silence. Willy paused and looked at me, and I knew that meant we should stop, listen, and look.

Ahead, just at the edge of the meadow, a large group of birds stood near a stream flowing into the meadow. I could see something black and white on the ground. We stood silently and watched as their cries filled the air. After the birds squawked loudly for about five minutes, the flock rose as one, soaring across the meadow. We walked over to see a dead magpie on the ground, its eyes closed, wings tucked near its body.

"That was a magpie funeral," Willy said. "They'll gather to mourn the loss of a fellow bird, just as we mourn our dead. Not many people have seen an event like this."

"Should we bury it?" I asked.

"Let's cover it with grass," Willy said. "His spirit is flying with the birds now, and its body will nourish insects and other animals."

"Will you say a prayer?" I asked after plucking meadow grass and covering the bird.

"Why don't you say one?" he asked, extending his arm to me.

I grabbed his warm calloused hand. "Please be at peace," I said, closing my eyes. "May your spirit roam free with the other birds." Then we were silent for a moment.

"That was good," Willy said when I looked up at him. "Death is part of life, Diana."

"I know," I said. "His spirit will be free."

Now, as Glenda carried us away from the meadow, I watched the jubilant crowd flying below the chariot. Once the usual jockeying for position was finished, they quieted down, with only an occasional bird objecting when another flew too close.

We progressed in comfortable silence, with only the wind and a periodic raspy caw breaking the stillness. I glanced back to see Indigo dozing in the corner of the bench. We were both tired after our adventures, and I was relieved I could trust Glenda to find her way back to the ranch.

When we reached the border of the Wind River Reservation, I noted the change in the terrain. Sagebrush-covered hills stretched for miles, reminding me of my first sight of the ocean last summer. Cresting and falling in broad sweeps, the ground below mirrored the pattern of ocean waves, expanding, rising, and cascading. From above, the grey-ish green sage looked small and close to the ground, but I knew from experience that it could grow to over four feet tall in some places, big enough to hide mule deer. The scent drifted in the air, reminding me of the sharp odor released when I crushed its leaves in my hand. Tender and tangy, the meaty leaves stored water. Although animals ate the sage, the real treasure was underneath because grasses and wildflowers nestled in the sandy soil below. Sage was the lifeblood of the west, providing cover for birds, animals, insects, and other vegetation. Willy had taught me to respect this plant.

A sense of peace filled me as I gazed east toward the Owl Creek Mountains. I thought about the history of the Eastern Shoshone people with a sense of hope for the future. In spite of all that the government did to destroy our culture, it was returning with the energy of young people who wanted to learn the Eastern Shoshone language from the elders. It is my culture, too, I thought. Just last summer, Grams and Willy told me that he was my real grandfather, making me part Eastern Shoshone and Crow, as he was. But it was still new to me.

A honk from above jolted me out of my reverie and I looked up in surprise. A large white bird flew ten feet overhead, carrying something in its mouth. A Trumpeter Swan. They nested in Yellowstone Park. I wondered why this one was here, over the reservation.

The magnificent bird looked down, keeping pace with the chariot. Moving lower, the swan opened its black beak, dropping its burden right above me. I automatically reached out to grab it before the wind took it. The bird honked and banked around. Looking down, I realized I clutched a long, graceful, white wing feather.

I turned to see the bird flying back toward the Gros Ventre Mountains and Yellowstone National Park. His wingspan was easily eight feet, and the pure white of his body gleamed in the sun.

Looping the reins around the center brass knob in the chariot, I examined the feather. A single white feather, soft and long. I wondered what it meant.

As soon as my thought formed, Indigo flew to the front.

"A white wing feather," she said. "Who would give up such a treasure?"

"A Trumpeter Swan dropped it on me," I said, gently touching it.

"I can't believe I slept through that," Indigo said.

"It's beautiful," I said. "I don't know what it means."

"I don't either," Indigo said. She sat with me for a few minutes, then returned to her nap. Holding the reins with one hand, I put the feather inside the special compartment in the front of the chariot. Before I closed it with a satisfying brassy snap, I looked one last time at the gorgeous white feather, fanned out and safe in the glovebox-like space.

With a contented sigh, I shifted the reins to my right hand, enjoying the smooth ride and the wind in my hair. Ahead, the Wind River Mountains waited as Glenda took us back to the ranch. I needed to process the meaning behind this gift. Maybe Willy and Grams could help me figure it out. Maybe I'm too old to always run to them with my problems.

"You'll need to tell Willy and Grams about this," Indigo said, returning to the front of the chariot as we flew over the boundary where an invisible line separated reservation land from the rest of the county.

"You're right. Willy might know what this means."

Glenda whinnied as she guided the chariot with her strong wings. The magpies remained below, hiding us from human eyes as we skirted Lander and continued the short distance to the ranch.

CHAPTER SIX
GRANITE AND GREENERY

A few days later, Persephone landed Hades' chariot in the horse pasture behind the barn, out of sight from the highway. I was intrigued from the moment I set eyes on Kya and Spruce, Persephone and Hades' young twins. Much like other gods, they were born as young adults, and it was jarring to see their maturity. Persephone hadn't come to the ranch sooner because she didn't want to interrupt my initial bonding with Daphne and Galene.

As I walked to greet the new gods, I was struck by how much they resembled their parents. Back on the ground, Kya looked around with interest. For some reason, I thought the girl would look like Persephone and the boy like Hades. But it seemed each child inherited the genes of the opposite-gendered parent. Rather than resembling her mother, she looked exactly like her father, possessing his angular features and dark hair. Her black, arched brows and delicate ears gave her an elfin appearance. Taller than her brother, she possessed Hades' blue-black eyes and bronze skin. The blue was more predominant in her eyes, and I noticed later that when she was happy, the sapphire blue of her name took over, creating brilliant blue eyes. Her jawline and high cheekbones reminded me of the first time I'd set eyes on Hades.

When Kya's eyes landed on me, I was overwhelmed by the feeling of the strength of granite and stone, and the trickle of ancient aquifers filled my head, the tangy smell of water on limestone in my nostrils. She was a creature of caves and towering cliffs, the very molecules of granite embedded in her psyche.

Spruce bounded gracefully to the ground, mirroring Persephone with his emerald-green eyes, brown skin, and black hair. His slender form, dressed in brown pants and an olive tunic, brought to mind a young sapling. Once his soft boots landed on the ground, he paused, observing his surroundings. His green eyes met mine with a direct gaze. This young god was different from his father and mother. I wasn't afraid of the power in his green eyes, but, rather, felt warmed with the hope of growing things and the energy of plant life.

Persephone enveloped me in a hug. "How are you?" I asked after she released me, referring to her difficult delivery. While I wrestled with an iceberg in March, she'd experienced a long and difficult labor. Her mother, Demeter, and Eileithya, the goddess of childbirth, attended her during the ordeal.

"I'm fine, now." She didn't volunteer details, and I didn't ask. "Kids, come meet Diana," Persephone said, gesturing toward Kya and Spruce. "We can think of her as your aunt."

They looked at each other before approaching. I was impressed by their manners as they greeted me politely, bowing from the waist.

"May we explore the barn?" Spruce asked, his voice deep and comforting. "Mother told us you grow and harvest alfalfa and bromegrass on the ranch. I'm interested in your process. My grandmother planted grass in mountain meadows around the world."

"I've seen that meadow grass, and I'd love to tell you about our fields," I said. "We'll all go to the barn so you can meet Galene and Daphne."

"It's interesting that you built so many structures using wood," Kya said as we made our way to the barn. "I build with stone and granite. How long does a wooden structure last? Mom said you have a stone fireplace inside your house. Could I see that?"

"Yes," I said. "What do you build?"

"She's still figuring that out," Persephone said, draping her arm over Kya's shoulder. "Both of the twins are discovering their strengths and passion while learning to control their developing powers."

"Oh?" I looked at Persephone. "Powers?"

"I'll tell you later," she said, looking over Kya's head.

"Mother is worried we're getting out of control," Spruce said. "I like to experiment with growing things, and Kya builds granite structures."

When we reached the barn, I paused outside the door. "I've told my twins you're coming today, and they're very excited to meet you. I've already completed my initial bonding with them. They sense my emotions, so be prepared."

I opened the door, and we went inside. Spruce looked up to the rafters, and then walked over to investigate the stack of hay in the corner of the barn.

"We've used most of the hay over the winter," I said, standing beside him. "It was stacked almost to the ceiling."

He touched one bale. As soon as his smooth brown hand connected with it, the hay turned green, sending roots out in search of soil. The roots turned to dust when he removed his finger.

"How did you do that?" I asked, moving closer.

"My plant power is strong," he said with a smile. He placed his palm on one of the giant support beams extending to the ceiling. I gasped when leaves sprouted from timber that I knew was almost one hundred years old. This barn was built by my great-grandparents when they first settled the ranch. He lifted his hand and the leaves turned brown, falling to the ground.

A high whinny from the stalls in the back of the barn reminded me of the twin horses. "Let's go see them. You can take them out to the pasture, and I'll put blankets on the mares so no one sees their wings."

We walked toward the large stall where Galene and Daphne stood with Glenda and Golden. The youngsters pranced around, eager to meet our guests. Pulling two lead ropes from hooks outside their stall, I opened the door and walked inside. They nuzzled my hand before I hooked lead ropes onto their halters. Turning inquisitive eyes on Kya and Spruce, my fillies bobbed their heads and whickered in unison as we walked out.

"Galene and Daphne, I'd like you to meet Persephone and her children, Kya and Spruce," I said, securely holding the lead rope of each horse. They felt my excitement at this meeting, their dancing hooves creating a little spring in their steps.

Spruce extended his hand for the foals to sniff. Kya followed. I appreciated the fact that they didn't startle them, but waited for the sniffing and prancing to subside.

"They're beautiful," Spruce said. He patted Galene's neck.

"Adorable," Kya said, rubbing Daphne's nose.

"They're so tiny compared to our horses," Spruce said. "Look at their wing buds."

Kya gently rubbed Daphne's neck, moving her hand to the small bump at the back of her shoulder. "We each have a filly to play with," she said, looking at her brother.

"May we go out to the pasture?" Spruce said, stroking Galene.

Two pair of brown eyes, one set of green eyes, and one of piercing blue eyes expectantly waited for my decision.

"Yes," I said, still not used to being in charge. I handed one lead rope to each twin. "Stay inside the pasture. I'll send the mares out." I picked up one horse blanket and handed the other to Persephone. "They'll keep an eye on the kids." I patted Glenda on the rump as she walked out of the barn, following the trotting foals.

Sitting on the bench outside, Persephone and I leaned back, watching the four new friends in the pasture. The twins removed the lead ropes, and the horses ran and kicked up their heels while Kya and Spruce chased after them. Then they reversed roles, and the fillies bolted after the goddess and god, racing across the pasture. Glenda and Golden whinnied nervously, and all four came back toward this end of the pasture. Kya jogged toward the fence at the base of Table Mountain, and the others followed. Persephone closed her eyes, the sun warm on her face.

"What is she doing?" I saw Kya bend down, grab some pebbles, and form a small pile at the bottom of the fence. She placed both hands on the pile, which began to grow. Soon it towered over her head. The pile turned into a wall, and, as she maintained contact with the stones, the wall grew taller and wider.

Spruce placed his hand on the surface of one large stone. Ivy sprouted from the cracks in the wall's surface. Bright yellow flowers bloomed on the trailing green plant. The wall formed two corners, creating a stall of sorts. Daphne and Galene trotted inside.

"Persephone, wake up," I said, shaking her shoulder.

By the time I looked up again, the three walls had become four, surrounding them all. The enclosure continued to grow taller, and I heard laughter and whinnies coming from within. As the stone shot upward, the sounds grew muffled. Out in the pasture, Glenda and Golden seemed not to notice.

"Persephone, help!" I jumped up and ran toward the structure. It rose above the barn. Somebody might see this from the highway, I realized. Worse, how was I supposed to get in? "Open up," I yelled, pounding on the stone. Glenda and Golden perked up their ears but remained in the pasture. Apparently, they thought we had this under control. I heard footsteps from behind and turned to see Persephone striding toward the new building.

She marched up to the now-impressive structure and knocked firmly on the stone directly in front of her. "Kya, tear down this wall. Spruce, stop growing plants. Both of you come out right now." She crossed her arms and waited.

A loud groan came from the stone. Fine dust appeared as the wall disintegrated, and the twisting, flowering vines dropped to the ground. With a final puff, the structure was gone, leaving a laughing Kya and Spruce inside the footprint of what had been a growing tower only moments before. They all looked at me in surprise, as if I had unnecessarily wrecked their fun.

"Children," Persephone said firmly, "no building and growing when we're on the ranch. Is that clear?"

"Why not?" Kya asked.

"It's dangerous. Remember, some of your structures have collapsed in the past," Persephone said.

"And someone might see it from the highway," I added. "We don't want anyone to come here unexpectedly and see the mares."

"Do you understand?" Persephone said sternly.

We both have youngsters to corral, I thought.

"Yes, mother," they said meekly in unison, but when they glanced at each other, I could tell they couldn't wait to do it again.

"Run and play with the horses. We'll be leaving soon," she said.

They all took off running, and the air filled with happy noise.

"They can do that all on their own?" I said.

"Yes," Persephone replied. "We're just now discovering their capabilities."

"They look like young adults. Will they keep growing older? Will their powers increase?"

"Well, we're not quite sure," Persephone said. "New gods and goddesses haven't been born in modern times. We're fairly certain they will remain this age, just like I remain my age, but we think their powers will evolve over time. My family on Mount Olympus is very excited to see what happens. These two seem to be able to control the physical world in ways Hades and I cannot."

"What does that mean?" I asked, watching Spruce run.

"We don't know yet," she said. "And now everyone wants to give them presents."

"I know Grams has been making a quilt for each twin. Not baby blankets, but adult quilts."

She looked at me and nodded. "Zeus wants to recognize his new grandchildren in some manner, and I'm sure it will be extravagant. Their birth has rejuvenated the gods and goddesses. Apollo is giving them harps. You know he's also the god of music and poetry."

"That's right," I said. "Nice gifts."

"Artemis is giving them moonbeams. They'll be able to call moonbeams to their side, even in the darkest cave," Persephone said. "But I want them to earn these gifts. You can't just hand things to kids."

"Right," I said. "I had to work while growing up."

"My mother has a special gift planned, but I don't know what it is." Persephone sighed. "And my uncle, Poseidon, wants to give them each a horse. It's all happening too fast."

"I know, right? I can't believe we're halfway through June already," I said. "When will all these gifts arrive?"

"We're still working on that. I'm trying to delay this as long as possible. Planting season takes up a lot of my time. I still have to help my mother. Do you like taking care of the fillies?" Persephone turned to face me.

"Yes, I like it," I said. "But it's a lot of work."

"Would you like a little help?" she asked.

"Why? Are you offering?" I took a good look at Persephone, noticing the tired droop of her shoulders and dark circles under her eyes.

"No," she said. "But I can offer help from the twins. They could stay here each day while I help Mom with planting."

"Why can't their dad take care of them?" I asked.

"His time is occupied by keeping the crust of the Earth intact," she said. "With all this fracking going on in Canada and the United States, he has his hands full."

"I don't think I can babysit your twins and mine," I said. "Aren't yours a handful?"

Seeming to hear us, the twins looked our way and smiled angelically. I knew it was a facade when green sparks twinkled in Spruce's eyes and blue daggers leaped from Kya's gaze.

"Oh, no, they're no trouble at all," Persephone said. "It'll be very easy. We'll live in the cave all summer, and every day, I'll bring them here on my way to help my mother with planting."

"No, I can't do that. What would Grams say? And what if my friends come to the ranch?" I shook my head. "I don't see it working out."

"Yes, it can easily happen. The twins will help you with the fillies. They'll keep each other entertained, and you can go about your business during the day," Persephone said. "I'm glad that's all settled. We'll be here at sunrise tomorrow morning."

"Wait," I said as she smiled brightly and strode off toward the chariot.

Ignoring me, Persephone called," Let's go, kids. Diana agreed to babysit so we'll come back tomorrow."

"No," I protested. But it was too late. The twins ran to the chariot, Persephone gathered the reins in her hands, and the horses trotted over the ground in the pasture, prepared for takeoff. How could she spring this on me and then leave? I vowed to confront her tomorrow. Then I thought for a second, and decided I could at least give it a try for one day.

"Goodbye," Spruce and Kya shouted in unison, turning back to wave at me. "See you tomorrow, Aunt Diana."

I was left standing outside the horse pasture, while inside, two very excited youngsters pranced around.

How was I going to tell Grams and Willy we had a stone mason and a gardener coming to the ranch every day?

CHAPTER SEVEN
GIFTS FROM THE GODS

The next day, I entered the barn and paused just inside the door when I saw Willy and the little ones. Morning sunlight poured in from the opening behind me, flooding the space with a warm glow and casting my shadow in front of me. Dust floated through the rays, kicked up by their hooves as the fillies pranced around Willy. Even in the confines of the barn, the sun highlighted their white manes and tails. High, happy whinnies filled the air.

Willy looked up and smiled at me but continued his play with the horses. Galene and Daphne trotted around him. It looked like they saw this as a form of tag. When each horse passed by, Willy reached out his hand, patting her on the back. When Galene eluded his touch, he laughed, and she whinnied in victory.

As Willy started a new game, I realized he was teaching them hand signals and verbal commands. He held up one hand and they stopped in front of him, one on each side. He dropped his hand and said, "Go," in a firm manner. Normally, Willy didn't teach our horses hand signals, but I liked the idea. What if I needed to communicate with them without speech sometime? It might come in handy.

The horses circled him, each moving in a different direction while keeping an eye on his movements. "Stop," he commanded, raising his hand, palm facing the front. When they stopped, their twitching tails was the only indication of their excitement. Finally, Willy grabbed each one by the mane as they faced me.

I could see they adored him. Willy's warm brown eyes pulled me into the circle of his love, and I basked in it, imagining that the way I felt must be the way a bear felt feeling the first light of day on her face after emerging from her winter den, holding her nose up, sniffing the air, once again above ground after a long winter nap, but now with cubs.

He led them forward, releasing them to me. They trotted the short distance, nuzzled my chest and waist, and leaned against me.

I laughed. "These guys are happy today."

"They're always happy," Willy said. "They're magical creatures, Diana. I feel their power. It's still undeveloped, and I don't know its full potential, but someday, we'll find out. Poseidon gave you a tremendous gift."

"I know," I said. "They sense my emotions, especially when I like something or someone."

A neigh from the corral in the back startled us. I looked at Willy as Galene and Daphne bolted toward the back door. "Wait," I shouted, but it was too late. They were out of the barn. I heard Glenda nicker, and the fillies join in.

Willy and I quickly followed, just in time to see a tall person step out of a one-person chariot.

"Hephaestus," I exclaimed.

"Diana of the Wind Rivers." His voice boomed across the short distance. His silver skin gleamed in the sun, turning copper as he walked closer, pausing to tower in front of us. "Good morning," he said, looking from me to Willy.

"This is my grandpa, Willy," I said. "Willy, this is Hephaestus."

Willy extended his hand toward the copper giant. "I've heard about you from Diana," he said. "The chariot you made for her is beautifully crafted."

"Thank you," Hephaestus said. "I'm glad you like it."

"What's going on?" I asked. "Is everything okay? I didn't expect to see you today." I was learning that he had a habit of showing up unannounced, which was fine, as long as nobody else was around.

"I came with more gifts," he said. "I know Persephone didn't want presents for the twins, but I brought something anyhow. I couldn't wait for the family celebration."

Persephone had said that she didn't want to spoil her children with all kinds of gifts from the gods. She also wanted them to find their powers on their own without influence from their royal relatives, the Olympians. Not even Zeus, their grandfather, had been allowed to deliver a gift yet.

Just then, a second chariot flew over the barnyard as Persephone arrived to drop off Kya and Spruce before going to help Demeter monitor the spring crops. Even though it was nearing the end of June, the young plants in the Midwest still required close watching. In addition, countless wildflowers and berries grew in the forests and fields, and those required attention as well. Demeter's bees were busy pollinating, and she monitored their health closely. The pesticides farmers used to kill insects also poisoned bees.

I could tell from the speed with which Persephone jumped from the chariot, leaving her kids behind to disembark on their own, that she wasn't thrilled to see Hephaestus here.

"Persephone. Sister of mine." he said, his skin turning a deep copper, somehow shinier than before.

I was glad Persephone slowed down and cleared the irritation from her face. He was so happy to see her that it changed her mood. She smiled and then glanced back to make sure the twins followed her.

Leaning down, Hephaestus hugged his half-sister. His skin retained its deep copper color, and then returned to silver as he stood, holding her arms. Her chin reached his chest. I admired the metallic-looking skin covering his muscles. I had expected him to feel like the tin man or a silvery culvert or chimney flashing, but I knew from our first meeting that his skin was warm and fluid.

They gazed into each other's eyes and then separated as Spruce and Kya approached, politely waiting next to their mother. "Kids, this is your Uncle Hephaestus," she said, clasping his hand. "Hephaestus, these are my children, Kya and Spruce." Taking a step back, Persephone watched as he smiled down on them.

"Greetings, Kya and Spruce. I come bearing gifts for you." After looking to their mom, who nodded her encouragement, the twins moved into his embrace. I was impressed with her willingness to accept this visit. She smiled at me, and I knew right away she felt as I did. Now that he was here, she didn't want to hurt his feelings. In spite of his size and metallic skin, we both knew Hephaestus was sensitive and kind.

"Hello." Grams' voice interrupted my thoughts. I turned as she walked through the back door of the barn.

Willy went to her and wrapped his hand around hers. "This is Helen, my wife, Diana's grandmother," Willy said.

"Hello, Hephaestus," she said. "Welcome to our ranch."

"He's here with gifts for the kids," I said. Persephone smiled at me, confirming that she wasn't going to object now that he was here.

"How nice," Grams said. "What did you bring?"

"You brought presents for us?" Kya said, too excited to remain quiet. "Are they magical? Can we open them now?"

"Hold on," Persephone said. "Let him give them to you first."

"Why don't we all sit down?" Grams said. "Let's sit outside the bunkhouse."

I knew she said that because the picnic table under the trees near the bunkhouse was secluded from the dirt road leading to the ranch. If anyone came, they still wouldn't see us, and the sun wouldn't reflect off the silver-skinned giant. Grams and Willy led the way through the barn.

When we reached the bunkhouse, everyone was already seated at the picnic table under the cottonwoods. I joined Grams and Willy on one side of the table, facing Persephone and the twins.

"I'll stand," Hephaestus said, too large to sit down.

"I'll get you a chair," Willy volunteered.

As he walked away, Persephone spoke. "Now, kids, I didn't want you to become spoiled by gifts from our family on Mount Olympus."

The twins dutifully nodded, but I could see Kya attempting to hide her excitement by folding her hands together on the table. Willy returned from the other side of the bunkhouse with a bench for Hephaestus.

When Spruce placed his palms on the picnic table, pine branches sprouted from beneath his fingers, the brown buds appearing at the ends just like they do when pines grow in the spring. The brown, papery buds broke off as fresh green sprouts formed. He quickly picked up his hands, folding them together so his palms and fingers didn't touch the surface. The greenery turned to dust, floating down on the table.

"What did you bring?" he asked while Kya brushed aside the green dust.

"I can't wait," she exclaimed. "We've never had presents from another god." She quickly snapped her lips together and smiled after Persephone shot her a warning look.

Hephaestus put his shoulder bag on the table and reached into it. "I love making gifts, especially for young gods," he said. "New gods haven't been born for almost three thousand years." We all watched his movements. "First, for you, Spruce, I have a special gift." He pulled out a long, narrow, green velvet box, extending it toward the young god.

I looked at Kya. She eagerly watched without jealousy. I knew it must be hard to wait her turn, but she looked at me and smiled with joy, happy for her brother.

Spruce's green eyes lit up as he reached for the box. Carefully opening the lid, he gasped as we all viewed its contents.

Inside, a small knife rested in brown velvet. Spruce carefully clasped the jade-green handle, holding it up for all to see. I inhaled at the beauty of the morning sun lighting up the olive-green surface of the knife handle. One beam of sunlight zoomed through the trees and landed on the blade. The silver glinted in the morning sun.

"What is it?" Kya asked. "That handle is Wyoming Jade. Dad told me it's a type of jade found only in Wyoming."

"A grafting knife," Spruce said softly. "I can bond one plant to another with this."

"It's a special grafting knife," Hephaestus said. "Normally, humans can only graft a tree within families, such as connecting an apple branch to another apple tree, or to a pear tree, because they are in the same plant family. With this knife, you can attach an apple to an oak. Or an aspen to a pine tree. Or a hydrangea to sagebrush."

"Why do that?" I asked. "It seems like messing with nature."

"I'll be able to grow unique and new varieties of plants," Spruce said. "I can even preserve a species that is dying out." Just last week, he told us, he'd spent the day with Demeter and Persephone as they began his training so he could help with planting in the future.

"Would you like to see it?" he said, looking at me.

I held out my hand. He reached across the table, extending the small knife toward me, handle first. It reminded me of the paring knife in Grams' kitchen. The jade was warm to my touch. Gaining heat, the handle pulsed in my palm, and I almost dropped it in surprise. "It's warm!"

"I infused the jade with the energy of growth," Hephaestus said. "Its power will never diminish."

"Should I pass it around?" I looked at Spruce, who nodded. I extended the small knife to Willy, remembering that Persephone told me the spruce tree represented constant, eternal life and was called the tree of birth. Spruce would indeed spark new growth with this tool.

"Thank you," Spruce said, looking at Hephaestus. "I love this knife."

Copper tinged his cheeks as Hephaestus said, "You're welcome. I'm pleased you like the gift. Beauty and function together as one." He looked at Kya and reached into his bag. "You have been very patient." Removing his hand, he extended a blue velvet box toward her.

Kya smiled at her uncle, her blue eyes connecting with his. Opening the box, she gasped, then removed its contents, holding up the gift so we all could see. A blue stone rested in the palm of her hand. As we watched, its surface changed from blue to black.

"A divining stone," Kya exclaimed. "I can use this to find minerals hidden underground."

"Exactly," Hephaestus said, his cheeks once again glinting with copper highlights. "Wherever you are, you can find what's underground or hidden in cliff walls. You can determine the content of rocks and locate gems underground. As a minerologist, you need to know these things. You never know when it might come in handy."

"Is that my power? Am I a minerologist?" she said.

"Well, I sense that's one of your strengths," he said.

"There must be some obsidian under the ranch," she said. "That's why the stone turned black. Does anyone want to hold it?"

I reached across the table, and she willingly placed the rock on my palm. I expected the stone to be cold and heavy, but it was surprisingly light. It turned blue again, the color of the Pacific on a sunny day. Then it changed to purple and then amber. "What's happening?" I asked, looking up at Kya, who looked at Hephaestus.

"It's sensing your power, Diana, and seeking a base color as it adapts to you," he said. "The only one who can truly make it locate gems and minerals is Kya, but the stone reacts to the power in others."

I passed the stone to my left, and watched it change colors with each of us. For Spruce, the stone turned olive green. Grams caused it to turn tiger lily orange, like the flowers in our yard, and Persephone stirred up fresh spring green tones. For Willy, the stone settled on deep red, like the iron in rock, and when Hephaestus had his turn, the stone became silver, barely visible on his palm.

He returned it to Kya, who smiled when the stone regained its blue hue. I remembered Persephone had told me the Greek word Kyanos meant deep blue.

"I have one more gift for each of you," Hephaestus said, reaching again into his shoulder bag. He glanced at Persephone, who nodded. He pulled two bronze flasks from the bag, much like the one Demeter gave me last year. "These will hold *Aqua Pura*, pure water from the mountains. First, this is yours," he said to Spruce.

"Thank you," the young god said. When he held up the flask, I saw a tree etched on the front, its branches reaching toward the cap. Suddenly, green leaves appeared, covering the bare branches.

"That's beautiful," I gasped. "It's alive."

Spruce placed the flask on the table, and the leaves puffed into dust. As if to verify my words, he reached out a finger and touched the front. Again, bright leaves appeared. When he lifted his finger this time, they turned golden and fell onto the picnic table, evaporating in a puff of gold dust.

Kya clapped her hands. "How clever."

Hephaestus extended a different bronze flask toward her. The surface was smooth, containing no adornment.

Kya carefully held the flask, first turning it to look, and then holding it up for all of us to see. "It's blank."

"You're still discovering your hidden strengths," Hephaestus said. "They will come to you in time, and the flask will form an etching. I don't even know what they are. Do you?" He looked at Persephone.

"I don't know," she said, shaking her head. "We just have to remain patient."

Kya nodded, but her face revealed her disappointment. Then, as if to brighten her spirits, the front of the flask turned a brilliant blue, like tile in an ancient villa. She gasped and smiled, pleased to see it reacting to her touch.

"Diana is also discovering her powers," Hephaestus said. "Yours will come in time." He patted Kya's shoulder.

"Thank you for the gifts," she said.

"I thank you, as well," Spruce said.

"Nice job, brother," Persephone said. "Now, I have to help Demeter. Want to come along and see her?" she asked, looking at Hephaestus.

"Yes, I'll follow you. I can only visit for a while, and then I need to get back," he said. "I'm forging extra lightning bolts for Zeus."

CHAPTER EIGHT
PANDO

"We're here, Aunt Diana!"

At the sound of excited voices overhead, I looked up just in time to see Spruce waving before the chariot disappeared behind the barn. Even though they'd been coming daily for several weeks, the young gods greeted me with new enthusiasm every day.

"Hello," Persephone said. "As you can tell, the kids are very happy about being with you today. I have a little time before I leave, so let's talk."

"Okay," I said. "I'll feed your horses." We led the horses and chariot into the barn and set them up with some hay. "This way, the chariot is hidden as well."

"Right," Persephone said. "Let's go outside."

I followed her, and we sat on the bench behind the barn. The worn boards provided a back rest, and I relaxed as the July sun warmed my face. Spruce and Kya went into the horse pasture, where they played a game of chase with the fillies.

"The twins seem more mature," I said, turning to look at Persephone.

"I've been talking to Mom about that," she said. "She consulted with Zeus because the kids have been learning so quickly. None of us have an answer, so we're just observing. But we do feel they'll physically remain forever young, as I do."

"They look like young adults," I said.

She nodded. "And they continue to work on their powers. We still don't fully understand what they are," she said. "Even though Hephaestus gave them gifts last month, we're still uncertain."

"Is Spruce able to grow plants on his own yet?" I asked.

"No. That's what's so curious. He can grow things from seeds and use cuttings from other plants, just like Mom and I do. You've seen him create live plants out of dead plant matter, such as bales of hay and old timbers. He's started to use his grafting knife, but just as an experiment." Leaning against the warm barn, she closed her eyes. "Tending the crops with Mom is hard work."

"Raising two kids must be a challenge," I said.

Opening her eyes, she laughed. "Yes, it's much harder than I thought it would be. But it's also brought us great joy. Especially getting to know them as individuals."

"You know," I said, "if Spruce could create plants, that could really help the planet. Could he grow an entire forest?"

"That's what we're wondering. He feels like he can, but anything he creates turns to dust after he takes his hands away," she said. "You've seen that happen."

"Right," I said slowly. "I never thought about having a god who could create plant life."

"We don't know for sure if he can do that, but it seems like that's where his power is. That would be amazing. Even my mother cannot create new life from old plant material," she said, turning to face me. "Imagine what we could do to help preserve water if Spruce had this power."

"That would be awesome." I stretched my legs in the warm sun.

"Next week, I'd like you to go with me on a trip with the kids," she said. "Mom and I are slowing down with tending the young plants, and she's giving me a little time off while she takes care of her bees on the Platte River."

"How are the bees doing?" I said. Last summer, I'd met Demeter on the Platte River where she kept bee colonies and sold honey at farmer's markets. I learned then that bees were in danger from nicotinoid chemicals used by farmers to kill other insects in an effort to improve crop production. Demeter was involved in a worldwide effort to save the bees.

"Her bees are holding their own, but farmers still use chemicals on their crops."

"So, you want to take a trip next week?" I said, returning to her original topic.

"Yes. I want to take you and the twins to see one of the largest living organisms on Earth," she said.

"What is it?" I asked, sitting up in interest.

"We're going to see Pando. I've been talking to the kids about it, and they're excited to go."

"Pando? I've never heard of it," I said.

"It's a grove of Quaking Aspen that covers over one hundred acres of land," she said.

"Whoa. That's a lot of aspen." I loved Quaking Aspen. In Sinks Canyon and on our ranch, groves of them dotted the hillsides and the area next to the river. Named for the way their small leaves shook in the breeze, the aspen turned brilliant yellow in the fall, a golden contrast to the green pines.

"The fantastic thing is that Pando is actually one large organism," she said. "Its forty thousand trees are clones, part of a unique network of trees, all connected underground."

"It's not a forest of individual trees?"

"No, all of the trees are clones of the original aspen," she said.

"That's amazing. Where is it?" I asked.

"Practically in our back yard, in Utah. We can fly there in one day," she said. "But Pando is dying, so we need to investigate. I'm hoping Spruce can lend some insight if we take him there, and we might get a greater sense of his powers. Are you up for a trip next week?"

"You bet," I said. "Which chariot will we take?" Inside, I welcomed the chance to focus on someone else's powers for a while, instead of my own. I still didn't know what they were, and I hadn't done much at all to save water on our planet since my trip to the Antarctic in March.

"We'll take Hades' chariot and horses," Persephone said, interrupting my thoughts. "It's large enough to hold all of us comfortably."

"You said Pando is dying? Why? What's wrong with it?"

"We'll know more after we go there. Mom and I have some theories, but we need to see it up close. It's been years since I've been there," she said. "We hope Spruce can help figure out how to heal it."

"I'm excited to see it," I said. I'd seen plenty of aspen groves, but never one so large.

Persephone rose and we walked to the pole fence encircling the horse pasture. Barbed wire surrounded the hay fields and larger pasture, but the smaller area next to the barn was enclosed in lodgepole pine, making it easier to train horses. Plus, it was convenient to lean on, which we did.

Kya and Spruce joined us. Spruce placed his hand on the fence, and branches began to form. I watched him caress the fence and close his eyes. More branches formed, sprouting new green pine needles. I gasped. This wood was old. Spruce opened his eyes and smiled, looking at me and then his mother. We watched the growth spiral up his arm, reaching his chin, where young, soft green leaves emerged, stroking his face. He laughed.

"Will it last?" Kya asked.

"I don't know. Let's try," he said. We watched as the fence pole continued to form new greenery for a moment after he removed his hand. Then it stopped, but didn't die.

"That's beautiful," I said, reaching out to the pole. "Can I touch it?"

Spruce nodded. "See what happens."

My touch must have been the kiss of death because the new branches turned to dust. "I'm sorry," I said.

"Oh, it wasn't you," he said. "It seems the new growth I create from old wood cannot live on its own. But I think one day it will."

"Don't worry," Kya said. "You'll get there."

"And next week, we'll see Pando. Mom just told you about that, right?" he said, turning his green eyes my way.

"Yes, she did, and I'm excited to go. I've never been there," I said.

"Plus, we'll see the Continental Divide," Kya said. "Rivers on the other side of the divide flow into the Pacific Ocean, and rivers on this side flow into the Gulf of Mexico and Atlantic Ocean."

"You'll be amazed to see that," I said.

"Yes," Persephone said. "You're going to love flying over the Rockies." She stood. "Let's go say hello to Helen before I head to work."

Every morning, Persephone made a point of talking to Grams. Demeter and Grams had known each other for decades, so it seemed natural that Persephone wanted to become closer to Grams. Demeter first came here when Grams took over the ranch after her parents died, at first claiming to be a tourist from California. Later, she revealed herself to Grams as a goddess, and they worked together to make Sinks Canyon a state park.

"Sure," I said. "Let me take care of the horses and then we can go. You enjoy the sun a bit longer," I said, climbing through the fence. "Come on, Galene and Daphne. Let's put you in the barn for a while."

Spruce and Kya followed as I opened the pasture gate. After we secured the horses in their stall, we left the barn and joined Persephone, who linked arms with Kya as we strolled to the house. Once inside, we found Grams and Willy sitting at the kitchen table.

"May I go look at the fireplace?" Kya asked. Even though she saw it practically every day, she still liked examining its construction. Made of small boulders from Sinks Canyon, the huge fireplace was a focal point of our living room. My great-grandparents had gathered the boulders from the canyon in the days before it was a state park. Nowadays, people weren't allowed to cart truckloads of rocks out of the canyon.

"Yes," Grams said. "You can look at it any time."

"We're working on polite conversation," Persephone said. "I want the kids to be able to function around humans without seeming too different."

"That's a good idea," Grams said as Spruce followed his sister to the living room.

"Look at this boulder." Kya's excited voice drifted to the kitchen.

"Helen, I have a favor to ask of you," Persephone said, sitting down at the table.

I joined them as Persephone described her plans for our trip. "What do you think?" I asked Willy and Grams when she finished. "Will you watch the horses?"

Grams looked at Willy, and they had one of those conversations without speech, looking into each other's eyes. I hoped I'd find someone like Willy, a person I could talk to with my eyes. I'd asked Grams about it earlier this summer, and she said they'd known each other for so long they could almost read each other's thoughts.

"We'd be happy to do that," Willy said.

"Thank you so much," Persephone said. "I've told the twins about our idea but said it's not a done deal until all of you agree."

Spruce and Kya entered the kitchen. "What did they say?" Spruce asked.

"It's a go," said Grams, standing up to hug Kya after she clapped her hands joyfully.

"There's Indigo and her babies," Spruce said, walking out to the deck.

"Hey, Indigo, want to go on a trip with us?" Persephone said as we followed Spruce.

"Where are you going?" Indigo landed on the railing and her five fledglings lined up next to her.

"We're going to see Pando, a huge grove of aspen in Utah," Persephone said, touching the head of the nearest baby bird.

"I'd love to take a trip," Indigo said. "But first I have to talk to Rock. I'm sure he'll take care of the fledglings while I'm gone. Come on kids, let's go see your dad." She flew off, followed by five obedient birds.

As I watched them leave, I hoped Rock would agree to our plan.

***

One week later, Persephone landed Hades' chariot behind the barn just after sunrise. I was already there, checking on the fillies.

"I'll get my stuff," I said, turning to run back to the house.

"Right behind you," Grams said, walking into the barn. "I brought your gear."

"Here's your bow and arrows," Willy said.

"Thanks," I said, reaching out to grab my backpack. Tucked inside was the bamboo and spider web rope Demeter had given me last summer, as well as my bronze *Aqua Pura* flask. I stuffed the pack in the bench under the seat and added the bow and arrows Artemis had gifted me with last summer. The arrows were made with Homing Pigeon feathers, so they magically returned to my quiver whenever I fired off an arrow.

"What about Indigo?" Kya said,

"Here I am." Indigo flew around the barn and into the chariot. "I wouldn't miss this trip."

"Good," I said.

As soon as we were airborne, a flock of Western Meadowlarks filled in the area below the chariot, hiding us from view as we soared over the rim of the canyon. Persephone directed the horses to fly southwest.

"I'll take us over South Pass City so we can see parts of the Oregon Trail," she said.

Spruce looked over the edge of his side while Kya looked down from in front. I scooted closer to the edge on my side, and the meadowlarks shifted to provide a view of the sage-covered terrain below. I saw the cabins of the historical gold-mining town. "We're right over South Pass," I said. "It used to be a gold-mining town."

Soon, we were above the Oregon Trail, deep ruts visible from the air where hundreds of thousands of settlers had traveled in the 1800s, searching for new land in the west.

A short time later, Kya turned back and pointed. "That's the Continental Divide below us," she said. "Rivers on the western side of the divide flow into the Pacific Ocean."

"Mom and Dad told us all about that," Spruce said as I nodded. "Pando is right in the middle of Utah."

"We're going to fly over the high desert area and then to the southwest corner of Wyoming," Persephone said. "We'll be in the air for about five hours before we reach Pando. Feel free to take a nap," she added with a smile.

I looked down to see Indigo had tucked her head inside her wing. "I think she was up early with her babies before joining us today." I chuckled and gently touched her back. She didn't stir.

"That's the Red Desert below us," Kya said, embracing her self-appointed role as tour guide. "It's a high-elevation desert."

"The main plant there is Wyoming Big Sage," Spruce said. "Did you know that it grows to over four feet tall?"

"I didn't realize that," I said, looking down. The meadowlarks shifted slightly, allowing me a view of the light-green and brown surface below. A herd of brown and white animals raced along the ground. "I see antelope."

"They're one of the fastest land animals in the United States," Kya said. "They thrive on sagebrush."

I laughed. "You guys are a font of information."

Kya smiled. "Mom wanted us to know about the area before we took this trip. Hey, look. That's the Green River."

I peered over the side to see water snaking through a broad plain, and then it was gone.

"Mom told us that's the major source of water feeding the Colorado River," Spruce said. "But the Colorado is drying up because humans pull too much water from it."

"Right," I said. "We really have to rethink how we use water in the West. People can't fill their swimming pools, water their lawns, and expect to grow crops in the desert now that we're in a megadrought. We have to rethink what we grow and where we grow it."

"Places like Pando can help conserve water," Spruce said. "That's another reason to keep it from dying." We flew in a companionable silence for a while before he spoke again. "Mom told me that trees communicate underground by sending chemicals to each other. Did you know that? They also send water and nutrients."

"I guess I didn't think much about that before now," I said.

"Pando has survived over ten thousand years on this planet," Spruce said. "His name means 'I spread' in Latin."

"That's interesting. I didn't know that. You think Pando is male?" I looked into his green eyes.

"I do. From what Mom knows, the entire forest was cloned from one tree. I want to understand the relationship all the clones have with each other," Spruce said. "Maybe I can communicate with him."

"This is going to be amazing," I said. "I've never seen any plant that huge and old."

"Me neither," he said. "This is an important day for me."

"I'm glad I'll be there with you," I said. We smiled at each other, his warm green eyes sparkling with hope.

Spruce was kind, thoughtful, and deliberate in his actions. I thought about the way he caressed fencepoles and old barn wood, seeming to appreciate the life once vibrant in the living tree. I'd watched him close his eyes while holding his palm against a spruce tree on the cliffs above Sinks Canyon, a calm smile lighting his face. His resilience in trying to grow things impressed me. I also knew he had a close connection to Artemis because the Greeks had dedicated the spruce to her.

"One day, you'll meet Artemis," I said, echoing my own thoughts. "She is powerful, but kind."

"Mom said we'll meet her sometime this summer," he said, turning to smile at me.

We flew for some time, only breaking the silence when we snacked. Indigo woke and joined us for lunch, gobbling up the honeycakes I crumbled in the seat between us. In the afternoon, the terrain below changed from sagebrush plains to green forest as we traveled straight south.

"We're getting closer," I said. "I know Pando is near forests in Utah."

Below, the dark green forested landscape had changed to the brighter green of aspens.

"We're going to land," I said, noticing Persephone gesturing to a small clearing below.

"We're in Fish Lake National Forest," she said after guiding us to a smooth landing.

Spruce started to rise.

"Wait," Persephone said. "Let's review the rules for this trip." She turned to face the bench where we sat, and Kya joined us. "What's the first rule?"

"Don't wander off," Kya said.

"Wait for you guys before running into the forest," Spruce said. "We'll stay together because we don't know how Pando will react."

"Very good," Persephone said.

Spruce bounded to the ground. "It's beautiful, but sad," he said. "I must find out why it's dying." He ran the short distance to the trees.

"Wait," Persephone yelled, jumping from the chariot.

Before she could reach him, Spruce leaned down to touch the ground.

"Why did he do that?" I said, jumping out to follow her.

"He's really excited to see Pando," Kya said, her feet pounding as she followed me. "He could barely sleep last night."

I reached them just in time to see Spruce lie down, poking his nose into the leaves on the ground. I watched, stunned, as he began to merge with the forest floor, which wrapped around his body. Persephone and I attempted to hang on to his shirt, but it was no use. I couldn't hold him. The last thing we saw was the back of his head as the loamy floor absorbed him.

"Spruce, come back," Kya yelled as she ran up. "Mom, he disappeared."

Persephone ran to the nearest tree, placing her palms against the smooth white bark. "Pando," she said loudly. "Release my son." Her words had no effect. The wind softly blew, and the aspen leaves rustled in the breeze, but Spruce did not pop out of the ground.

Shocked, I watched as Persephone placed her entire body against the tree, whispering against the white bark. Again nothing happened. "I need to communicate with Pando, and he won't listen," she said. "This has never happened to me. I can always talk to plants." She frowned. "I have to find the source tree. This is an ancient grove, *Nemus Antiquum*, and it's refusing to acknowledge me. We're on the far edge. I'm going to take the chariot and fly deep into the center to locate the source tree, the original aspen. Just as this is an ancient grove, the source tree is ancient, *Arbor Antiqua*. I might be able to communicate with it."

"What about us, Mom?" Kya said. "What can we do?" She wasn't crying, but breathed rapidly. Indigo joined us, fluttering around our heads. Kya tensed, and I sensed her panic increasing.

Persephone put her arms around Kya. "It's okay, honey. You stay here with Diana and Indigo, and I'll find out how we can help your brother." She looked at me over Kya's head. "You'll be okay here. I need you to focus and remain calm." She pushed her daughter away, holding onto her shoulders. "Can I count on you?"

Kya inhaled deeply and nodded. "Yes. I'll stay and wait."

"I'll be here with you," Indigo said.

"What should we do?" I asked.

"You stay right here in case Spruce surfaces. I don't know why Pando took him underground, but I'll find out. He could come up again, so don't leave," Persephone said. She got into the chariot and picked up the reins. "I'll be back."

Kya and I watched as the horses trotted through the clearing and became airborne. "Be careful, Mom," Kya shouted.

I grabbed her hand. "Let's go sit on the ground near the trees where Spruce disappeared. Maybe he can hear us talking or something. Indigo and I are with you," I added, pleased that the Mountain Bluebird now sat on Kya's shoulder, rubbing her face. We walked the short distance to where Spruce had been gobbled up by Pando and sat. I brushed my hand across the grass. "Spruce, come out," I said, even though I know it wouldn't work.

"The Ancients are stirring," a voice said.

Kya gasped and I turned to see a slender young woman in a white dress literally walk out of the tree behind us. One minute, the tree was smooth bark, and the next, a figure separated itself, moving forward.

"You're a tree nymph," Kya exclaimed.

"Yes," the young creature said in a smooth, silvery voice. "I am one of many nymphs protecting Pando. Sadly, we haven't been able to keep him completely safe. For over ten thousand years, I've done my job well, but now forces beyond my control have entered the ancient grove, the *Nemus Antiquuum*, and I need help."

"Did you take Spruce?" I asked.

"Did you take my brother?" Kaya echoed.

"Pando has taken him," the nymph said. "Pando is ancient, and he is stirring."

"What will he do to Spruce?" I asked. "Will he harm him?"

"No," she said, gracefully lowering herself to the ground next to me. "My name is Aspis," she said. "It means shield in Greek. I shield the trees from harm, especially when I'm inside them. The small trees aren't large enough to hold me, so I haven't been able to protect them from dying."

"My mother went to find the source tree," Kya said.

As Kya spoke, I admired the green color of Aspis' slender arms and their smooth, creamy texture. Her long, wavy hair was green and gold, a mixture of spring and autumn colors, highlighted against her white linen-looking gown.

"I rarely show myself to others," Aspis said. "But I came out today to reassure you that Pando is not vicious. He just needs to communicate, and he can do that with Spruce."

"When will he come back?" Indigo said, flying to sit on the nymph's shoulder.

"I don't know, little Mountain Bluebird," Aspis said. "Just be aware that he is unharmed."

"I'm Indigo," she said.

"I know who you are. *Tixi Pegos* sent the news that you are helping Diana of the Wind Rivers. Word travels swiftly on the wind and through the leaves," Aspis said, reaching up so Indigo could perch on her finger.

"And I'm Kya," Kya said, bowing her head in greeting.

"You are a strong young god. I sense the power of granite and stone within you. You are different from your brother. He connects with plants. You talk to stone," Aspis said.

"How do you know all that?" Kya said.

"Nymphs are quiet observers, and we sense many things. We are ancient. *Nympha Antiqua*," Aspis said. "Diana of the Wind Rivers is stirring the ancients."

Before I could ask what she meant by that, Indigo flew from her finger. "Here comes Persephone."

We all rose to our feet, turning to see the chariot racing our way from the center of Pando.

"Maybe she has Spruce," Kya said.

Suddenly, several things happened at once. The ground next to us opened to expel Spruce, thrusting him up from the ground, covered in wet ooze, appearing somewhat dazed. He shook his head and looked up, breaking into a smile when his mother landed the chariot.

"I spoke to Pando," he yelled. "Mom, I know why he's dying and how we can help."

Persephone leaped out of the chariot and ran to her son, enveloping him in a hug, in spite of the ooze covering his clothes and head. Kya joined them while Aspis and I looked on with a smile, but I couldn't avoid a small shiver as I saw the ooze spread from Spruce to his sister and mom.

CHAPTER NINE
THE BLUEBIRD REPORT
PANDO SPEAKS

I flew to Diana's shoulder and perched, gripping with my feet. As I watched Kya and Spruce hug, I realized I hadn't thought of my own little ones since this morning. Am I a terrible mother? My mom would probably say no; after all, she'd supported my quest last summer. And I didn't have to worry about my fledglings because they were with their dad, who was perfectly capable of caring for them. There was no reason to feel guilty about leaving them. At least, that's what I told myself.

"Yuck," Kya said as she separated herself from her mother and brother. "What is that stuff all over you?"

"It's gunk from the fungi," he said.

"What kind of gunk?" I asked.

"Before you say anything else, I want you to clean up," Persephone said. "Go to that stream and jump in."

"Clothes and all?" Spruce asked.

"Yes. I'll follow and help you dry off," she said.

"I'm coming, too," Kya said. "This stuff is gross."

Spruce walked into the shallow water and sat, then, at his mother's apparent urging, he leaned back and put his entire body under water. He suddenly jumped up, wrapping his arms around himself. Persephone waved her arms over her head, and Spruce's hair began to blow back. Whatever she was doing created enough wind for his clothes and hair to quickly dry. After watching from the bank of the stream, Kya jumped in, and her mom repeated the process. In a short time, they were coming back to us.

"That was interesting," Diana said when they got back.

"Mom made a warm wind," Spruce said. "It was really nice after that cold bath."

"I feel better," Kya said. "It was in my hair and on my clothes from hugging you." She smoothed her hair on the side of her head.

"What was it?" I asked, fluttering to Kya's shoulder.

"Weird, that's what it was," Kya said, jiggling me as she patted the front of her now-dry shirt.

"I know how it all works," Spruce said. "The centipedes use the fungi as food, and they also travel along the pathway created by the fungi under the forest floor. An entire ecosystem of fungi and centipedes exists underground, and the trees use it to communicate and send chemical nutrients to each other."

"But why was that goop on you?" Diana asked.

"The centipedes urged me to follow the path of the fungi so I could quickly reach the center of Pando because the original tree wanted to talk with me," he said. "The gunk helps them move along the path."

Persephone put her arm around his shoulders. "Are you okay? How was it talking with Pando? And why did you go underground?"

"It was out of my control," he said, looking up at her. "I wanted to lie down on the forest floor to be closer to the tree roots, and then the ground opened up and sucked me in."

Persephone faced her son, placing one hand on each shoulder. "Now that I know you're okay, let me shake some sense into you. Don't ever run away like that again, especially after I told you to wait for me." She shook his frame firmly. I could tell she was relieved he was safe, but still frustrated.

"I'm sorry, Mom," Spruce said, reaching out to hug her. "I was so excited that I forgot."

Persephone pulled him closer, muffling his voice. "I'm just glad you're safe," she said. "What did Pando tell you?"

"Wait," Diana said. "You mean the tree actually talked?"

"Yes," Spruce said, pulling back from his mother's hug. "At least, it seemed he talked. His voice came into my head through the fungi."

"Come on over here," Persephone said. She led us to a shady spot under the trees. "Let's sit down so we can listen."

As we all followed her, Spruce gasped. "A tree nymph."

In the excitement of the moment, I'd forgotten Aspis was with us. She quietly approached, her green and gold hair shimmering as she walked, while the sun highlighted her slender green arms. She bowed from the waist.

"Greetings, young god. I am honored to meet you. My name is Aspis."

He bowed in return, taking a couple of steps closer to her. "You're the first nymph I've met," he said. "I've seen others in Sinks Canyon, but they ran when I approached."

"Yes, my fellow nymphs are quite shy. Perhaps next time they won't run," she said, extending her slender arm to touch his shoulder. She jumped back in surprise. "You're very powerful, young god. I've never encountered this before."

"My grandmother is Demeter, goddess of agriculture," he said, standing taller. "Perhaps you have met her. And this is my mother,

Persephone, and my sister, Kya."

"Demeter has walked through Pando before," Aspis said. "You clearly inherited her power to grow things." She looked directly at Persephone. "This is good for our planet."

"Greetings, fair nymph," Persephone said. She bowed. "I am Persephone, Demeter's daughter."

"We are honored you have come to Pando," Aspis said. "We need the help of the gods, and the birth of your son brings joy to my heart. Pando is stirring, and change is in the wind."

"Come sit with us," I said, flying to her shoulder.

"I must leave now and check on the other side of the forest. I have a few young trees to comfort. They're afraid because many of their companions have been eaten by animals, and they don't know what to do," Aspis said. "But I will spread the word that the nymphs in your canyon can trust you."

"Thank you," Spruce said. "I'll mention your name and that might help next time I see a nymph."

She walked into the forest, her white dress blending with the bark of the aspen.

"Let's sit," Persephone said.

I flew to her shoulder. Spruce and Kaya sat on either side of her while Diana faced us, forming a small circle. Once everyone was settled, I flew to Kya's shoulder. She gently trailed her fingers along my back as I rubbed her cheek with my head.

Diana jumped up and ran to the chariot, returning with a supply of honey cakes, which she handed around. "Let's have a snack. I think we all need something right now."

Everyone said thanks and gave Spruce time to eat a few bites.

"Okay, Spruce, tell us what happened," I said.

Spruce swallowed the last bite of his honey cake while Kya held up a small piece in her palm. I gratefully gobbled it up. Such a thoughtful young goddess, I thought.

"As I said, I wanted to lie down on the forest floor and see if I could feel Pando's presence," Spruce said, looking around our small circle. "As soon as I was on the ground, I could hear his voice calling me, as if from a great distance. Then I felt the grassy area literally open beneath me. Someone tugged on my shirt, but the dirt covered me."

"That was me," Diana said. "I tried to pull you out, but the ground wouldn't let you go."

"How did Pando talk to you? He's a tree," I said. I flew to Spruce's shoulder as he talked.

"Pando is a sentient being," he said. "He told me that all trees communicate with each other, but it's rare for them to talk to other beings."

"Surely the gods can talk to trees," Kya said.

"I can understand them to a degree," Persephone said. "But hearing the voice of a tree is unusual." She looked intently at Spruce.

"It's like he was talking to me directly," Spruce said. "Do you think that's a power I have?"

"That would be exciting," Kya said. "I can't talk to rocks and stone, but maybe you can communicate with plants."

I jetted back to Kya and rubbed my head against her cheek. She was such a generous sister. She never wanted all the attention for herself and seemed happy to let Spruce have the spotlight.

"But how does he talk with you?" Diana asked. "He doesn't have a voice, does he?"

"The fungi and centipedes are key to the communication," Spruce said. "The fungi create long connected structures underground that act like a network of sorts. It's like a highway of information flowing along through the fungi's root system. Information travels much quicker that way than it does above ground. That's how he was able to send his voice to me."

"What happened next?" Persephone said.

"I somehow traveled along this fungi highway until I reached the center of Pando, the main tree, the original tree that cloned all the others over tens of thousands of years. After we greeted each other, he proceeded to tell me that he's dying because cattle are eating the new shoots."

"What about deer and elk?" I said. "They're pretty big animals and they come into Pando, too." I darted from Kya's shoulder to Spruce. He smelled minty and his shoulder was a bit bony. He was slender, while Kya was muscular. She wasn't stocky or overweight, but very solid.

Spruce yawned. "I asked him about that. He said that deer and elk graze in the grove, but they don't eat as much. In addition, cattle come through here in the fall and bite off the shoots just when they are getting ready for winter." He yawned again.

"I think we need to set up camp so you can get to bed early," Persephone said.

"What are we supposed to do about the cattle eating all the shoots in the fall?" I asked, hopping from his shoulder to his knee.

"Good question," he said. "Pando said we have to keep the cattle out of the forest so the shoots can grow. Right now, there are only old trees in Pando and very young shoots, which the cattle are eating. That's the problem. Nothing in between, which would guarantee the health of the grove."

Persephone said, "Let's set up camp and then we can eat dinner."

Spruce reached down and extended his finger so I could hop on. "Let's go help Mom," he said, gracefully standing while holding out his arm so I could ride along.

Soon a cheerful campsite nestled in the clearing, with one large tent on a platform that Persephone said she'd "found" in the forest. Kya set up a ring of rocks and Persephone started a warm blaze within it that seemed to pulse from the green stone she placed in the center of the fire ring.

"No need to burn wood when you're with Persephone," Diana said.

We ate soup Persephone prepared with water from the stream and dried ingredients she'd brought along. I even had my own little bowl which she placed on the ground for me. Spruce continued talking while he ate.

"Pando told me that part of my power will be to develop new varieties of plants," he said. "Remember my gift from Hephaestus?" He pulled his small grafting knife from his pocket. "This knife will allow me to successfully graft one species of plant to another. For example, if I need to create a plant that requires less water, I can graft sagebrush, which needs less water to grow, with another plant, so that the new plant has the qualities of both."

"How will you know what to do?" I asked, hopping from my empty soup bowl to where he sat.

"Pando said I have to experiment with different plants. I'll get better over time," he replied. "Great soup, Mom. Thanks."

I helped them clean up after dinner by picking up a few honey cake crumbs I found on the ground near the fire. The sun disappeared below the tree line and the forest became darker. A soft breeze whispered through the leaves on the trees at the edge of the clearing.

"We can all benefit from an early night," Persephone said. "I'll put out the fire, and let's go to bed."

"I have a couple more things to tell you," Spruce said. "Pando told me about a place called Fairy Creek Forest. Old growth trees live there. He said we should go visit because they know how to absorb more carbon than younger trees."

"And that could help the planet," I said.

"Exactly, Indigo," Diana said. "It's amazing the old growth trees hold more carbon. That means we should stop cutting down the old forests. Logging companies keep doing that, thinking it helps to plant new trees. We must shift our thinking on this."

"Right," Spruce said. "Pando wants me to visit Fairy Creek Forest on Vancouver Island and see how they retain so much carbont. We can learn something by going there."

"We'll have to go home first," Persephone said. "That's clear up in

Canada. Did Pando say this was an emergency?"

"No," Spruce said. "He said we could go anytime. The ancient grove, *Nemus Antiquum*, can teach us how to protect and store water. A logging company is trying to cut down these old trees, but right now protesters are preventing that. Pando said the protestors are doing a good job."

"Okay," Diana said. "Let's go home tomorrow and plan a time later when we can go to Canada and see the Fairy Creek Forest."

"Wonderful," I said, flying to Diana's shoulder. "I want to see a fairy forest."

Diana laughed. "We'll take you there with us."

"What else did Pando tell you?" Kya said.

"He told me that he's learned from the birds that humans are using too much water in the west. He knows about the drought and even feels it here," Spruce said.

"The birds talk to him?" I asked. "I didn't realize trees can understand birds."

"Pando has been on the planet for so long that he's learned to understand the chatter of birds in his clones," Spruce said. "He also said Diana is stirring the ancients."

"That's what Aspis told us also," Kya said. "What does that mean?"

"I'm not sure, but Pando is ancient. He feels the need to communicate with me."

"We'll find out more when we go home," I said. "Maybe Persephone can ask Demeter. She understands plants."

"I'll do that," Persephone said.

"There's one more thing," Spruce said, turning to his mom. "Pando told me that we can't keep growing things like almonds in California because they use up so much water."

"He's right," Persephone said. "Mom and I haven't been able to control human behavior, but maybe Diana can help us."

"I don't know how to stop that," she said. "People love their almond milk."

"We're going to find a way to work together and solve this problem," Persephone said. "I'll talk to Mom about it. We need your help to spread the word, Diana. But now, we all need some sleep." She leaned over the campfire and blew fiercely. The green light of the stone dimmed, and she reached down to pick it up. As she lifted the stone out of the campfire pit, it began to glow again, filling the campsite with soft green light. "Off to bed, everyone. The sun comes up early in the forest."

We followed her into the tent, and the green light illuminated the interior, revealing four soft beds covered with white blankets. "Bamboo blankets," Diana said with a laugh. I remembered last summer when

Demeter told us about the benefits of using bamboo instead of cotton because it required less water to grow.

"My mother's specialty," Persephone said. "Soft, light, and warm."

We all settled in, and I curled up next to Diana's head, resting on the puffy pillow she shared with me. As the others drifted to sleep, I heard the comforting gurgle of the creek coming out of the forest.

Listening to Diana's soft breathing, I thought about my fledglings and Rock. I missed them, but I also enjoyed being on an adventure with Diana. Was it wrong to change my mind about having children? All my life, I wanted to be a mother. The nesting instinct was strong in me, and last summer all I wanted to do was lay eggs and raise adorable baby bluebirds. Instead, I'd walked away from a potential mate in order to help Diana on her quest,. Now that I had a family, I wondered if I wanted to keep having two batches of babies in a row.

What if Rock and I had only one batch next summer? Would he be willing to fight against our nesting instincts, and, instead, go on adventures with Diana? Rock was such a stable force in my life.

What would my mom say? She did her duty as a bluebird parent by raising two batches of hatchlings throughout her entire adult life. If she objected, I could remind her that Grandma, her mother, had only one batch of bluebirds for several years in a row while she helped Grams influence people into turning Sinks Canyon into a state park.

I once asked Mom how Grandma did that, and Mom told me that she persuaded the entire flock to go down into the canyon often and make themselves visible to people. A few brave bird souls lost their lives because they were unfamiliar with the bird-killers, those things Diana called cars, that traveled on the highway which looked just like a snake winding its way through the canyon. Mom said that seeing Mountain Bluebirds in Sinks Canyon helped convince humans that it was a special place.

As the murmuring of the forest stream lulled me to sleep, I realized what was wrong. I kept trying to separate my life into categories: life with Rock and life with Diana. Rock versus Diana. It shouldn't be that way. I opened my eyes, listening again to the stream whisper over the rocks. I needed to merge these two areas of my life, not separate them.

I knew how to do that. I'd tell Diana that I wanted Rock to see the River Oceanus and the Birds of Dawn. If Rock saw pure water at its source, he would understand my desire to help Diana protect clean water on the planet. With a happy sigh, I closed my eyes, mentally thanking the babbling brook for helping me figure out what was wrong and how to fix it.

CHAPTER TEN
A COLD HEART

We settled into our routines on the ranch by the third day after returning from Pando. Indigo was back with Rock and her fledglings, Persephone monitored crops with her mom, and the twin gods and I spent our days together. I was glad to be home again.

As I left the bunkhouse in the early morning sun, I called out to the fillies. Excited neighs greeted me as I walked into the barn. We kept them inside during the night just in case. In case of what, I'm not sure, but it made me sleep easier, knowing they were safe in their stalls with the palomino mares.

After leading them to the pasture, I watched the little ones run after their moms, who trotted to join the other horses. By now, our string of riding and pack horses accepted the winged ones. I figured the horse blankets concealing their wings helped.

I secured the gate and leaned against the railing of the corral. Inhaling the fresh scent of morning dew on the pasture grass, I closed my eyes and relaxed. Persephone would be arriving soon, so I had a few minutes of peace. Even though I loved watching the twins all day, it was nice to have the corral and morning sunshine to myself. Grams was in the house, and once Kya and Spruce arrived, we'd go inside for breakfast, our normal morning routine.

A loud beating of wings and an obnoxious squawk interrupted my quiet reverie. I opened my eyes to see a large magpie sitting on the fence next to me. It squawked as if trying to tell me something. Figuring I had no time to call Indigo to translate, I pulled the necklace from under my shirt and removed my moonstone ring. Putting it on, I looked at the magpie, who was eye level with me on the fence railing.

"What's going on?" I said. "Is something wrong?"

The magpie bowed his head and extended one wing to the side and back in a dramatic gesture. "Hello, Diana of the Wind Rivers. I'm Jones, an American Magpie."

"Hello, Jones. I see you know my name. I'm pleased to meet you." I bowed my head in a solemn gesture, sensing this bird wanted a formal greeting.

"I have heard about you, Diana of the Wind Rivers," he said, looking at me with dark brown eyes. As he came a few steps closer, the morning sun caressed his black back, turning the feathers brilliant blue-green.

"You really are quite beautiful," I said, knowing he would appreciate my comment. Most people in the west hated magpies because they were scavenger birds who hung around ranches, swooping down, stealing bright objects, and making lots of obnoxious raspy squawking noises. However, I found them attractive birds with their black bodies and wings, which turned iridescent green in the sun, highlighted by the white on their wingtips and backs.

"Thank you, Diana," Jones said with another polite bow. He regarded me with solemn eyes. "I am here on an urgent errand."

"What?" I asked.

"Tixi needs your help."

"Tixi? On Younts Peak?" I was surprised.

"Yes. She sent me with an important request. She wants you to come today and help her," Jones said.

"With what?" I asked, mentally rearranging my day. Persephone would be here soon with the twins, so I'd have to see if they could hang out with Grams today.

"She needs help with a glacier nymph in Montana."

"At Glacier National Park?"

"Yes." Jones leaned down to preen his chest. Then he swiped his bill twice across the fence rail.

"What's wrong?" I asked. I'd have to take my chariot and leave right away, I realized.

"I don't know all the details," he said. "I was told to come here and relay the message. But she wants you to come as soon as possible."

"How did you get here so early in the morning? That's such a long way."

"We had a messenger chain going. Other birds flew all night long. I was the last bird on the chain, and I've been flying by the light of the moon."

"Okay, you can relay the message back that I'll be there today. I just have to take care of a couple of things and then I can take off," I said. I knew it must be serious if Tixi wanted me there immediately.

"I'm going to fly back and start the reverse message chain," he said. "But first, I need to eat something."

"I've heard from other birds that our grasshoppers are very sweet," I said, thinking about how much Indigo liked the grasshoppers in our fields. I knew it was because insects ate the grass that we irrigated with pure mountain water.

"I see some now," Jones said, spreading his wings. "I'll grab a few of those little goodies and then be on my way." He flew off with a squawk.

I returned the ring to my necklace and hurried into the house to talk to Grams. By the time Persephone arrived with the twins, I was already in the barn, hitching Glenda to my chariot. Golden would stay with the little horses while I flew to help Tixi on Younts Peak.

"Diana, we're here." Kya's excited voice told me they had arrived.

"I'm in here," I said loudly.

"What's going on?" Persephone asked as she followed Kya and Spruce into the barn and automatically started helping me with the harness.

"I've had a messenger magpie tell me Tixi needs my help. I'm leaving right now, so Grams will hang out with you guys today," I explained, looking up at Kya and Spruce, who stood near Glenda's head. I filled them in on the details as they followed me back into the warm sun.

"Can we go with you?" Spruce said.

"No," I said. "I have to hurry, and I don't know exactly why she needs my help. It's something to do with a glacier nymph in Montana."

"Okay," Spruce said after a stern look from Persephone.

"We'll be waiting for you," Kya said. "It must be very serious if she wants you right away."

"That's what I thought," I said. By now, Grams was down at the barn, and they all followed as I led Glenda into the horse pasture, where we had room to make a running start and fly off.

Suddenly, Indigo flew up and landed on the chariot. "What's happening?" she said. "Where are you going?"

I quickly explained and added, "I wish you could come, Indigo, but I have to leave right now, and I don't know how long I'll be gone."

"That's okay. I understand," she said. But I could tell she was a little sad she couldn't just take off with me. "I have to stay here with Rock and the kids anyhow."

"You're a good mom, Indigo," I said. "We'll go on more adventures together this summer."

"Be careful," Indigo said. She flew to my shoulder and touched her head to my cheek before flying to Kya.

"Take care," Grams said, hugging me. I'd already stashed my gear in the bench seat: my bamboo and spider web rope, my flask with *Aqua Pura*, and, to be safe, my *Aqua Fortis* flask as well. I hung my bow and arrows over my shoulder and pushed them toward my back. I wanted to keep them close.

Soon we were airborne, and I curved the chariot around to fly north and slightly west.

Throughout the morning, a flock of Western Meadowlarks screened my progress through the sky. Only once during the flight did I leave the front of the chariot, going to retrieve my flask and some honey cakes.

At midday, I arrived at the base of Younts Peak. At this point in the summer, the glacial runoff still trickled to the tarn. As soon as my feet touched the grass, Tixi appeared.

In the winter, Tixi's periwinkle skin, blue with hints of lavender, gleamed against the snow as her ice wings carried her across the glacier. Now that summer was here, Tixi's ice wings had melted and her winter periwinkle skin had turned a lovely moss green for the summer, which helped her blend in as she ran with tree nymphs through the forests and mountain meadows.

"I'm here," I said, realizing I was stating the obvious. "What's wrong?"

"Poseidon and I decided to abandon some glaciers that are dying," she said. "But that's created a problem we didn't anticipate."

"You're abandoning the glaciers?" I said. I faced *Tixi Pagos*, Guardian of the Headwaters. This *Aqua Pura* on Younts Peak, the headwaters of the Yellowstone River, which the Eastern Shoshone and Crow people call the Elk River, was the source of my power.

"We're not leaving all of the glaciers," Tixi said. "Just the ones we can't save."

"What?" I heard the alarm in my voice.

"Some glaciers are beyond the point of return," she said.

"What do you mean?" I said, automatically smoothing my hand down Glenda's neck before moving closer to Tixi. I realized I always touched the nearest horse in times of stress.

"When a glacier diminishes in size to a certain point, glacier nymphs can't prevent the final meltdown," she said. "This depletion is happening in several places around the world, so we're doubling up on glacial guardians in the places we can still save."

"You and Poseidon made this decision?" I asked. My brain seemed to have trouble processing this information. Things were happening too fast.

"He actually came here," she said. "He doesn't like to leave the warmth of the ocean for a visit to glaciers, but he had no choice. I'm one of the oldest nymphs on this continent, so he came to discuss this idea with me."

"But it's horrible to think you guys are just giving up," I said. "We need to protect them."

"We don't have much choice with some glaciers," Tixi said.

"Isn't there anything Poseidon can do?"

"Yes, he does have some ideas. One thing he's doing is working with the merfolk to create a seaweed film that we can place over glaciers."

"How will that help?" I said.

"The film coats the glacier and delays melting for a while. It will at least give us some time to develop other solutions. Plus, the film might keep microplastics from drifting down on the glaciers."

"So the two of you have decided to focus on certain glaciers?"

"Yes," Tixi said. "We're actually relocating an additional nymph to help me because the Yellowstone is that important."

"The longest free-flowing river in the continental United States," I said, reciting what I'd learned from Persephone last summer. Listening to Tixi, I realized how hard it must be for the glacial nymphs to leave their mountaintops, knowing the glacier they'd nurtured for tens of thousands of years—or more—was going to die alone.

"They can't even remain behind to lament the passing of their glaciers," Tixi said, seeming to read my thoughts. "They can't ease their grief with hot tears, which would also hasten the passing of the glacier, and thus reduce its suffering. So we have to secure the future of as many glaciers as we can." She sighed. "But we've encountered serious problems that I didn't anticipate. It was my idea to concentrate on glaciers we can save, and Poseidon agreed. We sent bird messengers to mountaintop glaciers around the globe so the others could learn about our decision."

"What did the others say?" I asked.

"Almost everyone agreed, but some glacier nymphs are having a lot of trouble leaving their glaciers. Think about it. For tens of thousands of years, nymphs have successfully built up and protected glaciers. Now they must abandon their life's work. It's causing severe mental health issues. That's why I need your help."

"Why didn't you think about their grief?" I asked. Last summer, I'd finally come to terms with my grief over my mother's death, but the process had taken years. "How can you expect them to just give up on their glaciers?"

"I was so focused on duty," Tixi said, "that I didn't think about their feelings, and Poseidon is a god. He doesn't understand."

"What can I do?" I asked. I wondered if I were up to the task. How could I, a college kid, help nymphs, creatures thousands of years old?

"Well, because my ice wings have melted, I can't get around as I do in the winter," Tixi said. "I want you to help me with the Guardian of the Headwaters in Glacier National Park in Montana."

"I've been there," I said. "My family took a trip there when I was in high school."

Tixi nodded, her moss green face highlighting her cerulean blue eyes, the exact color of Indigo's wingtips and tail feathers. "The nymph's name is Caligo. We've realized that the melting on her glaciers can't be stopped. They've depleted to point of no return, and without colder weather and more snow, they won't be replenished."

"And she's having trouble coping with the loss?" I remembered reading headlines stating that scientists had determined they could not save the glaciers in that park. I couldn't save my mother when she drowned, either. I knew how Caligo must feel.

"Yes," Tixi said. "I haven't been up there, but my bird messengers tell me Caligo is inconsolable and refuses to leave her glaciers."

"She has more than one?"

"Yes," Tixi said. "That area has been so cold for so long that we didn't require more glacier nymphs up there. After over seven thousand years, she won't leave. We reassigned her to come work with me, but she wouldn't come this past winter when she still had wings to fly. And now her wings have melted for the summer."

"What can we do?" I asked.

"I want you to pick her up. She's very light, so you can easily bring her back here in the chariot."

"Right now?" I said. Everything was moving too fast. "I should tell Grams I won't be home right away."

"We don't have time for that. I'm very concerned about her state of mind. I'm worried she'll dive right off the cliff because she can't bear to watch her glacier die. I've already had some nymphs in other parts of the world do that," Tixi said, shaking her head.

"What do you mean?" I asked.

"Well, in the winter, we enjoy a good game of cliff-diving. With our ice wings, we can fly off our cliffs and take a nosedive down the side, pulling ourselves up before we reach the ground. It's very fun, but it is dangerous."

"Have you done that?" I said. Now that she described it, I could easily envision this daredevil side of Tixi.

"When I was younger, I was the best cliff diver around," Tixi said with a smile. "These days, I leave that sort of activity for the younger nymphs. By the time you've been around for ten thousand years, it just doesn't give the thrill it did when you were young."

"I'm glad you gave up cliff diving," I said. "But do you mean nymphs are cliff diving in the summer instead of running through the forest with the wood nymphs?"

"Yes," Tixi said. "Rather than watch their glaciers die, a few nymphs have chosen to dive to their deaths. We live long lives, but we are not immortal. Caligo says she is going to dive because she can't save her glacier."

"Oh, no." I said. "You mean they deliberately end their own lives?" I'd never known anyone who'd done that.

"Yes," she said. "The isolation of glacier life and the feeling of doom brought on by the inability to stop the melting causes deep depression, resulting in a total loss of hope. Some glacier nymphs would rather die suddenly than watch the slow, torturous melting of their glaciers."

"We can't lose hope," I said. "We have to believe we can save pure water. I want to help. Your plan seems to be a good one, trying to save what can be salvaged."

"Even if Caligo refuses to leave, you have to pick her up. She might argue or refuse, but just bring her here, whatever it takes," Tixi said. "I'm very worried about her."

"The question is, do we give up in the face of despair, or fight to save the glaciers?" I didn't realize I'd spoken out loud.

"I think the birth of new gods and the emergence of Diana of the Wind Rivers creates hope for the future," Tixi said. "Poseidon and I agree we can still salvage something from this tragic mess."

"Why me?" Even as I boarded the chariot, I was still unsure that I was up to this task.

"You've experienced grief at one of its highest levels," she said. "You have a strong sense of empathy. You will be sensitive to her frailty in a way the gods can't."

"Is that part of my power?" I said.

"The whole planet is grieving," she said. "Empathy can be powerful, and you know how to use it with all creatures."

"Just like all living things deserve clean water, they also deserve empathy and understanding," I said.

"Well said," Tixi added.

"I'll go right away." I picked up the reins.

"Thank you," Tixi said. "The birds tell me Caligo seems more desolate every day."

"I'll bring her back," I promised, remembering how Persephone had helped me with my grief last summer.

"I'll be waiting," Tixi said.

Glenda trotted forward as I waved goodbye. When we became airborne, a flock of Western Meadowlarks surrounded us, obscuring Tixi from my view as we flew north toward Montana and Glacier National Park. As the wind ruffled my hair, I wondered if we'd arrive in time to prevent Caligo from taking her final deadly dive.

CHAPTER ELEVEN
GLACIER NO MORE

When I reached the cliffs of Glacier National Park, I scanned the area, looking for the nymph. At first, all I saw was tall grey granite spiking into the sky. Starting at the base of the cliff, what looked like a river of dirty snow snaked around the bottom, snuggling up against the rocks. The river of ice curved down the valley, literally flowing away from the cliff. It abruptly stopped, and I knew from before and after photos I had seen in articles that this glacier used to be much larger. It was, indeed, receding beyond the point of no return. Coming closer, I saw rough spikes of snow protruding upward.

I'd forgotten to ask Tixi what the Glacier National Park nymph looked like, but I soon spotted her at the top of the cliff, mostly because her bright orange hair stood out against the surrounding grey rock. I called her name, but she didn't look up. She appeared mesmerized by the dirty glacier below. She leaned forward, her head over the edge of the cliff.

Before I could stop her, she dove headfirst. Her bright orange head leading the way, she pressed her arms to her sides, looking like an orange-tipped bullet.

"Glenda," I shouted, "take me to Caligo,"

Faster than I thought possible, we were suspended just above the glacier, waiting for the bullet to hit.

I looked up to see the orange tip headed my way. Without thinking, I held out my arms. At the speed she was traveling, I had no idea if I could stop Caligo's progress. All I could do was hold out my arms and hope. Please, Artemis, help me catch her, I thought.

As if in response to my plea, my elk tooth necklace grew warm against my skin, sending a glow of strength through my arms. I closed my eyes, not wanting to see what would happen when the orange-haired nymph crashed into me. Although I was expecting the worst, all I felt was a soft breeze pass by my face as a feather-light weight landed on my outstretched arms.

Opening my eyes, I looked down. Caligo's eyes were closed, and her skin was cold. Curly hair hung limply against her aquamarine face.

"Glenda, back to the clifftop," I whispered, looking down at the ethereal creature in my arms. She felt solid, but effervescent, like bubbles floating in champagne. When we landed at the top of the cliff, I carried her out of the chariot and sat carefully on the ground.

At first, all I did was hold Caligo in my arms. Her body jerked as if she were sobbing, but without sound or tears. I held on, pouring my heart into hers, silently beseeching her to accept my sympathy. Finally, her body stilled, she opened her eyes, and began to talk.

"Glacier nymph tears reduce pain and improve mood," Caligo said.

"Even though you've been sobbing, you haven't cried tears," I said.

"Tixi told me I didn't have time to cry for the loss of my glacier. She wouldn't allow me to mourn because she knows I'll want to stay for a year or more until it dies. But, if I eventually cry, my tears will literally ease my glacier's suffering. Both of us will feel better," she said, sitting up after I gently set her on the ground.

We sat side by side, but I kept my arm around her shoulders, looking down at her face. "Maybe she's just worried about you being here alone and ending your life."

Caligo said nothing.

"Why did you decide to dive off the cliff?"

"If I can't save my glacier, I see no reason to live," she said. "It's reached the point of no return, and so have I. Nothing I do will stop the receding, and it will melt away. I cannot bear to see that happen."

Rimmed by a black circle, her irises were the most brilliant aquamarine I had ever seen. Her eyes implored me to understand, and I felt her begin to accept my sympathy.

"Legends say our names indicate our final state on Earth," she said.

"What does your name mean?"

"Caligo is Latin for mist," she said, shrugging. "I can think of worse ways to die."

"You're still needed. You can't die."

"Tixi wants me to leave my glacier before I can cry to ease its suffering. All it takes is a few of my tears to ease the pain and hasten its melting," she said, glancing from me toward the edge of the cliff. "My tears of grief are immensely hot and will burn permanent tear tracks onto my face. All nymphs who meet me thereafter will bow in respect for my great loss."

"Haven't glaciers melted before?" I asked.

"Not since the end of the last ice age," she said. "The tracks will be a symbol of my suffering and the tragic loss of an ancient glacier, *Glaciarium Antiquuum*. I want to become mist created by the heat of my own tears melting the glacier."

"The time for you to dissolve into mist is not here. We need your help now, Caligo."

"Why? You have other nymphs." She clenched her hands into fists, pushing them against her lap.

"Tixi can't do this on her own. No other Rocky Mountain glacier nymph has your experience." I grabbed her hand, which was now cold and limp.

"Yes, my experience in killing glaciers," she said, pulling her hand from mine.

I leaned forward and cupped her chin. The black rings around her irises became more prominent as she opened her eyes wide.

"Snap out of it," I said. "This is no time for self-pity. There will be time to mourn later, but now we need your help. Are you with me?" I grabbed her shoulders, gripping them firmly as I looked into her eyes.

But she shook her head and looked down.

"Can I offer *my* tears?" My words came without thought.

"You would do that? Grieve for my glacier?" Caligo looked at me, a new emotion brightening her face.

"Yes." I nodded, seeing the hope in her eyes. "I'll cry for you. Will that help?"

"Even human tears will ease its suffering," she said, looking toward the cliff edge with a sense of purpose. "I will go with you to help Tixi on Younts Peak, but only if you cry to ease and hasten my glacier's demise."

"I will," I said, putting my hand over hers. "You won't jump again, right?" I thought she seemed better, but how could I know for sure?

"I won't jump. Let's do this." She stood and faced the edge. "Let's say goodbye to a magnificent force that's been here for over seven thousand years." She held her hand toward me, palm up.

I stood, placed my hand in hers, and was almost knocked to the ground as the full force of her sorrow engulfed me. She gripped tighter, nodding as if she understood my reaction.

"Let's do this together, Diana of the Wind Rivers. Your empathy will sustain me," Caligo said. "Are you ready?" Her eyes held steely determination.

I nodded, forcing myself to stand taller, but keeping my knees flexed. I hadn't anticipated the extent of her pain. It threatened to consume me entirely, caught in an undertow in the ocean, pulled into a sea of sadness so deep, I could never resurface. I wasn't sure I had the internal strength to deal with this. "I will help you carry this burden," I said, in spite of my doubts.

"Your empathy is strong," Caligo said. "Maybe you *can* help me do this."

Just when the force of her grief was too much to bear, an inner peace stabilized the pressure on my chest. I broke free of the undertow and raised my head, squaring my shoulders. I thought of all the grand moments throughout history when living things had confronted and overcame their greatest challenge, emerging victorious on the other side of the task.

In a movie, I thought quickly, this situation would include robust music that inspired the characters to succeed. But there was no music as I stood on the edge of the cliff with Caligo, only birdsong on the wind.

I gripped her hand, half wondering if she would jump again. "Will I have burn marks on my face, too?" I asked as we stood under the clear blue sky, looking down on the ragged glacier.

"No, your human tears won't be as hot as mine. But your tears will help. Are you ready?"

I nodded, not quite sure what to expect. She looked deeply into my eyes, and for one moment, I caught the strength of spirit that had sustained this glacier for over seven thousand years, lost in time, a glorious stretch of frozen life on a living planet.

"Glaciers contain the majority of fresh water on our planet," Caligo said as we stood side by side on the edge of the cliff, her damp skin and drooping hair a contrast to the new resolve in her eyes. "We mourn the loss of this magnificent being, a glacier that sustained the planet."

Then she broke into a clear, wordless song in a haunting contralto. The power of her voice brought tears to my eyes, and my heart flooded with pain for the loss of my mother. Last summer, I'd learned to move beyond that sorrow, but now it returned, in an overpowering rush, bringing sharp tears to my eyes. They fell from my face, down, down, down to the glacier below. A quick burst of steam erupted from the surface.

Caligo gasped and I glanced to the side when she stopped singing.

"Tixi told me not to cry, and yet you do this for me," she said.

All I could do was nod, still overcome by sorrow. Sorrow for the death of my mother, sorrow for the loss of this glacier, and sorrow for the nymph before me, who was overcome by grief, just as I had been at the loss of my mother.

Caligo once again began to sing, and tears streamed down her face, falling to the glacier below. As the first hot tears hit the surface, a loud hiss and pop accompanied the cracking of ice, and a stream gushed from the glacier.

Searing pain threatened to crack open my chest, and the only thing supporting me now was the strength of Caligo's grip. My tears dropped to the glacier, popping and crackling on the ice. A new, smaller stream erupted, its blue water shimmering in the sun. We stood together as her anguish hit me in waves. Finally, I could stand upright no more, and my knees buckled.

This time, Caligo pulled me up. "There," she said. "I'm ready to go.

This process will take time, but the end of this glacier will come, and I will feel it, wherever I am on this planet."

I stood, hearing myself gasp. Angry red welts bisected her cheeks, the scars of her mourning evident for the world to see. But already her tears began to dry, leaving her eyes brittle blue and resolute.

"Let's go help Tixi," she said grimly. "I can't save my glacier, but, together, we might save the glacier on Younts Peak."

I looked in her eyes, gaining strength from her. "You're amazing," I said.

"The power of your empathy gave me great strength of spirit," she said. "Truly, you are strong, Diana of the Wind Rivers."

"And you made me stronger," I said, realizing that was true. I felt something within me, soft as sandstone, but immovable as granite. "How long will it take the glacier to die?"

"It will happen over the course of the next year," she said. "In human terms, that seems like a long time. But to a glacier nymph, that is but one brief season." She faced me. "Let's leave. I cannot bear to watch."

We boarded the chariot, and I directed Glenda south. It would take many months for her tears to slowly burn their way through the ice. All the while, the beautiful blue water would stream off the glacier, pouring into the rivers, valleys, and lakes below.

After one last look at the sizzling stream arising from the glacier, Caligo faced the front. She didn't look back again

CHAPTER TWELVE
RETURN TO YOUNTS PEAK

We neared Younts Peak, and as I scanned the grassy slope for Tixi, a spot of purple appeared next to the stream feeding the glacial lake at the source of the Yellowstone River. I guided the chariot toward the tarn, and we landed a short distance away. Tixi came toward us, her moss green skin blending with the grass, while her pastel purple spiked hair pointed toward the sky.

Caligo disembarked, standing in front of Tixi. To my surprise, Tixi dropped down on one knee, bowing her head in front of the slender aquamarine glacial nymph. I realized I was witnessing the first show of respect toward Caligo for the loss of her glacier. Caligo reached down, placing her palm on Tixi's head.

I half expected Tixi to be angry, because she'd directed Caligo not to cry. The evidence that Caligo had ignored her was carved in her cheeks. When Tixi didn't admonish the other nymph, I figured she'd decided that Caligo had suffered enough.

Tixi rose and embraced Caligo. Only then did the other nymph soften her posture, bending into Tixi's hug.

"I'm going to fill my flask," I said, thinking they should have time alone.

"Let me see it," Tixi said, releasing Caligo from her arms, but keeping one around the smaller nymph's shoulder.

"No," I said. "Last time you held my flask, my elk ran away." When Artemis brought me to Younts Peak last summer to refill my flask with *Aqua Pura* from the source of the Yellowstone River, I had allowed Tixi to hold it. That's when the tiny copper creature jumped from my flask, enlarging to a full-size elk as she leapt through the air and bounded into the forest.

I walked toward the lake and leaned down on a boulder, submerging my flask in the water. After it filled with *Aqua Pura*, the source of my strength, I tipped my head back to drink, enjoying the cold drops running down my neck. I lowered the flask and gazed around. Suddenly, I felt pressure on my palm. Looking down, I saw my elk no longer grazed, but pushed her nose against my hand while bobbing her head and pawing the ground.

"All right," I said. "You can go for a run through the forest, but promise you'll come back soon, okay?"

She nodded and pawed the ground again, so I held up the flask and watched as she leapt through the air, growing into a full-sized elk before her feet touched the ground. She bounded across the grassy slope and disappeared into the trees in the distance. Confident she would return, I walked back to the nymphs.

"She'll come back," Tixi reassured me.

I nodded. "How are you doing?" I asked Caligo.

"Better," she said, hugging me. "Thank you, Diana of the Wind Rivers. I told Tixi how you saved me."

"You're coming into your own, Diana," Tixi said, her pale purple spiked hair moving as she spoke.

"I am stronger after helping Caligo," I said. "Her grief was overwhelming, but we conquered it together."

Caligo squeezed my hand. "I'm ready to help Tixi now."

"I'll show her around a bit," Tixi said. "Are you going to wait here for your elk, or do you want to come with us around the cliff base?"

I looked toward the forest to see my elk emerge from the pines, accompanied by a graceful, grey-haired woman.

Walking toward me with her hand on the shoulder of my elk was Running Elk Moon, my great-great-great grandmother. As they drew closer, my elk ran toward me, leaped into the air, and diminished in size as she headed toward the flask, which I held out. She jumped onto the flask, once again a tiny copper etching.

"My dear Diana of the Wind Rivers, welcome back to Younts Peak." Running Elk Moon embraced me in a fierce grip, and I reveled in the strength of her arms encircling me. She was the first owner of the elk tooth necklace I wore. She'd ensured the necklace was handed down through our family so I would eventually receive it from Willy, her great-great grandson and my grandfather.

"I'm so happy to see you again."

"Your elk found me in the forest," she said. "She's telling me something, but I don't fully understand. She keeps repeating the words, 'Find the *Avia Antiqua*,' but I'm not sure what that means."

"Ancient ancestor," I said. "It's Latin." I understood the term because we'd studied some basic Latin in my biology class last year.

"Why is she saying that?" Tixi said. Instead of walking around the cliff, Caligo and Tixi had remained with us.

"I don't know," Running Elk Moon replied. "She's trying to get a message to me, but she's so young she doesn't know how to tell me. Evidently, we're supposed to find this ancient one."

"How do we do that?" I said.

"I have an idea," Running Elk Moon said. "I think you should go to

Squaretop Mountain. You might find her there."

"There's an ancestor up there? She's female?" I said. Last summer I'd met Artemis on Squaretop Mountain, which towered above the Green River Lakes, the source of the Green River, the major tributary of the Colorado River. More *Aqua Pura* in Wyoming, I thought.

"Yes," Running Elk Moon said. "For tens of thousands of years, indigenous people lived throughout the Wind River Mountains. I haven't met this ancestor, but I think she is on Squaretop. She might know something. Many old mysteries have been lost to time, but knowledge remains hidden with her in the mountains."

My elk rubbed her nose against my palm again and bleated. "What is she saying?" I asked.

"Now she is saying the *Cerva Antiqua* guards *Aqua Antiqua*," Running Elk Moon said.

"That means ancient female elk and ancient water. Where is the ancient water?" I asked.

"It could be anywhere," Running Elk Moon said. "Most of Wyoming used to be an ancient sea. Plus, there are lakes all over the United States. There also used to be many kinds of elk across North America."

"Really?" I was genuinely surprised.

"Yes," she said. "Mountain elk roamed the Rockies and Smoky Mountains. Prairie elk lived out on the plains, and desert elk thrived. You can ask the ancient ancestor. She might know what your elk is talking about. We know Hephaestus gave the elk to you for a reason, but I think you must find this ancient one and let her talk to your elk."

"How do I find her?" I wondered if I really wanted to do this.

"All I know is that she might be on Squaretop above the Green River Lakes. You'll have to go there. I do think she will come out of hiding if you, Diana of the Wind Rivers, call for her," Running Elk Moon said.

My elk bleated again, and I looked enquiringly at Running Elk Moon.

"She said her name is Little Elk."

"Little Elk," I repeated, looking down. When I said her name, she looked up and bobbed her head, her square nose facing me.

"You know, a wild elk has appeared in South Carolina for the first time in three hundred years," she said.

"Yes," I nodded. "Artemis told me about that last summer."

"That's a good omen," she said.

I again felt the inner resolve I'd experienced when I'd helped Caligo. Maybe the ancient elk will add to my abilities, I thought.

"I'll go back to the ranch and then go to Squaretop," I said. "I don't really want to search for the ancestor on my own. Maybe Persephone can help me."

"As you develop your power," Running Elk Moon said, "don't forget the new young gods. I sense they will help you save *Aqua Pura.*"

"I'll talk to Persephone," I said. "Kya wants to see that mountain."

"You'd better go soon," Running Elk Moon said. "Little Elk seems to feel it's an urgent situation."

"Okay," I said. "I'll be back to see you sometime when I can stay longer." I embraced my great-great-great grandmother, the softness of her buckskin dress warming my palms.

"Thank you for coming to help," Tixi said, after our brief hug.

"I'm grateful," Caligo said. "You and I will meet again, I think."

"Yes," I said, climbing into the chariot and storing my flask under the bench. "*Aqua Pura* on Younts Peak is a source of strength for me, so I will be back. Thank you for coming to help Tixi save this glacier."

I clicked my tongue, encouraging Glenda to move. She pulled us across the grassy slope, and I turned back to wave at the figures standing next to the tarn: two glacier nymphs and one River Crow ancestor. I knew I had powerful allies.

CHAPTER THIRTEEN
ANSWERS ON SQUARETOP

"Instead of telling me what my powers are, it seems as if I'm being tossed about at the whim of the gods. They're sending me on mysterious errands for their amusement," I said to Persephone the day after I returned from Younts Peak.

"I honestly don't know your powers," she said. "If my father, Zeus, is doing this as a joke, I'm part of the entertainment. My mother would be furious if she thought he was wasting our time during growing season."

We sat at the oak kitchen table with Grams while Kya and Spruce played in the corral. Grams brought a carafe of coffee, and I smiled my thanks before pouring myself a cup and adding creamer. Persephone shook her head when I offered a refill.

"Thanks," Grams said, sitting as I filled hers. "I don't think they're playing games with you," she said. "I talked to Demeter about it when you were gone, and she's as puzzled as you are. But I'm glad you've learned empathy is an important tool you possess."

Last night, I'd told Grams and Willy about my experience with Caligo at Glacier National Park, and this morning, I informed Persephone and the twins and filled them in on my new task: find the ancient ancestor on Squaretop Mountain.

"I didn't know this person existed," I said after taking another sip of my coffee. I enjoyed these mornings when Persephone came inside to talk to Grams before leaving for a day of monitoring the plants with Demeter.

"I'm intrigued by the elk on your flask," Persephone said. "We knew Hephaestus could create magical gifts. After all, he's the one who prepares thunderbolts for Zeus. But his use of copper is legendary. He's created a magical flask, indeed, if your elk can come to life and talk. I think there is more to this copper creature than we know."

"You should ask him," Grams said.

"That's a good idea. I will," I said, sipping my coffee.

"Why can't you just put on the ring and talk with the elk?" Grams asked.

"I tried that on the way home," I said. "I just can't understand what she's saying, but I can make out the words *Avia Antiqua.* So now I'm supposed to find the indigenous ancestor and see if she can understand my copper elk. I think I'd better leave tomorrow."

"I also have a change in plans," Persephone said. "We just had word this morning that Pando wants to work with Spruce for a while."

"You mean like an apprentice or intern?" I asked, sitting up. "How long will he be with Pando?"

"A couple of weeks," Persephone said. "I'll take him there tomorrow and I wondered if Kya could stay with you when I go there. Spruce will be with Pando to learn more about the giant clone. If we can figure out how to help the young trees survive the onslaught of cattle grazing in the fall, we might help prevent it from dying."

"She can stay here," Grams said.

"Maybe she could help me," I said.

"Help you on Squaretop?" Persephone said. "That's perfect. I want to take her there, but this second trip to Pando has delayed my plans. She's very interested in examining the granite cliffs. She could learn about Squaretop and be there if you need help."

"What can I help with?" Kya's voice floated in from the deck before she entered the kitchen with Spruce right behind her. "Am I going somewhere? I'd love to help Diana."

The young gods now looked like adults in their twenties. Tall and graceful, Kya wrapped her slender arms around me in a strong grip. Spruce smiled as he came into the kitchen, moving quietly as he always did. Persephone had told me earlier that she and Demeter were convinced the twins would remain as young gods for the rest of their lives but continue to gain maturity in their understanding of the world and their powers. Like me, they were still on this quest. Unlike me, they didn't seem to provide amusement for the gods.

"That's settled then," Persephone said. "Tomorrow, I'll take Spruce back to Pando, and you can go with Diana to Squaretop Mountain to find the indigenous ancestor."

"Hooray," Kya shouted, grabbing her brother and twirling around in the kitchen. Suddenly, she stopped. "Wait. We've never been apart for such a long time," she said, looking into Spruce's eyes. "This will be our first real separation."

"Well, sis, it had to happen sometime," Spruce said with a grin, putting his hands on her shoulders. "We can handle this."

"You're right," she said after a moment. "I'm just being silly."

"No, it's a real thing," I said. I looked from one to the other. "You haven't been apart this long before, but you'll be okay. Plus, I'll be with you, Kya."

"Okay. That's good," she said soberly. Then her face brightened. "What adventures we will have to tell each other when we get back together."

"That's right," Spruce said, patting her shoulder. "We can fill each other in when we return. Double the fun." He pulled her in for a hug.

"What's double the fun?" Indigo flew into the kitchen and back out again to join her children, who were now lined up on the deck railing. I always admired how well-behaved the little Mountain Bluebirds were. They followed Indigo's directions whenever she gave commands. Grams often commented that human children weren't as obedient when they were young. Indigo once said that if baby birds didn't listen to their parents, it could be a matter of life or death. Hawks and eagles loved a tasty blue morsel anytime, no matter how small.

As Kya explained our new plans, we went outside to join the fledglings. I progressed along the railing, patting all five baby bluebirds. I enjoyed the way they pushed their little heads against my finger, almost cat-like.

"I'd love to go on this adventure," Indigo said. "I have to talk to Rock. Come on, kids."

***

The next morning, I was up before dawn, inhaling the cool morning air as I walked from the bunkhouse. I opened the barn door quietly, and, before I could speak, the soft nickers of the mares greeted me. I heard hooves scrambling on the wooden floor, softened by straw, as the little ones got to their feet. Since everyone was awake already, I turned on the overhead light and walked to the large stall where the four horses spent each night, secure in the safety of the barn.

"Good morning, little ones," I said, opening the stall door and stroking the neck of each filly as they rubbed against my chest and engaged in some double-time hoof action on the barn floor. "You're happy this morning. But that's silly to say because you're happy every morning, aren't you?" I kept up a running chatter as I tossed fresh hay into the bin, welcoming the contented crunching sounds that followed. I brushed Golden while she ate, comforted by the suckling sounds as the youngsters nursed. I didn't know if the little horses could understand me, but I knew the mares could. I'd developed a lifetime habit of talking to horses, and now it served me well.

"You're like the elk on my flask," I said, rubbing Daphne's rump while she nursed. Her short white tail whipped around, letting me know she listened. "When I put on my ring and try to talk to you, it's like a foreign language. When will I be able to understand you?"

It was a rhetorical question because none of us knew the answer, just like we didn't know what my powers were.

"I'll be leaving today," I told them, "but Grams will take care of you guys, okay?"

When Eos brought the sun over the horizon, the rosy light of dawn touched my new chariot, highlighting the amber glow of the bamboo and the shiny finish on the titanium rim. Hephaestus did indeed make fine gifts, and I benefitted from his talents. I hadn't even begun to use the full power of this chariot.

Following the sunbeam, I opened the lid on the bench seat. I knew my bow and arrows and my spider web and bamboo rope were tucked inside, but wanted to make sure before leaving, just like every good pilot checks out her plane before flying.

By the time the sun was up, Kya, Indigo, and I were airborne. Kya waved goodbye as we circled the ranch and glided overhead. I called for birds with a clear, wordless tune, and a flock of Western Meadowlarks flew up, hiding us from any hikers or campers in the canyon below. Kya joined me at the front, and Indigo chirped from her special perch right under the front rim.

"This chariot is amazing," Kya said.

"It's fun traveling with just the three of us, isn't it?" I glanced at Indigo and smiled at Kya, noticing the piercing blue of her eyes. I realized that I now played the role Persephone had filled with me last summer: I was the guide and Kya was the student. Even though she would one day become an impressive goddess, I suspected that her fresh honesty and eager approach to life would never disappear. Right now, she was more like a younger sister than a goddess in the making.

"We'll fly over the Continental Divide and head slightly southwest toward Squaretop Mountain," I said. "You'll be impressed by its majesty. Did your mom tell you much about it?"

When she nodded, I looked forward again, controlling the reins with one hand.

I knew she was excited about stopping there because for the first time, she would see the highest mountain in Wyoming, Gannett Peak. I planned to fly over the glacial source of the Green River before landing on Squaretop. From our view in the sky above the Wind River Mountains, water seemed plentiful. But I was worried about Minor Glacier, which wrapped around the base of the mountain. When we reached it, I hoped we'd spot the summer form of the nymph who guards the headwaters of the Green River, the major tributary of the Colorado River.

The Green River still flowed strong and pure from this glacier, but the Colorado was drying up from overuse, and already the federal government rationed water in the deserts of the west. It was my job to convince humans to change their agricultural practices because the rivers of the west could no longer provided enough water for crops, cattle, and people. Changing human behavior was not going to be easy, especially when it came to raising cattle in the west and growing almonds in California.

We were quiet for a while, lost in our individual thoughts as we traveled above forested land on the western side of the divide. "That's the Bridger National Forest," I said. "We're going to fly toward those mountain peaks." I pointed toward granite jutting into the sky, just beyond the green conifers.

As we got closer, the meadowlarks flew away. "Why are they leaving?" Kya asked.

"They probably figure nobody will see us up here, except the occasional mountain climber," I said. "Who would believe it if they came out of the mountains and reported seeing a chariot pulled by a horse? The story would be blamed on their lack of oxygen at high altitudes."

"Is that it?" Kya asked, pointing ahead. "I think I see the tallest one."

"Yes," I replied. "That's Gannett Peak." As we looked where grey rock towered into the sky, a brisk wind cooled my face.

About halfway down the highest point, greyish-tinted snow clung to the side. As I guided the chariot around the peak, it was clear the glacier was disappearing.

"I read about the reduction in the size of Minor Glacier," I said. "Especially on the eastern side. It's almost gone there. From the photos I've seen, it's definitely shrinking. That's not good."

"Will the Green River Lakes dry up?" Kya asked.

"Not right away. They're still deep and store large amounts of water," I replied. "But if we don't change the amount of water people use in western states, it will continue to be a problem. For tens of thousands of years, these mountains have provided enough snow to maintain the glaciers. Now, human behavior is changing that."

"What can we do?" Kya asked.

"We have to convince people to stop using so much water. We don't have enough to irrigate almond groves in California, water lawns, and fill swimming pools," I said. "Let's get over to Squaretop, which is a bit southwest of here. In fact, you can see it in the distance now."

"Look at the color of the lakes," she shouted as we drew closer. "They're blue-green."

"That's from the minerals in the water," I said. "This is *Aqua Pura*, the kind of water that gives me power. Although my main source of energy is from the glacial lake at the source of the Yellowstone River, any water from mountain lakes is pure and strong." I pointed to a flat, grassy area. "We'll land over there." No other humans were in sight when we touched down. "Good thing no one is here," I said. I felt vulnerable without a bird flock to cover our passage through the sky.

"Will you call up another flock when we leave?" Kya said, seeming to read my mind. "Maybe you can call out for some big birds that can fly over Gannett Peak with us."

"Eagles?" Indigo said. "You know they might eat me." She flew to Kya's shoulder.

"You'll be okay with us," Kya said, pulling her closer to her neck.

We disembarked and walked around after unhitching Glenda from the chariot. "We can let her graze a while," I said.

"Have you been here before?" Kya asked.

"Yes," I said. "This is where we met Artemis last summer and she officially named me Diana of the Wind Rivers."

"What a fine place for that event," Kya said, linking her arm through mine. "This is a magnificent mountain." She gestured with her other arm as if this were a viewing of a grand estate in *Architectural Digest* or some other magazine photo shoot.

Standing in companionable silence, we looked out over the peaks of the Wind River Mountains. I liked the way she could appreciate something without talking.

The sharp call of an eagle brought Indigo to my shoulder. "You'll be okay," I said. "Let's have lunch." I retrieved our basket of food and walked to the grassy area where I spread out a blanket to sit on. "These are new," I said, after removing two copper cups from the food basket. With clever little handles, the drinking cups tinkled against each other.

"I can tell my Uncle Hephaestus made these," Kya said. "He said copper is so lightweight, it's good for picnics. I like the beautiful color," she added, holding her cup up to admire the shiny surface.

We sipped, enjoying the brisk taste of the *Aqua Pura* I poured from my flask. After drinking, I held my cup up to my face and saw my reflection in the shiny surface. "It works," I exclaimed, laughing. Looking back at me was a little girl's face. She looked just like photos of me when I was in kindergarten. "Hephaestus told me these cups would reflect the past of those who drink from them. He said it would help us connect to our inner selves."

"Let me see your childhood image," Kya exclaimed.

"You can't," I said. "The cups only reveal that to the person drinking."

"Darn it," she said. "I'll bet you were a cute little girl." She giggled after looking at her own copper cup.

"Have some lunch," I said, handing out the grapes, cheese, and bread Grams packed for this trip. We ate quietly, sharing pieces of bread and cheese with Indigo.

"Food always tastes so good in the mountains," Kya said.

"Cheese is my favorite," Indigo mumbled through the food in her beak. "If I'd never met you, I wouldn't know about cheese."

Kya and I looked at each other and laughed. "You're right," I said.

Just as we finished eating, a loud squawk interrupted our quiet perusal of the scenery. A large American Magpie landed on the blanket next to Indigo. I put on my ring, wanting to understand the black and white bird as it spoke.

"Greetings," the magpie said. "I'm here to introduce myself to you. My name is Marty."

"Greetings," I echoed. "We are honored you stopped here to meet us."

"I'd like to take Indigo with me for a tour, if I could," the bird said. "I'll tell her about the history of my species in this area, and she can relay that information later."

"Would you like to go?" I asked Indigo.

"Yes," she said, fluttering to my shoulder and rubbing against my cheek.

"Have fun and be careful," I said, remembering the times when she ventured off with other birds last summer. She'd flown over the Pacific Ocean with Wanda, the Wandering Albatross, and over the southern seas with the Birds of Dawn at the edge of the world. I knew she would come back. I took off my ring as the birds flew away, returning it to the chain on my elk tooth necklace. "I'm going to take a little walk," I said after we packed up the remnants of lunch. "I really want to see if I can find the Green River glacier nymph. Now that it's summer, she might be here instead of on Minor Glacier."

"I'll go with you," Kya said. We walked in silence for some time before she spoke. "Diana, I'm worried I'll never find my true power."

"You will," I replied. "I'm still trying to figure out mine. Don't forget that Indigo worked all last summer to find her blue."

Before I could elaborate, a young woman emerged from behind a large boulder a few feet away. Her hair was bright purple, long and curly. Her blue-green skin almost clashed with her green dress, the shade of new grass tendrils poking through snow in the spring. As she got closer, I could see her eyes were deep blue, the same blue I experienced when I first saw the ocean last summer.

"You're a glacier nymph," I said. "You must be the Guardian of the Headwaters."

"Yes," she said, pausing when she stood a short distance away. "Greetings, Diana of the Wind Rivers. Tixi told all the glacier nymphs about you."

"Greetings, Guardian," I said, bowing. "I am honored to meet you."

"My name is Limni, the Greek word for lake," she said, extending one blue-green arm.

I reached out to clasp her hand and gasped as we touched. A jolt of pure energy flowed from her hand to mine. If she hadn't been gripping my hand, I would have leaped back in surprise. "You're amazing," I said.

Her laugh rippled like water over rocks. "Yes, I am. I've been guarding the headwaters of the Green River for over half a million years. The Wind Rivers are the oldest mountain range in the Rocky Mountains. Time spent with granite will have that effect."

When she said the word granite, a deep calm descended on me. I felt a visceral connection to that word, and something soft inside hardened. I was grounded to the mountain, part of the molecules of the very rock beneath me.

"Hello, my name is Kya," said a voice next to me.

I was so mesmerized by Limni that I'd forgotten about Kya. "I'm sorry. I forgot to introduce you," I said. "Limni, this is a young goddess named Kya, daughter of Persephone and Hades."

"Greetings, young goddess," Limni said, bowing from the waist. "I have heard you will help Diana save pure water on the planet."

"Greetings, Limni," Kya said, bowing in return. "Who told you about me?"

"The birds spread the news of your birth around the globe," Limni said. Moving forward, she held her hands out toward Kya, palms up. "Welcome to Squaretop Mountain."

"Thank you, Guardian," Kya said. She clasped Limni's hands in her own, inhaling deeply when they touched. "I feel your inner strength."

Limni laughed, and her voice filled the air around us like chimes in the breeze. She extended one hand to me, and the three of us stood, clasping hands. Cold air briefly surrounded us, and I inhaled the scent of water on granite, biting and strong. The moment ended when Limni broke the connection and raised her arms to the sky, twirling slowly. "You seek answers on Squaretop," she said. "I sense you need help."

"We are looking for the ancient ancestor," I said. "My magical elk keeps telling us something we cannot understand, and we hope the ancient one can understand her." I returned to our picnic blanket and picked up the flask. As I walked back to the other two, Little Elk pushed against my hand with her nose. Looking down, I watched as she nodded up at me.

"I recognize the work of Hephaestus," Limni said as I held up the flask. "May I hold it?"

I extended the flask. "Her name is Little Elk," I said when Limni gazed at the front of the flask.

Limni nodded and held it up. Just as had happened when Tixi held the flask, Little Elk jumped out, growing as she bounded through the air. By the time her hooves hit the ground, she was the size of an adult female. With one bleat, she took off across the grassy area, disappearing behind a boulder.

"Will she come back?" Kya asked.

"Last time she did," I said.

"Oh, yes, she will always return to you," Limni said. "I can tell Hephaestus bonded her to you."

"Do you know the ancestor who dwells in this area?" I asked.

"Many spirits dwell here," she said. "This is an ancient place. But I know the ancestor, and our paths have crossed many times. We both inhabit these granite peaks. I guard the glacier, and she guards the memory of indigenous peoples who lived here for tens of thousands of years. We have both witnessed the changes brought on by humans, just as we both waited for the birth of a young girl named Diana, as foretold in the prophecy. We knew you would one day come here, seeking our help. We need you as well, Diana. You will protect water in these mountains."

"How will I do that? Do you know my powers?"

"You must discover that on your own," she said. "Tixi sent bird messengers to tell the guardian nymphs how your empathy helped save Caligo. For that, I am grateful." She extended her hand again.

I automatically wrapped my fingers around her blue-green hand, again jolted by the burst of energy surging up my arm. I tugged, but Limni held on, seeming to seek something in my eyes.

"Your connection to granite bonds us," she said. "Someday, you will understand how its force works within you."

"How am I connected to granite?" I said. "I've felt its strength, but don't understand."

"I do not know the answer," she said. "But you will, someday. In the meantime, I'll help you find the ancient one who dwells with me in the mountains. I have not seen her for a long time."

The bleat of an elk caused us all to turn, just in time to see Little Elk walk around the boulder, accompanied by a tall figure. Her graceful form belied her wrinkled face. Bounding ahead of the grey-haired woman, Little Elk leapt into the air and returned to the flask.

The woman paused in front of us, her brown eyes gazing into mine. I inhaled deeply when she touched my face, marveling at the softness of her fingers. She seemed real. "Diana," she said. "Your elk found me."

"I guess you don't need my help," Limni said. "That elk of yours is extremely powerful, if she can find the ancient one so quickly." She turned to the other woman. "Greetings, great one. I haven't seen you in a long time."

"I didn't expect to locate you so quickly," I said. "Running Elk Moon told me about you, but even she wasn't sure if I'd find you." A tiny bleat from my flask reminded me to give Little Elk credit. "If it weren't for Little Elk, we might not have found you." I smiled down at the flask, and she nodded before lowering her head to once again graze on copper grass.

The ancient one surveyed me with serious eyes. "You are indeed holding a special gift in the form of this little elk. Treasure what you have." She held my gaze silently before speaking again. "I see you travel with the young goddess. Welcome to Squaretop Mountain." She offered her hand to Kya.

"I'm Kya," she said, wrapping her hand around the slender fingers of the woman.

"You can call me Bia," she said. "That means mother in Eastern Shoshone. I am the mother of all people who once roamed the Wind Rivers."

"How did you know about me, Bia?" Kya said.

"The eagles brought news of your birth," she said, her brown eyes roaming over Kya's face. "You and Spruce will help Diana save pure water." She turned to me. "But your task will not be easy. Why have you come here today?" She smiled, seeming to already know the answer.

"How do you know Kya and Spruce will help me? Can you tell me that?" I asked.

"I know many things, All of you will learn more about your powers," she said. "But now, answer my question. Why do you come?"

"Running Elk Moon told us to seek your help in understanding my little copper elk. We don't know what she's trying to tell us. Can you understand her? She keeps talking about an ancient female elk and ancient water," I said. "*Cerva Antiqua* and *Aqua Antiqua*."

"I understand Little Elk," the woman said. "She told me you need the help of the Red Desert Elk. I know of what she speaks. However, the secrets of the desert are precious. We do not give them up lightly. What will you offer in exchange for this knowledge? Just because you ask does not guarantee success."

"You mean I have to give you something? What should I give you?" I asked. This was unexpected. What did I own that she would want?

"That is tricky," Limni said. "Trading for secrets can be dangerous." She looked sharply at the old woman.

"Why do I have to give you something?" I looked at Bia. "I'm helping the world by trying to save clean water on the planet."

"Indigenous people have given up everything. Their land, their culture, and their lives," Bia said. "You should give up something to prove your dedication to your cause. Again, what will you offer?"

"Be careful of what you surrender," Limni said, turning to look at me.

"Diana must make her own decisions," the ancestor said. "Whatever she gives in trade must be of her own volition. Perhaps you should leave us and tend to your glacier."

Surprised at the apparent animosity between the two, I watched as they eyed each other with seeming hostility. Finally, Limni bowed at the waist in apparent surrender. "I will leave you with the ancestor, Diana." She turned to Bia. "I'll see you after Diana and Kya depart. We have old friction between us, but perhaps now is the time to begin working together again."

"I agree," Bia said. "We will discuss our issues later in the hope we can begin working with Diana and Kya."

With that, Limni pirouetted and walked away, fading into the landscape.

"What was that about?" I looked at the ancestor. "What old friction is she talking about?"

"Never mind that right now," she said. "Let's figure out how I can help you."

"What can I give a being such as you?" I asked. "I'm just a human."

"That's for you to decide," she said. "In order to learn about the secret wealth of the desert, you must offer something of great value. What do you have?"

"I don't know," I said. "I guess I have my necklace, but it protects me." I pulled my elk tooth necklace from under my shirt.

"I have no use for a necklace," she said. "I wear my own." She reached under her buckskin dress and withdrew a silver necklace.

I gasped, and heard Kya's swift intake of breath.

Ten large elk teeth were strung on fine silver filament. Interspersed between each elk tooth were polished olive-green oval stones, slightly smaller than the ivory-colored teeth. A large, deeper green polished pendant graced the center of the necklace, its round shape pierced through by the silver filament. Recognizing the warmth of jade, I automatically reached out to touch the stone, but pulled back my hand, realizing I should ask first.

She smiled and lifted the necklace over her head, offering it to me. Looking into her deep brown eyes for confirmation, I gingerly clasped it between my fingers after she nodded.

My elk tooth necklace protected me. Only two elk ivories were on mine, interspersed with three polished tiger eye rectangles. The energy of her necklace told me it was potent, with its ten ivories strung with magnificent green polished stones, but when I touched it, an incredible sense of well-being flooded my veins. Then a deep calm descended upon me, and I automatically closed my eyes. The smell of water on granite permeated my nostrils. My mind filled with a sense of time, ancient and deep, transporting me back through centuries of human existence. I felt the very essence of the granite in the mountains, the deep compression of rock over time, the thrusting of the earth's crust when the Rockies were young. Deep, deep, deeper, my connection to granite pulled me into the new mountains. My lungs filled with clean air as I inhaled with bright hope. The piercing call of an eagle brought me back to the present.

"What happened?" I asked after opening my eyes.

The woman smiled, lifting her palm in a wordless request for the necklace. "You felt a connection to the earth through the jade," she said. "It is ancient. I sense your power lies within the granite of the Rockies."

"How does it give me power?" I asked. Kya clasped my hand, and I glanced at her. We both wanted to know more about our potential powers, and she understood my intense desire to understand this moment.

"I can't answer that for you," the woman said. "It's something you must discover on your own. I do know granite is strong within you, but more than that, I cannot say."

"I've felt it before," I said. I remembered the time last summer when Artemis described me as a lone tree growing from a cliff, gaining power from the granite where its roots took hold, defying gravity and the wind by growing from rock.

The woman nodded as if she knew my thoughts, and then placed the necklace around her neck, tucking it under her soft buckskin dress. She threw her long grey braids over her shoulders. "You must tell me what you will give in exchange for the secrets of the Red Desert, the secrets your elk talked about."

"How does the elk know these things?" Kya asked, still holding my hand as if sensing my need for something familiar.

"Hephaestus made her with the magic in the copper flask," the woman said. "I feel its power, but cannot fully explain it. The gods have visited me before, seeking to understand the mysteries of Earth's past. I am familiar with his work. More than that, I cannot say."

I remembered Demeter telling me that Hephaestus had included a lock of my hair in the magical flask, and Tixi, the glacier nymph on Younts Peak, had told me he'd collected granite dust from the cliffs there when he made the flask. I vowed to ask him about all of it the next time he came to the ranch.

"What can I give you in exchange for the knowledge of the Red

Desert?" I asked. "My flask?"

"You must decide what is most valuable to you. That will be a fair exchange. If you want to find the Red Desert elk and learn how they can help you, you'll think of something. I will return here tomorrow for your answer." She turned and walked away, her solid form dissipating. Little Elk bleated from inside my pouch where I tucked the flask.

"That was Wyoming Nephrite jade on her necklace," Kya said, releasing my hand. "It's stronger than regular jade."

I turned to face her. "How did you know that?" I said, then realized it was a silly question because her father was Hades, god of the underworld.

"Dad told me when we were studying Wyoming rocks and gems," she said. "He said Wyoming jade was formed in the Wind River Mountains, among other places. Her jade was very old. I can tell from its deep green color."

I nodded. "That makes sense. She is the ancient ancestor. Let's go set up camp and have something to eat. I need time to think."

"Good idea," Kya said, following me as I walked back to where Glenda grazed contentedly on mountain grass planted by Demeter. Last summer, Persephone taught me how to identify the highly nutritious grass Demeter planted in the mountains so that her flying horses would have ample food wherever she landed her chariot.

After we set up camp, heated the soup, and ate the bread Grams sent with us, we sat around the blue glowing flame Kya had established in the little circle of stones we'd gathered for our campsite. Traveling with gods meant I didn't have to burn trees for a campfire, and we always dismantled the ring of stones in order to leave no trace of our presence in the mountains.

"What do you suppose you'll have to give in exchange for learning about the mystery of the Red Desert elk?" Kya asked as I poured hot tea in her copper cup. We were once again using the magical gift from Hephaestus. "Did you notice that she told us the elk were in the Red Desert? That's just south of here."

I looked at the image of my childhood self, illuminated by the eerie light from the blue flame. "I don't know. I've been thinking about it. Let me bounce some ideas off you."

"Sure," Kya said, giggling as she looked at her cup. "I see myself playing with Spruce when we were younger. What does your cup reveal?"

"I'm laughing and playing with Grams," I said, smiling. My dark curly hair was tousled and untidy. My jeans were dirty, and my tennis shoes scuffed. I'd always liked being outside more than inside, and I could tell it must have been a challenge to get me in the bathtub at night before bed. We knew by now that only the person drinking from the copper cups could see the image, so all we could do is tell each other why we giggled.

"What ideas do you have?" She chuckled again before sipping hot tea, turning from her cup to look seriously at me. Her blue eyes reflected the light of the fire.

"I thought maybe my necklace was a valuable thing to give up, but Bia doesn't want it. Maybe I should offer my favorite saddle that Dad gave me when I was in high school."

"No." Kya shook her head. "There has to be something more important. What about Daisy, your horse?"

"I would hate to give her up," I said. "And what use would my mortal horse be to Bia? Daisy would die long before the ancient and be of no use. How about my favorite mythology books? That's where I learned about your relatives."

"How about your soul? Don't humans give up their souls in great literature? Mom told me about that theme," Kya said.

I thought about the many stories of humans giving their souls to obtain something they desired. "I don't know. Can I really give up my soul? What about my title as Diana of the Wind Rivers?"

"Who will save *Aqua Pura* if you do that? Besides, is that yours to surrender? Wasn't there a prophecy about your birth? You can't go against a prophecy. The Greeks knew about that. Remember Oedipus?"

I remembered the story of Oedipus, who tried to defy the prophecy that he would kill his father and marry his mother. In spite of the fact that his parents sent him away at birth to be killed by a shepherd and therefore avoid the prophecy, he lived, and eventually did what was foretold: he killed his own father and married his mother, the Queen of Thebes. Once he learned the truth about himself, he gouged out his eyes with his mother's broach.

"No, let's not try that," I concluded. "I don't know. Let's go to bed and maybe we'll have an idea tomorrow."

I laughed once more after finishing my tea. "Now I'm playing with my mom and dad," I said. "What are you doing?"

"I'm chasing Spruce through the forest," she said. "He keeps hiding behind trees and blending in."

We rinsed our cups, put out the blue flames, and crawled into the tent we'd set up earlier. I had expected Indigo to return by dark, and wondered where she was. I assumed she would be safe with Marty, but she had never been gone this long before when she'd gone off with another bird.

Kya must have wondered also because she spoke first. "Where is Indigo? Shouldn't she be back here by now?"

"I was just thinking the same thing," I said. "I trust that she's okay with Marty, but I'm not sure. All we can do is wait until the morning and see if she returns. I don't like it, but what else can we do?"

"Marty seemed like a nice bird, and he is bigger than Indigo, so he could protect her from eagles, hopefully," Kya said. "I'm going to give her a lecture when she returns."

"Me, too," I said, yawning. "I think we can trust Marty to bring her back safely tomorrow. If she doesn't come back, we'll send out some birds to find her."

Soon I heard Kya's soft, even breathing as she drifted to sleep. I tossed and turned, listening to Glenda eating grass right outside the tent. Then that comforting sound ended, indicating that even the mare was asleep.

Putting Indigo to the back of my mind, I wondered what I should give up in order to learn the secrets of the Red Desert elk. Running Elk Moon said it wouldn't be an easy task, and I realized the ease with which we'd found the ancestor was deceiving. I couldn't give up my necklace. I needed its protection. Besides, how could I give up something Willy gave to me? How could I betray my ancestors who'd held onto the necklace in order to pass it down to me? It didn't matter anyway; Bia didn't need my necklace. Plus, I knew I must someday pass on my elk tooth necklace to the next person who would carry on my legacy of protecting clean water. At least I hoped I'd leave a legacy.

What about my new little fillies? Could I give up that gift from Poseidon? What about the magical chariot Hephaestus created? The ancestor didn't need a chariot. It seemed her spirit could transport her anywhere. What if I promised my firstborn child, like they always did in fairy tales? I didn't even have a boyfriend, much less a future mate. How could I give up something I might never have? Maybe I wouldn't ever have children. I knew I wanted kids someday, but I could see from Indigo's experience that it was a lot of work. I wasn't ready for that yet.

What if I gave up my powers as Diana of the Wind Rivers? Of course, I didn't even know what they were yet. Maybe I should just get up and have some tea, I thought. But I needed Kya to start the blue fire and I didn't want to leave the warm tent. I closed my eyes, willing myself to sleep. Suddenly, an image popped into my brain, the image of my younger self in the copper cup, playing with Mom and Dad. I opened my eyes, understanding now what was one of the most valuable things in my life.

Last summer, I'd not only continued to mourn my mother's death, but also mourned the loss of my memories of her. I couldn't remember the sound of her voice, and I was losing my memory of her face. If not for the photo next to my bed, I wouldn't have recalled any of her features. The joy I saw on my face in the copper cup made me realize what I treasured most: the memory of my mom.

Through my adventures with Persephone and our growing friendship, I learned to accept my grief over Mom's death. I learned to recall the good times from my childhood. And more importantly, I'd met my mother again when I dove into the ocean to rescue Persephone from the deep waters where the oil monster dragged her down in our battle in the Gulf of Mexico.

"I'll be with you always," my mother told me after appearing in the ocean in her new form, that of a mermaid. "I'll be the breeze on your cheek when you sit on the deck at the ranch. I'll be the butterfly you see in the garden at the back of the house. I'll be the sparkle in the snow when you ski down the frozen Sweetwater River in the winter." I knew then that I would never forget her face or the sound of her voice. I didn't need copper cups to remember her, even though seeing myself as a child brought back the joy of being with my mom.

I almost wanted to wake Kya with the news that I'd realized what I must give up in order to learn the secrets of the Red Desert elk. I didn't shake her awake, however. Instead, I closed my eyes again.

"No, not your magic cups," I imagined Kya saying when I told her.

A loud flash of lightning lit up the interior with sharp white light. Glenda whinnied loudly just before a boom of thunder shook the ground.

"What happened?" Kya sat up, her blue eyes alarmed. "I heard Zeus."

I sat up also, grabbing her hand. "I know what to give the ancestor," I said. "I've realized what she means by a sacrifice. And Zeus just signaled his approval by sending down a lightning bolt. I'm giving her the cups."

CHAPTER FOURTEEN
THE BLUEBIRD REPORT
I AM THE MAGPIE

After saying goodbye to Diana and Kya, I flew after Marty, flapping quickly to keep up. Just above his wings, a bright white patch highlighted his black head and body. His white belly contrasted with the deep blue tint of his wings, which sparkled in the sun. Fanning behind, his long tail gave him a graceful look as he zoomed through the air over Squaretop Mountain.

"Wait up," I said. "I can't fly as fast as you." This magpie wasn't as large as other birds I knew. I'd successfully followed Wanda, the Wandering Albatross, over the ocean last summer, and she was much bigger, but keeping up with Marty was a challenge. He glanced back when I shouted, slowing down so I could catch up.

I looked below where the sharp cliffs of Squaretop towered above two lakes glimmering in the sun. We swooped down, flying above the smooth surface of the water, which reflected the nearby cliffs. The upper and lower lakes gave way to the river, snaking its way through the open grassland spreading in the valley below.

When we reached the lower elevation, Marty landed in a tall pine at the edge of a meadow. "There's the mighty Green River," he said, pointing his black beak toward the fresh flowing water. "My family has lived in this area for generations. I am the keeper of our sad history." He fluffed his black wings and looked at me with serious dark eyes. "We'll rest for a minute."

"Okay," I said, settling in next to him at the top of the tree. "I'm trying to keep up, but I can't fly as fast as you."

He looked critically at me, moving his head up and down as he surveyed my body. "Well, you're a mousy little thing, but you've got spunk."

I puffed out my chest. "I might not be completely cerulean like the males of my species, but I know the power of my inner blue." I wasn't going to let this confident bird get away with a remark like that.

He whistled and laughed. "Like I said, you've got some spunk. I can see why the eagles told me to find you."

"They did?" I asked. My blue courage evaporated. "Are they going to eat me?"

"No," he said, turning his head to preen his wing. I admired the way the sun emphasized the deep blue-green of his feathers. "Tixi sent an eagle to tell me I should give you a tour of the area. Apparently, you're well-known in the Wind Rivers. They told me you helped Diana last summer."

I stood tall on the branch, my confidence returning. "I did help bring down the oil monster in the Gulf of Mexico," I said. "And now I have a mate and fledglings on the other side of the Continental Divide on Diana's ranch near Sinks Canyon." I sat again, securing my feet in the bark of the tree.

"Oh, you live on a ranch? Magpies despise ranchers," Marty scoffed. "They tried to kill my species years ago, but didn't succeed."

"Kill you off?" I was shocked. "Why would ranchers try to kill birds? Diana's grandpa and grandma helped Mountain Bluebirds by building nesting boxes on the ranch. They don't try to kill us."

"They thought we plucked the eyes of their cattle. We don't do that. Then they said we ate the cattle alive because some magpies plucked at the raw skin after cattle were branded. But it also has to do with the magpie's revenge," Marty said grimly. "Let's fly to my nest and I'll tell you about it. As I said, I am the keeper of the American Magpies' history."

"Okay," I said. "I'm ready to go again."

Marty trilled and took off. He flew too fast at first, but slowed after slanting his head back to see if I kept pace.

Just when I grew tired, we turned to the right and flew toward the forest at the edge of the grassy meadow next to the river. He landed in a tall tree. "There's our nest," he said, pointing down with his beak.

"Wow," I said. "That's some nest." A large domed structure occupied the intersection of branches next to the trunk of the tall pine. Twigs and sticks stuck out all around, and I could tell it was a safe fortress for nesting.

"My kids are out hunting right now, along with my mate. They'll be back later. Let's settle in and talk. Do you want some ticks? Are you hungry?"

"You have ticks here?" I asked. "In the tree?"

"Yes, we do keep a supply on hand," he said. "Do you like them?"

"Well, I usually eat grasshoppers, but I can try one."

Marty flew to the edge of the nest and reached in with his beak. "Here," he said, flying back to join me on the branch. "Try some ticks." He dropped several on the branch next to me.

As the small critters scurried along the bark, I quickly reached down, picking up a few with my beak. "Interesting," I said. Mother taught me to be polite with other birds, so I didn't tell him I wasn't fond of the bitter taste.

"These came from the backs of cattle," Marty said. "They're not as sweet as the ones my ancestors plucked from buffalo in the old days."

"You ate ticks from the backs of buffalo? Those animals are huge."

"You've seen buffalo?" he said, turning bright black eyes on me. "Where? They are gone from here."

"On the Wind River Reservation near Diana's ranch," I said. "Diana told me that the Eastern Shoshone and Northern Arapaho brought some from Yellowstone National Park, and I've seen them."

"The Eastern Shoshone are gone from this area also," he said, shaking his head. "I've never seen a buffalo outside of Yellowstone National Park, but my ancestors lived with them. In fact, our history is intertwined."

"Tell me about that," I said, ignoring the few ticks escaping in the bark on the branch. I settled down, anticipating a story like the ones my mom used to tell in the nest when I was a young fledgling.

Marty warbled and settled closer to the branch. "My mate and I are descendants of the ancient magpie. Our species survived the buffalo slaughter."

"Who killed them?" I peeped but closed my beak quickly after his stern glance. I taught my children never to interrupt at story time, and here I was, interrupting Marty.

"First came the French fur trappers," he said. "They didn't disrupt the peaceful coexistence of the magpie and buffalo here on the banks of the Green River because only a few trappers came through. Magpies plucked ticks from the backs of the mighty buffalo, and all was fine. My ancestors pulled hair from the generous buffalo, who grazed while we tickled their backs with our beaks and feet. Then we flew to our nests, taking buffalo hair to combine with mud. We made nests of twigs and sticks, but deep inside, we created a warm and safe pod to raise our young, lining the nest with buffalo hair. In that manner, the smell of the buffalo hair was imprinted on our young so that we could always find the great beasts, no matter where they roamed."

He inhaled deeply, looking off in the distance as if remembering. Then he turned to look into my eyes. "We also lived in harmony with the Eastern Shoshone who killed what they needed and shared the bounty. We ate while they skinned the animal and threw some scraps our way. They laughed at our antics as we attempted to steal more. They wasted nothing of the large beast, including the hide and innards. They made pouches from the bladder and gained strength from the heart of the animal. They left some bones for us to pick clean. Ours was a peaceful relationship as the sun rose and set over this land."

He paused again, and I waited silently. "Then a trickle of white men came through from the other side of the mountains. At first, all was well, but after the white men joined the French fur trappers in killing the beaver, a steady stream of settlers came through, headed west."

I realized my feet hurt from gripping the branch tightly. I tried to relax.

"Moving through the valleys, they flooded this land with a steady stream of people. When the beaver was depleted through trapping, the white men still passed through. But then they began to stay, bringing their big guns. The never-ending booming, booming, booming. The buffalo dropped in huge numbers as the white men shot with guns that were so hot we could feel the heat as we flew by. The shooting never stopped and on went the killing, killing, killing of buffalo. The ground thundered as they fell."

I squeaked in horror.

Marty looked at me in sympathy before continuing his story. "The thundering boom of guns was followed by great bellows as the giant beasts of the west, the buffalo, our symbiotic friends, fell to the ground, groaning as they died. Dust flew up, merging with their pain."

"Look at all this food," our young ones cried. "We can eat forever."

"But the elders among us knew this rotting flesh would not last long. Too many buffalo had died at once. We knew the final buffalo would melt into the earth as its flesh rotted."

I gasped. I'd never seen animals die in great numbers.

Marty lowered his head to his chest. He closed his eyes briefly and then continued. "We could no longer pluck their hair to line our nests because, even though the white men left the meat to rot, they skinned the buffalo and took away the hides. We couldn't pick ticks from their backs. This glorious animal had not been able to survive the coming of the white man. My ancestors wondered: would we?"

Marty stopped talking and I remained silent, stunned by his story. Finally, I worked up my courage and spoke. "How do you know this? Wasn't it long ago?"

"Yes, little Indigo, this happened long before my time. However, my species decided to pass on the stories so our young would never forget. Even though we no longer line our nests with buffalo hair, we keep the old stories alive. Our young don't know the smell of the hides or the feel of the strong creature under our feet; our young have not imprinted the smell of the buffalo on their brains." He shifted on the branch and briefly spread his wings. "But now you tell me the Eastern Shoshone have buffalo on the reservation. Maybe there is hope for a return to our old ways, our symbiotic relationship with the buffalo and Natives."

"How did your species survive?" I asked.

"We gained our revenge, the magpie's revenge," he said with grim satisfaction, once again gazing into the distance.

"Revenge? How?"

"When the white men killed the buffalo, they created ranches and filled the land with cattle. My species plucked the ticks from elk and cattle. The hair of a cow doesn't keep our nests as warm as buffalo hair, but we used it nonetheless, mixing in the warm hair of the elk. We continued to build nests and raise our young, living near the dwellings of ranchers, tormenting them by swooping down and tugging at their hats. Soon, they tried to kill us with poison and their guns, but some of us flew away too quickly. To survive, we taught our young the smell of poisoned meat and told them not to eat it."

"They tried to kill you as well?" I was shocked. Nobody tried to kill Mountain Bluebirds, at least as far as I knew. In fact, Grams and Willy made us welcome on their ranch. I thought about my fledglings safe at home with Rock.

"The ranchers hated our mimicking ability. We can bark like a dog or sing like wind chimes. We can be far too clever for our own good, and some of our young died while attempting to annoy the ranchers. Remember that they thought we plucked the eyes from their stupid cattle and ate them from within while they lived? That was not true." Marty shifted his feet.

"Why did they think that?" I asked. "You didn't really pluck the eyes of living creatures, did you?" I backed away, suddenly concerned that he was four times my size.

Marty shook his head. "We would never do that. Maybe one horrible bird tried, and the ranchers thought we were all like that, so they were determined to kill all of us. But we flew quickly when they shot at us and built nests on the edges of meadows away from the ranches. In this way, the American Magpie has survived, waiting for the return of the buffalo, whose coarse hair is much warmer than inferior cattle. And now, you bring hope with your tale of buffalo on the Wind River Reservation. Perhaps I should fly there one day to investigate. Have you seen magpies on the backs of the buffalo?" He looked at me with hope in his intelligent black eyes. "Do they pull hair to line their nests, as my ancestors once did?"

"I haven't seen magpies do that," I admitted. "But I have seen magpies on the backs of horses. If you come to the ranch, I can take you to see the buffalo."

"I'd like that," he said as trilling voices filled the air.

"My family returns," he said. "Come meet my mate and our children." He flew from the branch down to his nest just as a group of birds approached.

Raucous calls filled the air, and I watched as he noisily greeted his family, rubbing his head against a very beautiful bird that I knew must be his mate. Suddenly, I missed Rock and wondered how my fledglings were doing—and if they missed me.

CHAPTER FIFTEEN
FRICTION FROM THE PAST

Looking at my flask, I addressed the copper creature engraved upon it. "Find the ancient one and Limni." She stopped eating and looked up. Dropping the metallic grass from her mouth, she nodded and lifted her right front hoof. I wasn't sure she'd leave on my command, but I extended the flask, and she jumped from it immediately.

I wondered why Bia had challenged me by requiring a gift. I didn't understand her attitude. Didn't it matter that she was also my ancestor? This area was once part of the Eastern Shoshone hunting grounds, and our people had roamed here in pursuit of buffalo. I felt my resentment building. This was the first time since my battle with the oil monster last summer that someone had challenged my efforts to save pure water. I didn't like it.

And where was Indigo? She hadn't returned last night, and I was becoming concerned. She was never gone this long after flying off with other birds last summer. Maybe Bia and Limni could help me find her.

While we waited, Kya and I filled the time by taking down the tent, packing up the chariot, and returning the fire ring rocks to the surrounding grassy area. The only trace of our camp was the scorched grass next to where we'd set up the tent, evidence of last night's lightning strike from Zeus.

"I think the grass will grow back," I said, scraping the area with the bottom of my bamboo boot.

Kya nodded. "It seems Zeus approved of the idea for your gift."

I was confident Little Elk would soon return, and she didn't disappoint me. After tucking the last of our equipment inside the bench seat on the chariot, I looked up to see Bia and Limni materialize in the distance, seeming to appear from a fog. Little Elk ran ahead, barreling toward me. I knew by now to hold out the flask as she leapt from the ground, reducing in size, and jumping onto the front. "Thank you," I said when she resumed grazing. I wondered if the copper grass had any flavor.

Limni and Bia approached, but before I could ask about Indigo, I noticed they were speaking sharply to one another, continuing their disagreement from yesterday.

"Your laziness caused the glaciers to diminish," Bia said. "You could have prevented this."

"It's your fault the buffalo and beaver are gone. My glaciers wouldn't have melted so quickly if beaver ponds were still holding back the water in the mountains and on the lower slopes," Limni said, her voice rising as they approached.

"I couldn't prevent the French fur trappers from killing the beavers," Bia said. "And then the whites came in great numbers."

"But the Native Americans joined them," Limni said. "You're the ancient ancestor. You should have made them protect the beavers."

"How could I do that?" Bia said. "The white men had guns. They killed all the buffalo, and then the Natives had to trade pelts for food. I had no power over that. Why didn't you do something to stop the melting? You could have piled rocks in front of the glaciers or done something." Her voice grew shrill. "Why is this my fault?"

"You didn't stop the flood of people who came to settle. That's why it's your fault."

"You didn't do enough to protect the glaciers."

"You should have helped Natives protect their culture and way of life," Limni snarled, her lip curling. "The French fur trappers and other white men took over the hunting grounds and decimated the beaver. You let the whites destroy them."

"Please stop fighting," I said firmly, but both women ignored me, continuing to raise their voices and blame each other.

"It's your fault," Limni snapped.

"No, your laziness is to blame." Bia pointed her finger at Limni. "You sat around, wringing your hands while the glaciers melted. You did nothing."

Limni stood her ground, raising a green arm over Bia's head.

"Just stop," I yelled. "What's done is done, and we can't afford to fight. We must work together, and I need your help." My spine became granite and my voice boomed across Squaretop.

Two faces looked at me in surprise, one brown and one blue-green.

"Way to go, Diana," Kya said.

Ignoring her praise, I grabbed each woman's arm, pulling them apart and shaking both of them. "Neither one of you could have stopped humans from destroying the buffalo and beaver. Now the water runs out of the mountains too soon. There is little left after the ranchers pull water for irrigation. Bia, you couldn't change human behavior to protect the beaver and prevent whites from killing them. Limni, the planet is warming so quickly that you couldn't stop glaciers from melting, no matter how many rocks you piled to protect the ice."

"Listen to Diana," Kya said as she approached the women. She rested her hand on Bia's brown arm, then did the same with Limni. Her touch seemed to calm them and they stood quietly.

"I need your help," I repeated firmly. "We can't change what has happened, but maybe we can prevent further damage. I'm here to help the planet."

"How?" Limni said. "My largest glacier is half the size it used to be." Her piercing blue eyes blazed.

"She's right," Bia said. "The beaver are gone, the Natives are gone, and the buffalo are gone. All decimated by white men. Now, my Native children are confined to the reservation and whites own the land that isn't protected by the Forest Service." Her shoulders slumped in defeat. "I don't know what to do."

"Little Elk keeps talking about *Cerva Antiqua,* the ancient elk," I said. "Why? And I've figured out what I can give you in exchange for telling me how to find the elk."

"What do you have?" Bia said. She faced me, raising her eyebrows.

"First, let's agree to work together," I said. "I want you two to forget this ancient friction and help us."

"Okay. Fine. We'll stop," Bia said. She stood taller, regaining control of her anger.

"I'll stop," Limni said, her lips forming a grim line.

"Kya, will you bring the gift?" I didn't want to leave them, relieved the goddess was here to help. She walked to the chariot and returned with my pouch.

Nodding my thanks, I opened the pouch and removed the two copper cups we had used last night. "This is my gift in exchange for the secrets of the ancient elk."

Bia looked scornfully at the cups. "That's nothing. Why do I need those little things?"

"Just wait," I said. "Each of you take one and hold it up to your face. I'll pour some *Aqua Pura* for you to drink." As they each clasped the handle of a cup, I took out my flask and poured water from the source of the Elk River. "Even though you didn't ask for a gift, Limni, perhaps Bia will share a cup with you."

As the water from my flask filled their cups, I hoped they would be charmed by my gift. Would they have childhood memories like I did? Was there something from the past they had forgotten? Perhaps an ancient joy lost to granite as the Rockies formed? I looked at Kya, encouraged by her smile.

"Now take a sip and then hold the cup up to eye level. Look at your reflection and wait."

As the powerful women followed my directions, I held my breath, hoping Hephaestus would forgive me for surrendering this magical gift.

At first, nothing happened, and the two women looked at their cups silently. Then, Bia gasped, a beautiful smile illuminating her face. Limni's swift intake of breath followed, and I exhaled, watching their faces. Tears filled Bia's eyes, but she turned to face me with joy.

"I see myself as a child," the old woman said. "I'd forgotten my mother and father. I forgot the people of my village." She looked back at the cup, giggling like a girl.

"I'm young again," Limni said. "I used to be a lighter green when I ran on the edges of the glacier. I see my mother and father also." A soft sigh escaped her lips as she turned back to the cup.

"What a wonderful gift," Bia said, drinking again and peering into her cup. "How does this work? How did you come across this magical copper?" She continued to look at the cup.

"My uncle Hephaestus made this for Diana," Kya volunteered. "Anyone who holds the cup and drinks sees herself as a child. Forgotten memories return to you."

"How did he do it?" Limni asked. "I've heard of him, and I knew he made lightning bolts for Zeus, but didn't know he made things like this."

"He used his magic and some of my baby hair," I said. "Both Kya and I saw ourselves as young girls."

"You truly give this of your own free will?" Bia asked, her brown eyes searching mine. "You will miss seeing yourself as a child if you surrender these cups." Her gaze turned back to the copper surface, and she smiled softly. "I had forgotten my mother's face. Since the birth of the Rockies, I have roamed alone. If you surrender these cups, I will not return them."

"I freely give them to you," I said. "I must fulfill my duty to save clean water on the planet, and Little Elk led me to you so I can learn the secrets of the ancient elk." Inside, a soft pang of regret hardened to metaphoric granite that strengthened my mental spine.

"Very well, Diana, I accept your gift," Bia said, inserting her cup into the pocket of her buckskin dress. "And Limni, I give the second cup to you as a pledge of my willingness to work together."

"Thank you, Bia," Limni said, bowing from the waist and pocketing her own cup. "I will treasure this and drink with you often."

I sighed in relief. Maybe now I'd learn how the Red Desert elk could help me.

"You will find the elk next to the Oregon Buttes in the Red Desert," Bia said. "I don't know how they will help you, but that's where you'll find them."

"I've seen the Oregon Buttes from the highway," I said. "But I've never been in the desert."

A raucous squawk drew our attention skyward. The magpie,

followed by Indigo, landed on the edge of the chariot. "I'm back," Indigo announced.

"Good timing," I said. "We're going to the Red Desert. On the way, you can explain where you've been all night. We've been worried."

CHAPTER SIXTEEN
THE BLUEBIRD REPORT
THE POWER OF BLUE

I followed Marty as he flew from the base of the cliff and back to Diana on Squaretop Mountain. What a journey. I'd spent the night in his family nest, cuddled up with the magpie fledglings. Their big black wings kept me toasty, and their unique magpie scent filled my nostrils all night. After eating a tick for breakfast, I realized why their feathers gave off a metallic blood odor. I was glad my babies smelled like grasshoppers and dragonflies instead of ticks.

Eager to tell Diana that Marty had taken me on a tour of the Red Desert, I was surprised to see she and Kya were packing up, preparing to leave the mountain just as Marty and I reached the top. I landed on the chariot, and Diana announced we were going to the Red Desert.

"We've been worried about you, Indigo," Kya said. "Where have you been? We're already close to the desert, and since Mom is with Spruce, we're going to go directly there right now before heading back to the ranch."

"I know where the desert is," I said, hanging on to the titanium edging around the front while watching Diana. "I just flew over it with Marty." I nodded at Bia and Limni, who stood nearby.

"You did?" Kya asked. "Why did you go there?"

"I wanted to show Indigo the Blue Forest. It's west of Eden, a small town on the edge of the desert," Marty said. He landed on the chariot bench before flying to Glenda's back, and then he looked down at her golden rump.

"Don't look for ticks," I said. "Glenda is a special horse."

The mare looked back at Marty and whinnied just as he prepared to peck her.

"Okay," Marty said, straightening up. "I just thought maybe she had some lunch in her hair."

"Besides, they brush her all the time, so she probably doesn't have any." I was relieved he sat politely, no longer searching for ticks.

Glenda neighed again and tossed her head while Marty remained on her back.

"I know about the Blue Forest," Kya said.

"And I've heard about the Red Desert," Diana said, patting Glenda on the shoulder before placing the reins along her back, causing Marty to jump back to the chariot. Diana threaded the reins through the titanium circle in the front of the chariot. She turned to look at me. "I've never been there, except to see it from a distance when we drive to Rawlins on the way back to school."

"How do you know about the Blue Forest?" I asked Kya, ruffling my feathers. They still gave off a metallic blood smell from my night in the nest with Marty's family.

"My dad told me all about it," Kya said.

"What did your dad tell you?" Marty said.

I noticed Diana putting on her ring so she could understand what Marty was saying. "What about my babies?" I interrupted Marty, thinking out loud. "I guess I could send a message to Rock, so he knows where I am."

"I can send a magpie," Marty said.

"Would you do that?" I asked. "I know Rock won't mind if I'm gone a bit longer, but I want him to know."

"You know what?" Marty said. "I'll just go myself. It's not too far from here as the crow flies, so I could get there easily. After I talk to Rock, I can fly over to the Wind River Reservation and see those buffalo you talked about. I'll zip home now and let my mate know."

"I'm sure the magpies around the ranch can tell you where to look on the reservation," I said.

"Your news about the buffalo gives me hope for my species," Marty said. "I'm honored to have met you, little Mountain Bluebird. And you, too, Diana of the Wind Rivers." Marty bowed his head. "Goodbye, young goddess," he added, nodding to Kya as well. "I'll see all of you again someday, I hope."

"Tell Rock I love him," I shouted to Marty as he flew off.

"Well, that worked out well," Kya said. "What did he mean about hope for his species?"

"I'll explain later," I said. "It's a long story. Why are we going to the Red Desert?"

"You're going to find the Red Desert elk."

"Where exactly will we find them?" I asked. "And how will they help us?"

"I cannot reveal the secrets the elk keep," Bia said. "That is their story to tell. But I told Diana where to look for them."

"Where?" I asked.

"Go to the Oregon Buttes," Bia said.

"I know where that is," I said. "I saw them when Marty and I flew to the Blue Forest."

"Was the forest really blue, the way my dad said it would be?" Kya asked. "He said the forest was once a swamp with palm trees and giant ferns that grew long ago on the banks of an ancient lake. But now it's petrified. Did you see blue wood?"

"The petrified wood is buried," I said. "It's not an actual forest anymore. It's a large area of petrified wood, buried underground. Marty knew where to find some exposed pieces, so we went to look at it." I sat up taller, pushing against her hand as she continued to caress my back, pulling gently on my tail feathers in the way I loved.

"I want to see that someday," Kya said.

"I'll tell you about the Blue Forest on the way to the buttes," I said. "Maybe when we finish in the desert, we could go there."

Diana looked at Bia and Limni, then picked up the reins. "I'll come back and let you know how things go."

"We'll be here," Bia said.

"Good luck," Limni added.

I flew to the front of the chariot and perched near Diana, prepared to help guide her to the buttes. A flock of Western Meadowlarks converged underneath the chariot.

"You guys leave some space in front so I can guide us to Boar's Tusk," I shouted at the birds, who obligingly moved apart. Now I could see the ground directly ahead as we flew off Squaretop. Below, the Green River Lakes, headwaters of the Green River, shimmered in the sun, their glassy waters reflecting the surrounding cliffs.

"Do you know why the petrified wood is blue?" I asked Kya.

"Dad said that when the ancient lake flooded the forest, the trees fell into the water," she said. "The wood was preserved in the sediment at the bottom of the lake, and, over time, the sediment mixed with minerals that gave the wood its blue color."

"What kind of minerals?" Diana asked.

"Manganese, copper, and titanium," Kya said, looking ahead where the great expanse of the Red Desert filled the horizon.

We followed the path of the river below as it wound through meadows and onto a broad plain. The banks of the river were green with grass, but beyond that, the bright green turned to pale sagebrush, which soon became the dominant plant below us.

"It's hard to believe this was all once a huge lake," I said.

No trees grew here, but as far as the eye could see, the pale green of sagebrush contrasted with brown sand and rocks. We traveled in silence after I directed Diana to go south.

Looking up at her, I thought about the way Diana was changing. Last summer, she'd hesitated to make choices on her own, and we both relied on Persephone to help us in our travels. Today, Diana was in command of the chariot, taking charge, and making decisions without Persephone here to guide her. I admired Diana's strong hands on the reins, and the way she stood tall and straight, seemingly unafraid to take us on a new adventure. Would we find the desert elk? How would they help us? Diana seemed unconcerned, and, instead, focused on the task at hand, getting us to the Oregon Buttes.

The scope of Diana's influence was growing, it seemed. I respected the influence she had over glacier nymphs. They came when we landed near glaciers and willingly helped us. Bia, the ancient ancestor, was willing to help her. In addition, we might find the ancient elk. Things were moving in ways I didn't yet understand.

Unbidden, the Birds of Dawn came into to my mind. "Diana," I said, "I want to take Rock to meet the Birds of Dawn. Can we do that?"

She glanced down at me, her young hands firmly on the reins. "We can do that sometime. Why do you want him to go there?"

"I want him to see the River Oceanus. I want him to understand the importance of saving pure water because, at some point, he might come with us on our adventures." I looked up to gauge her reaction.

"That's an interesting idea," she said, looking ahead as we flew. "But why take him to the River Oceanus?"

"I think he'll love flying in the spray," I said. "Just like I did last summer." My experience flying to the River Oceanus and diving into its spray with the Birds of Dawn was transformative. I learned that the spray granted a bird's greatest desire. For me, that meant my entire body became cerulean, just like the males of my species. When my wings dried as we flew away from the river, my body turned back to its mousy grey color, leaving only my wingtips and tail covered in brilliant blue. I later learned that my lack of outer blue didn't matter because my inner blue was the source of my courage.

"I think he'll understand the importance of pure water if we go to the River Oceanus. After all, it's the source of all freshwater rivers, lakes, streams, and aquifers," I said. "But I also want to check up on the Birds of Dawn." I paused. "I'm worried about what's happening now that microplastics are in water all over the globe, even in glaciers at the top of the world."

"I remember you said that the Birds of Dawn gain energy from the spray of the River Oceanus," Diana said. "I agree we should check on them; we don't know what might happen if microplastics in the water coat their wings."

"That's what worries me," I said. "The Birds of Dawn accompany Eos on her journey as she brings up the sun each morning." I looked up at Kya, not sure she knew about that.

"Mom told me about Eos," Kya said. "I'd like to go with you and meet her."

I thought about the goddess with beautiful white wings. "If the Birds of Dawn cannot fly, Eos might lose her ability to bring up the dawn. They told me that just like legend says the English monarchy will crumble if the ravens leave the Tower of London, it might happen that Eos will lose her power without the Birds of Dawn."

"I saw her in March," Diana said. Diana had told us about her efforts to prevent the iceberg chunk from destroying the feeding grounds in the water off South Georgia Island in the southern seas. "I'd like to go back to the island of Eos sometime." She sighed. "I don't know what we'll do about microplastics. Sometimes I feel like it's too much for us to solve. How can we stop the production of plastic? How can we keep people from dumping it in the ocean?"

"I don't know," I said. "I just know we have to find a way."

"We'll tackle it together," Diana said, her resolve returning. "The United States makes large amounts of plastic. We have to let people know that and then stop this massive production that leads to so much pollution."

"Right," I said. "We can also ask Grams and Willy for ideas."

"We don't even know what impact microplastics have on humans," Diana said, "but we'll figure it out."

"So, another time, we'll decide when we'll take Rock to meet the Birds of Dawn?" I asked.

"Yes," Diana said. "I promise we'll do that."

"Thank you," I said, rubbing my head against her fingers as she held the reins.

I daydreamed about taking Rock to the edge of the world as we glided through the air. We might not be able to go until next summer. Maybe we would have only one batch of babies, and after they were old enough to live on their own, we could travel with Diana to meet Eos. I thought Rock might agree to that plan.

Our flock was growing so quickly that I didn't have to worry about producing two batches. Rock and I had left the meadow because there weren't enough nesting sites. Plenty of other birds already fulfilled the task of keeping our numbers growing. Still, I wasn't sure Mom would approve. Old habits can be hard to break.

I glanced up at Kya, who looked down at me and smiled. What a good companion she has become, I mused. Both of us depended on Diana, but Kya possessed her own strength, the solidity and endurance of rock and stone, fearless against wind and water, the power of crystal kyanite in her veins.

We are connected by our blueness, I realized. My inner blue gives me courage, and her inner blue does the same. I fluffed my feathers and looked ahead as I stood between the young goddess and Diana of the Wind Rivers. We made a good team, three strong females soaring through the sky.

CHAPTER SEVENTEEN
BIG WYOMING SAGE

We left Squaretop and flew away from Green River Lakes, traveling southwest for a bit in order to fly along the base of the mountains, leaving the forest behind. When we reached the lower elevation, I directed Glenda to the southeast. The terrain turned to grass, and then sagebrush rooted in reddish sand as we approached the Red Desert, a high-altitude, sagebrush steppe landscape dotted with formations that early settlers had used to find their way along the Oregon Trail. Far in the distance, the towering rocks of the Oregon Buttes stood silent against the sky.

"That's where we're going," Indigo piped, looking ahead from her perch on the chariot rim. It registered on me that she seemed to have gained a new sense of importance with the information she learned from her magpie friend.

Ahead, two flat-topped buttes rose from the ground, framed by the sage terrain. Oregon Buttes, jutting from the sage and red sand, had once been the landmark telling settlers they were at the edge of the Oregon Territory. Now, they signaled we were at the edge of the desert.

The vastness of the Red Desert was overwhelming. I'd seen prairie grasses blowing in the wind in the Buffalo Gap National Grasslands far into the distance. I'd seen cliffs echoing across the horizon from high mountain peaks in Wyoming, and, last summer, I'd seen the ocean for the first time and fully understood the power of water. But none of that prepared me for the immensity of the Great Divide Basin, a giant concaved landscape stretching to the edge of the earth, its only boundary the sky meeting the horizon.

My dad told me that although it was called a desert, some water flowed under the surface, pooling into shifting, seasonal lakes. Depending on the winter snowfall, temporary lakes and streams cropped up in depressions and draws, a glittering contrast to the red sand from which sprang the lifeblood of the desert, Wyoming Big Sage.

Grasses and flowers thrived under the sage, feeding countless animals, big and small, from elk towering ten feet into the sky to diminutive ground squirrels scurrying from one sage plant to the other, seeking sustenance and cover.

"Marty told me he's seen elk near the Oregon Buttes," Indigo said as we flew closer.

"I've heard that Red Desert elk are taller than mountain elk," I said. "Dad's friends hunt out here because of that. Their antlers are bigger, their bodies are much bigger, and their hair is darker red and curly."

"What?" Kya said. "Curly hair?"

"Well, not extremely curly, but it's longer and curls a bit, compared to hair on mountain elk." I studied the terrain below as we flew closer to the Oregon Buttes. "I'll land at the base of the butte, and we can look for some elk."

"We aren't going to just magically find them," Indigo said. "You might have to search a bit."

"I have a plan for that," I said. I guided the chariot to the ground after making sure no travelers were in sight. After landing, we quickly pulled the chariot to the side in a gully, concealing it behind a four-foot tall grouping of sagebrush. "This stuff is huge. It will hide the chariot perfectly while we look around."

"I know about this sagebrush," Kya said. "Spruce told me it's called Wyoming Big Sage. It grows out here in the desert and provides cover for animals. Most sage is half this size or smaller, but the Red Desert elk can lie down behind it and stay cool throughout the day. They also browse on the grass that grows at its base."

"Well, we've got a lot of sage to search through," Indigo said. "Maybe I should fly around and see if I can scare up some elk." She fluttered up to perch on a large sage branch.

"I have a better idea," I said, reaching up to pinch some succulent, green sage leaves. I pulled them off the branch, rubbing them between my fingers and raising it to my nose. "I love the smell of sagebrush. I wish they made a sagebrush perfume. I'd wear it."

Kya laughed. "Right. You'd be a hit at parties with that perfume." She grabbed some leaves to pinch and sniff. "It does smell good."

"What's your plan?" Indigo said, hopping from the branch to my shoulder.

"I'm going to send Little Elk out to find her desert cousins," I said.

"That's a good idea," Indigo said. She flew from my shoulder to the chariot. "She seems to have the ability to find important things."

"Yes," I said. "She found Running Elk Moon on Younts Peak last summer, she found Limni on Squaretop, and she found Bia there as well. I'm beginning to realize she's more than a copper decoration on my flask." I reached under the bench and retrieved my pouch, pulling out the flask. My elk tooth necklace became warm against my skin. I was on to something.

"How will she find them?" Kya asked.

"They might hear her bleating, or maybe she can smell them," I said.

"Honestly, it's probably magic from Hephaestus. After all, he made the copper cups."

"I think she might hear the elk also," Indigo said.

I felt pressure on my palm and looked down to see Little Elk pushing her nose against my hand. "Can you find the Red Desert elk?" I asked. She pawed the copper grass and nodded. "When I let you go, find them and come back, okay?" I didn't really know what else to tell her. She bobbed her head.

I held up the flask and watched as her copper legs carried her into the air, growing in size as she leapt. She didn't even stop to look back as she started around the base of the butte.

"Well, all we can do is wait and see," I said as she disappeared into the Wyoming Big Sage. "Might as well get comfortable in the chariot."

"Okay," Kya said, climbing back inside. She retrieved our food pouch from under the bench and sat.

I sat next to her and Indigo perched on the rim next to me.

"Will Little Elk return?" she asked, pressing against my fingers.

"Yes, she will, and she'll have an elk with her," I said with more confidence than I felt.

"When did you first realize Little Elk could find people?" Kya asked, reaching into the pouch and pulling out some honey cakes.

"I love those," Indigo said, flying to Kya's side of the chariot. We were silent for a while, eating our cakes and inhaling the pungent scent of the desert. I felt safe and secure, tucked in among the sage, eating and waiting for Little Elk to return.

"So, when did you first realize Little Elk could help you?" Kya said again, brushing crumbs from her lap.

"I was on Younts Peak last summer, and Tixi asked to hold my flask. I didn't give it a second thought and handed it over. Right away, the little copper elk jumped from the flask, turned into a full-grown animal when she hit the ground, and disappeared in the fog. She soon returned with Running Elk Moon. That's when I first met my great-great-great grandmother, the original owner of my elk tooth necklace." My neck warmed under my shirt where the necklace rested against my skin.

"I was with Marty when Little Elk jumped from the flask and found Limni, and later, Bia," Indigo said, lightly jumping from the bench to my leg. "But I was there last summer."

Out of habit, I tugged gently on the cerulean blue tips of her tailfeathers. "At first, I thought only a nymph could send Little Elk on search missions, but I learned I can do it as well."

"I hope she comes back soon. I'm getting tired," Indigo said, rubbing her head against my hand.

"Me, too," Kya said. "It's pretty lucky you have the elk flask. Can I lean on you, Diana?" She slid closer and placed her head on my shoulder.

I inhaled the clean scent of her hair. "That's fine," I said. "I think Hephaestus knew I would need help and that's why he gave me the flask. But I realize things aren't always going to be easy."

"Well, you did have to give something to Bia," Kya mumbled softly, falling asleep.

Bia needs some happiness, I reflected, recalling the way the cups had made her smile. After witnessing the destruction of Native culture and the deliberate murder of her people, she deserved something good in her life.

I probably should expect some trade-off for getting help from the Red Desert elk. I just didn't know what it could be. Last summer, I'd had to give up on the idea of a pack trip, and this summer was the same. Becoming Diana of the Wind Rivers had its obligations, and I'd come to realize that a year ago. I also had the added responsibility of the winged fillies. Would it be like this for the rest of my life? Giving up my time to save pure water?

Even on spring break, I'd given up skiing with Dad to help avert disaster in the Antarctic when I worked with the gods to steer the iceberg chunk away from South Georgia Island. That seemed so long ago, but it had only been a few months. I'd better expect more things like this to disrupt my life, I realized. I wondered if I would ever again cross-country ski by moonlight with Dad on the Sweetwater River. Saving pure water on the planet entailed more than joyous chariot rides.

Stop being so selfish, I chided myself. It was a small price to pay in order save pure water. I just was not sure I was up to the task. I still didn't even know what my powers are, or if I had any at all. At least I had the gods, Indigo, and Little Elk.

The others dozed in the warm sun. The desert wasn't unbearably hot, and a breeze floated through. "The high altitude keeps this from being a hot, hot desert," I said, aware the others probably didn't even hear me. "It actually gets cold here at night, I've heard."

Suddenly, Indigo sat up and peeped. From behind the large sagebrush beyond the chariot, Little Elk emerged. Directly following was a large bull elk that towered over her. But in spite of his size, I wasn't afraid because my elk tooth necklace warmed my skin. Four other elk came out of the tall sage, standing at attention directly behind the bull. Little Elk paused next to the chariot and bleated joyfully, letting us know she was proud to have achieved her goal.

Kya straightened, and Glenda whinnied nervously, shifting her hooves in the red sand before settling down.

"Thank you, Little Elk," I said. "I knew you could do this." I held up the flask so she could jump back on it, but was surprised when she didn't immediately follow our routine.

Instead, she turned to nuzzle the neck of the spectacular animal at her side. He turned his head, reaching down with his muzzle to gently sniff her face. I watched as they rubbed noses and rested their foreheads against one another. Would she refuse to return with me?

Finally, she blew softly through her nostrils and looked at me. For one moment, her eyes were wild, full of freedom and life. Then she shook her head as duty apparently won out, and she leapt into the air, returning to my flask, once more a small copper creature.

"Thank you," I whispered, grateful she had returned. I put on my ring so I could speak with the bull elk who patiently watched. "Greetings. I am Diana of the Wind Rivers. I seek the help of the Red Desert elk."

"Hello, Diana. We had knowledge of your coming." He bowed his head. His massive body towered over the chariot as I stood to greet him. His impressive antlers extended into the air, and the sunlight danced across his red coat.

"How did you know about me?" A deep calm descended upon me as I looked into his brown eyes, wise with the patience of time and wind blowing across the sagebrush, shaping the desert and its plants.

"Just as the prophecy said a girl-child would be born in the place where water enters the earth, so does the elk prophecy say that one day, this young warrior will come for water, and we must show her the deep lake, the treasured remnants of ancient Lake Gosiute," the bull elk said.

"What? You knew I would come here? You knew I would help save pure water on the planet?" I said. How could that be?

"Yes. The prophecy foretold of your coming. We guard the entrance to the secret underground chamber of ancient Lake Gosiute," he said. "We have for tens of thousands of years."

"*Lacus Antiquus* means ancient lake," I said. "The indigenous ancestor, Bia, told me you might help me. We didn't know why Little Elk kept mentioning an ancient lake, but you tell me there is significant water in this desert."

"Yes," he said. "We have funneled water into this chamber for as long as my species existed. This entire area was once a grand lake, and we protect the remnants of that ancient water. Minerals, oil, and gas are not the only valuable treasure hidden under the desert. Water is the most cherished resource, and, like oil, it is an underground finite resource."

"Are you saying Diana can use this water to help humans?" Indigo asked.

The magnificent elk turned his brown eyes on the little grey

Mountain Bluebird, her courage evident in the proud stance she took while perching on the edge of the chariot, bravely looking up at the massive creature whose eyes were almost larger than her entire body. The elk leaned down to gently sniff Indigo, creating a tableau of contrasts: his massive head versus her tiny black beak; his long eyelashes on brown eyes next to her beady black ones; her little feet gripping the chariot, dwarfed by his massive hooves. She didn't flinch as he sniffed, his breath ruffling the feathers on her head.

"Yes, little bluebird, Diana has the power to use the water we have protected for many millennia." He turned to look at me. "I will show you the lake, but the others must remain behind."

"I'll wait here with Indigo," Kya said. "But where are you taking Diana?"

"Greetings, young goddess," the bull elk said. "The birds told us of your birth."

"I'm Kya," she said with a bow. "I'm pleased to meet you."

"Where is the lake?" I asked.

"I will take you to see the water and to meet our leader. She will explain many things to you. However, you cannot reveal the entrance to our underground location."

"I won't," I promised. "Wait," I said. "I can't leave Kya behind. I told Persephone I'd take care of her on this trip." I looked at my charge, realizing the absurdity of worrying about the safety of the young goddess.

"I'll be fine," Kya said . "Indigo and I will look out for each other."

"But what if someone comes along and sees you? Or what if other elk come and charge at you? These are big creatures," I said.

"We have the chariot, and we can fly away," Kya said, laying her hand on my arm. "Don't forget I'm a goddess. I don't know what my full powers are, but I can fling large boulders at any intruder." She pointed to an area a short distance away where boulders rested among the sage.

"And I can peck their eyes out," Indigo said, flying to Kya's shoulder.

"None of that will be necessary," the elk said. "I'll leave two strong bulls to guard your friends. They will protect them." At his nod, two huge young bulls came toward us.

Glenda snorted and shook her head but calmed when I spoke.

"It's okay." I was impressed by their size as they loomed over the chariot. "You two be careful." I turned to Kya and Indigo. "Follow their directions if anything happens."

"We'll be okay," Kya said. "Watch this." She pointed to the boulders. Raising her hand, she laughed as a huge one floated up from the ground. Suddenly, it shot into the sky, and, as Kya flicked her fingers, zoomed across the sage. With another flick of her fingers, it stopped in the air a short distance away, hovering briefly before dropping to the ground with a thud. Dust spiraled into the air and the elk near us jumped in surprise. "See?" she said. "I can take on anything."

"You sure can," I said. "I've never seen you do that."

"I've been practicing up Sinks Canyon," she said. "Just testing myself."

"Good enough," the elk said. "Let's get going, Diana. The other two will wait here, protected by my bulls, even though Kya seems perfectly capable." He nodded at the young goddess.

"I'm ready," I said. "Is it far away?"

"Everything is far away in this desert. However, it won't take long because I'm going to give you a ride."

"You mean I get to ride on an elk the way elves do in books?" I said, feeling a little apprehensive. I'd ridden horses for most of my life but getting on an elk was a different story.

"Yes," he said. "I'm not sure what elves are, but you'll ride on my back. Come here." He lowered his head, bent his front legs, and kneeled.

I hopped onto the ground, and walked below his large antlers. I stood next to the large creature, suddenly fearful. But once I put my hand on his shoulder, I was instantly calmed by his warm body and strong scent, which was somewhere between musky and sagebrushy, earthy, and not completely unpleasant. The hair on his back was smooth and shiny, not the least bit dirty. I grabbed his neck and leaped on, just as I did when riding my horse Daisy bareback on summer mornings.

As soon as I was aboard, he stood, making me realize that he was definitely much larger than a horse. I gripped tightly with my knees. "I will trust you to keep secret the location of our underground lake."

I sat up straight. "I promise."

"Good," he said. "Let's go."

At first, he walked sedately, but then his pace picked up, sending up dust from the ground as we zig-zagged through the sage.

"Can you hang on if I run?" he asked.

"Yes," I said, gripping harder with my knees.

"Let's go," he said. "Hold tight."

He sprang forward, and at first I thought I would fall as my body bent back while he surged forward. He gave a little hop that aligned my body with his, and then it felt like we were flying. Of course, I knew we weren't because his hooves hit the ground with smooth thumps, and I heard the other bull elk following behind. Sage brushed my legs, but with a soft caress, not the deep scratching I expected. He ran for some time, and the rhythm made this feel like an easy journey, even though his deep breathing and warm body alerted me to his efforts. I didn't even have time to look around as we bounded through the sage.

When I began to tire of gripping his ribcage, he slowed to a trot, and then a walk. The soft footfalls of the others behind us reminded me we weren't alone. The smell of sagebrush became stronger, and dust no longer swirled around us.

"Now you will walk," the elk said, coming to a stop. "The trail to the lake is steep."

I held on to his neck as I dismounted, found my footing, and stood. I steadied myself against his back for a moment longer until my land legs returned.

"Keep one hand on my back and I'll guide you as we walk," he instructed. "We're going underground, but our cave has a high ceiling and wide path. You won't hit your head."

"Okay," I said, reaching out to him again. He shifted closer, making it easier for me to walk.

"Good. You'll be fine." His hooves clanged against rock and I saw granite under my feet. "Just trust me."

I had no choice but to do just that as we rounded a large boulder skirted by sagebrush. The light disappeared as we entered the cave. Cool moisture touched my arms and cheeks, and caressed my neck. We walked down a steep trail that snaked back and forth.

"You have now entered a cavern where no human has been before," he said.

"Just like Sinks Canyon Cave," I said. The tang of water on limestone filled my nostrils and I inhaled deeply, remembering the first time I'd entered Sinks Canyon Cave last summer. Soon, dripping noises accompanied the cool breeze that drifted past my cheek. I heard the flow of water far below. "Is that an underground river I hear?"

"I cannot tell you about this place, but we will soon speak with our queen, the Guardian of Lake Gosiute."

"You have an elk queen?" I said as the cave trail widened to a broad room.

"Yes," another voice said. I had never before heard a deeper, older, wiser voice.

As I breathed deeply, my eyes adjusted to the light flooding the area. From overhead, sunbeams shot through a hole in the cave ceiling.

"This skylight gives us light during the day," the elk before me said. "Welcome to the chambers of our lake, *Lacus Antiquus*, which means ancient opening, ancient pool, ancient lake. I am the queen of the Red Desert elk."

"Hello," I said, compelled by her presence to bow from the waist. "I am Diana of the Wind Rivers."

"Welcome to our cave," she said, lowering her head slightly. "Long have we waited for your coming, Diana." Her wise eyes held ancient knowledge, an awareness of time and desert sand shaped by wind and water.

I heard water rushing nearby, even though I couldn't see it.

"The prophecy states a girl-child would be born in the place where water enters the earth," she said.

"That's Sinks Canyon," I said. "The river there disappears into a limestone cave." I again inhaled the tangy smell of water on limestone, just as it smelled in Sinks Cavern. But this cave seemed much, much older.

"Just as it was foretold that you were born to save pure water on the planet, so does the elk prophecy say that one day this young warrior will come to us for water, and we must show her the deep lake. We guard the treasured remnants of ancient Lake Gosiute, some of the purest hidden waters on the planet," the queen said.

"You guard the entrance to this cave?" I said.

"Yes," she replied. "Our elk herds around the Oregon Buttes are the decoy herds, distracting humans from the entrance to our underground lake."

"What do you mean? How are they decoys?"

"We capitalize on the fact that humans like to hunt and eat us," she said. "The duty of my warriors is to lure humans away from our secret location deep in the Great Divide Basin. Much as in medieval Europe, when every family gave a son and daughter to the church to continue the line of monks and nuns, each elk family gives a young bull or cow to the diversion herd."

"They intentionally volunteer for this job?"

"Yes," she said. "The best and wiliest runners survive in the sage, weaving in and out, hoping that no rifle scope pins them down during hunting season."

"People talk about spotting elk herds near the Oregon Buttes," I said.

She nodded. "Our diversion herds hide in the sagebrush, and when humans come near, they run to draw attention to the elk. Unfortunately, it's a dangerous job because some elk lose their lives during hunting season."

"You mean they are killed?" I knew the answer, but my thoughts came out anyway.

"We are tasty because we eat Wyoming Big Sage," the bull elk interjected. "We capitalize on the human desire to hunt and eat us. For some reason, humans then like to pose with our dead bodies, not caring that our tongues hang lifelessly from our mouths when they prop up our dead heads."

"I've seen that," I said, recalling trophy shots of hunters with their fresh kill, proudly holding up the heads of animals to display the size of the antlers. I decided not to mention that my dad and Willy guided hunters in the mountains.

"We will now take you down to the lake," the queen said. "You have the power to draw upon this water."

"I do?" It seemed as if all I could do was ask questions.

"Yes," she said. "But you must remember this is a finite source. It took thousands of years for this lake water to accumulate, and we have guarded it with our lives so that you can use it as needed."

"But who will decide when it's needed?"

"You have that power," she said.

"I do?" This was too much to absorb. What if I used it in the wrong way or at the wrong time? What if it ran out? What if it's not enough? Then it really hit me. How was I supposed to make a decision like this? I was on my own, without anyone to guide me.

CHAPTER EIGHTEEN
GUARDIANS OF THE ANCIENT LAKE

"It's hard to believe this much water is here," I said to the elk queen.

"Like Killdeer, who pretend to have a broken wing to lure foxes from their nest, elk divert humans from the entrance to the cave by running across the desert, luring humans away with the promise of bagging a rare Red Desert elk," she said. "For thousands of years, we have done this."

"I'm amazed humans haven't found this water source," I said.

"What better hiding place than in the desert?" she said. "The Great Divide Basin rims a wide expanse of land: hills, rocks, shifting sand, big sage, lakes, and creeks that appear and reappear elsewhere over time."

"But how is it the water remained in this chamber?"

"There used to be a sea here, but it evaporated," she said. "Then the sea floor hardened, and, over time, the indentation filled with water, eventually becoming ancient Lake Gosiute, *Aqua Pura Antiqua*. What you see is the remnants of that lake. For a very long time, water has trickled underground. Now we must leave the chamber and return to the surface."

I nodded, and she turned, leading the way as we hiked up the trail. The slow drip, drip, drip of water faded the higher we climbed, and soon, dry air caressed my face. The warmth of sunshine and the afternoon wind touched my cheeks as we left the cave to find a small herd of bull elk waiting.

"You're going to ride for a while. I'll come along to say goodbye," the queen's voice vibrated near my ear. It was unnerving the way she'd moved so silently to my side.

"Okay," I answered, as the bull elk I'd ridden before came up next to me. I put my hand on his shoulder after he kneeled, and climbed on his warm back, gripping with my knees. The queen led the way as we bounded over the ground, the pungent smell of sagebrush filling my nostrils. After a long ride, the queen trotted and then paused. The small herd that was our escort milled around us.

"You can climb down now," the queen said.

The bull elk carrying me knelt so I could dismount, and I joined the queen where she stood a few feet away at the edge of a cliff, looking over the vast sagebrush desert endlessly stretching to touch the sky.

"There are great natural resources deep underground," the queen said, turning her head to look over the Great Divide Basin.

"Oil?" I said. "Humans will be after that."

"Water," she said, facing me.

"What?" I inhaled sharply.

"Reserves of ancient water," she said. "And you have the power to bring it to the surface. The water can only be used by those truly working to save *Aqua Pura*. Diana, you are one such person."

"But what happens if I use this water?" I asked.

"Just be aware that what you withdraw will take a long time to replace," she said. "You'll have to decide if you want to use it now."

"Well," I spoke slowly, my voice gaining speed as the ideas churned, "if I withdraw water now, it might help humans and animals in the short term, but will it make a difference in the long run?" I thought about the beaver drops I planned to do in August. Adding extra water now could make a difference, buying time until I could relocate new beavers in the mountains. The extra water would help this summer and the beavers would create mountain ponds that would slow the progression of water from the mountains next summer.

"The plants and animals here have learned to survive with less water. Wyoming Big Sage has roots growing six feet into the ground. Humans must do the same," she said. "Our ancient elk culture is dedicated to preserving and protecting the lake. Just imagine the water from rain and snowmelt flowing into these crevices between the rocks. For tens of thousands of years, the Great Divide Basin has been saving water for you." She turned her head, focusing her large brown eyes on me.

"I don't know what to say," I said. The magnitude of their efforts was astounding, and I couldn't digest it right in the moment.

"Humans should follow our example and change the way they live in order to conserve water, just as the elk have done," she said, her direct look making me feel it was my responsibility to make this happen.

"I know it's my job to influence humans," I said. "But I'm only one person."

She stared steadily and silently at me.

"I'll do all I can," I said, keeping my doubts inside. "I'm going to call it forth. I just hope that withdrawing water now will be a one-time deal."

She didn't speak.

"If I draw from this water source, how do I get it to the Green River?" I said.

"You'll have to figure that out," she said. "But don't forget the powers of the young goddess, Kya. She can help you."

"What can she do?" I asked.

"She can move stone, correct?"

"I think so. Her dad is Hades, god of the underworld."

"You two talk. My elk will take you back now," she said. "We've traveled far from the secret location and you're almost near the others."

"I'm going to call it forth," I stated firmly.

"Very well, Diana. But remember that you must use this water sparingly," she said, turning and walking away until she disappeared in the cover of Wyoming Big Sage.

The bull elk returned to me and kneeled, my signal to climb on board. He bounded forward, and I held tight with my knees as we returned to the base of the Oregon Buttes, where Kya and Indigo waited with the chariot.

When I dismounted, they eagerly rushed forward.

"What happened? What did you find?" Kya asked while Indigo fluttered around our heads.

"You'll never believe what I saw," I said, and proceeded to tell them of my experience. "The queen elk said I should talk to you."

"So, you've decided to use some water?" Indigo said when I finished. She perched on Kya's shoulder, her little black feet hanging tight to the young goddess.

"Yes, Indigo," I said. "I will use the pure water collected by the elk." I turned to Kya. "The queen said I should talk to you about how we can get the water into the Green River."

"I'm not surprised at this underground water source," Kya said. "For tens of thousands of years, the Great Divide Basin has funneled water into the bed of the ancient sea. The many fossils out here are proof that sea creatures once lived here in great abundance long ago. The Continental Divide travels down the spine of the Wind River Mountains, and splits in the desert, only to come together again miles away. This area is called the Great Divide Basin, and all water flowing in remains here."

"You know a lot about it," I said. "I'm impressed. Between us, we should be able to figure out a solution."

"My dad told me about this feature," Kya said. "All the water in the Great Divide Basin remains in the Red Desert. A place called Picket Lake is only one source of the water there."

"Marty told me that's why so many animals migrate to the desert in winter," Indigo said. "Elk, moose, deer, and antelope travel from the mountains in Yellowstone and the Wind Rivers, staying in the desert to find food throughout the winter. They like the tasty grass under the sage."

"Well, let's do this," I said. "We're going to figure out a way to get the water out of the underground lake and into the Green River. But we have to make sure people don't notice the increased flow of water."

"Won't they just figure it's additional snowmelt?" Kya said. "My mom told me they don't always measure the mountain snowpack exactly, so maybe they'll think the extra water is a result of that. Inaccurate snowpack measurements."

"That's a good explanation," I said. "It might work. In fact, we don't have to explain anything. We'll just let them assume the extra water is due to their faulty measurements."

"Good idea." Indigo said. "Humans always try to count exactly how many birds are on a lake, but sometimes they're wrong, my mom said. Maybe that will happen with water levels. We don't have to worry."

"I have an idea," Kya said.

"What?" I asked.

"My dad taught me how to create tunnels through stone."

"He did? Why?" Indigo piped.

"He's creating tunnels to relieve pressure underground in North Dakota in order to channel the toxic water away from aquifers. They use harsh chemicals to fracture the oil out of the ground, and he's trying to prevent those chemicals from polluting underground water."

"How will that help us?" Indigo asked.

"I'll create a tunnel in the rock leading from the elks' underground water supply, and we'll channel it directly into the Green River," Kya said. "That flows into Flaming Gorge near the Wyoming border with Utah. When the levels in the gorge rise, they'll chalk it up to mountain snowmelt."

"That just might work," I said.

She nodded. "I am worried about the instability I might cause when I create the tunnel. As I displace rocks, it could cause problems because I'll be shifting things around underground," Kya said. "And I definitely don't want to hit a gas pipeline. Humans have pierced the earth's crust to find the treasure of gas and oil. What they don't realize is that this desert contains something far more valuable—vast amounts of water."

"A friend of mine from high school found a petrified turtle shell in the Red Desert," I said, looking at the twisting and curving gully of hardened sand near us.

"That's because this place is the remnants of an ancient lake, Lake Gosiute," Kya said. "When the lake dried up, the sand on the bottom hardened. Strong rains created streams that carved trenches into the earth and shaped these sandy islands sticking up. My dad told me about that."

"He also told you about the Blue Forest," Indigo said. "We're going there on the way home, right?"

"Yes," I said. "We'll stop there and then report back to Bia before returning to the ranch."

"Good," Indigo said.

"Now, we've got to figure out how you'll make a tunnel to get the ancient lake water into the Green River," I said, turning to Kya.

"I've already thought about how I can do that," she said. "Let's sit down and I'll tell you."

Once we were settled in the chariot, Kya pulled a silver chain from under her shirt. "Dad taught me how to use my kyanite necklace to manipulate stone." She looked up, her youthful face serious.

Kya was small and wiry, but tough like hardened stone. In fact, her name came from the mineral kyanite, which formed blue-grey crystals, through the deep, heavily pressured process that formed metamorphic rock. The immense pressure on the bedrock under the Earth's surface as sections rose and fell over time generated enough friction and heat to create an entirely new rock, kyanite. From this, the young goddess had received her name.

As Kya looked up at me, my eyes roamed her familiar features. Diminutive, but angular, her face was like the cliffs created when the Rockies were born. Patrician and petite, her strong profile rose above slender lips. Her high cheekbones drew slight hollows in her cheeks, adding to the beauty of her wide sapphire eyes. Her ears were almost elfin, with slightly rounded points at the top that emphasized the elegance of her angled face.

She scowled, and, for a moment, I saw what she might look like as an old woman. I knew I would never see that because Kya would forever appear young, just like her mother, and she would never age into the appearance created by her scowl. The image vanished instantly when she arched her eyebrows and opened her mouth to speak. "This stone makes me feel strong."

"I forgot about your necklace," I said. "Mine makes me stronger. It warms my skin when I'm around elk or when I think about doing something hard, like last summer when I fought the oil monster in the Gulf of Mexico."

"Mom told me it protects you, also," Kya said.

"It does." I reached inside my shirt and pulled it out. "Even now, it gives me strength."

We looked at each other and smiled. Kya was so easy to be around. We both looked down at our necklaces.

"Yours is beautiful," I said.

The fluid chain of her necklace gleamed. The silver connected links merged with fine silver filigree that gripped the top of her dark blue crystal, shaped by Hades into an obelisk.

"Dad had this made when I was born," she said. She rubbed her thumb along the surface of her necklace.

Indigo hopped onto her leg, reaching over to peck at the blue crystal.

"Dad said this kind of rock splits along the planes of its structure, so he held it in his hand at the exact moment of my birth, causing the planes to bond together and merge with me. I've never tried to use it without him, but I want to now." Kya looked up at me confidently. "I know how to do this."

"I remember you told me kyanite is found in Sinks Canyon," I said, touching the blue-grey obelisk. In certain light, it turned grey, but was vivid blue when viewed from the front. It looked like a polished sapphire, but I knew it wasn't. A shock ran through my hand when I touched the smooth surface. My spine hardened and I sat up straight, the image of a tall cliff flashing in my head.

"Granite is your stone," Kya said, explaining what had happened. "My kyanite helps me sense that."

"That's amazing," I said. "Are you sure you want to try tunneling? We're new at this warrior thing and we might mess it up."

"You're right." Kya laughed darkly. "We might do something wrong."

"I'm here to help you," Indigo trilled. "We have the power of blue."

Kya laughed again, this time with a happier note. "We *do* have blue courage."

Even though the elk told me to keep the underground lake secret, I had to tell the others so we could travel back to draw water. We boarded the chariot and I directed Glenda across the desert to the cave. I knew she'd find it. Outside, two bull elk guarded the entrance, and I knew more were nearby, hidden in the sage. "Let's go inside," I said. The others followed me, and we walked down the trail to the lake, where the queen waited. I introduced Kya and Indigo, who both offered polite greetings.

"This location is secret," the queen said. "Diana brought you here to help her, but this lake must remain a secret."

"I promise," Indigo vowed.

"Me, too," Kya said in a somber fashion, her sapphire eyes wide.

"Very well," The queen said with a nod. "Let's begin." She addressed Kya. "You know what to do?"

Kya looked at the necklace in her hand. "I do now." She walked toward the cave entrance. "I'll drill a tunnel from the cave to the Green River. Let's go."

She stopped at the edge of the lake, looking from there to the cave wall. "I'll bore the tunnel through the wall at a higher level than the lake, so you can control how much water goes through the tunnel. If I build it lower, we might not be able to stop the flow. This way, you can bring the water up to the level of the tunnel and stop it when you've pulled enough out."

"Okay," I said. "Begin tunnelling." Indigo and I watched as Kya approached the wall, holding her necklace in one hand. She reached up and caressed the damp wall.

"Right here," she said, as if coming to an agreement with the rock. She cradled the necklace in her hand and gently blew on the blue stone. Touching the point of the stone against the wall right above her head, she commanded, "Find the Green River."

A soft scraping came from the kyanite where she held it against the rock. The stone began to spin, soon moving so quickly that it routed out a hole much wider than its circumference, dragging the chain behind. Now just a blur, the stone disappeared, sending dust back to the entrance as it carved a passage for the water.

I looked at Kya, who stood to the side, focusing all her attention on the widening tunnel. Dust continued to come out of the hole, but she ignored it. Her eyes turned dark blue as all her energy focused into the wall, following and commanding the stone. The minutes seemed to stretch into an hour. Suddenly the dust stopped, and a swift intake of breath from Kya told me something had happened.

"We reached the river," she said. "My stone did its job." The blue stone shot from the tunnel, and Kya reached out, catching it in her hand. She quickly placed the necklace around her neck. "Now you have to draw the water up and into the tunnel. I've bored below the surface of the river so that the water from here goes into the river without others seeing it." She looked directly into my eyes. "But you have to quickly start water flowing into the tunnel from this end so that it doesn't flow back this way. My tunnel gradually descends toward the river, but soon enough water will fill the tunnel that the force of the flow will come this way."

"How will we stop it?" I asked.

"I can use some boulders to block the tunnel," she said, pointing to large rocks at the base of the wall. "I'll do that when you tell me you've pulled out enough water."

I returned to the edge of the lake where the queen of the elk waited. "Bring up the water," she said. "The power is yours."

Not sure what to do, I looked at her. "How?"

"Draw upon your experiences," she said in her deep, gentle voice. She rubbed my shoulder with her muzzle in an encouraging and comforting manner, as if recognizing my feeling of inadequacy.

Her breath touched my skin, and the elk tooth necklace grew warm under my shirt. Then I knew what to do. Closing my eyes, I remembered last summer when Poseidon had turned me into a molecule of water so I would understand the water cycle and its power on earth.

I took myself back to that time when I'd joined other molecules to become a drop of rain, descending from the sky to the earth in a crescendo of excited voices, plummeting into the Middle Fork of the Popo Agie River in Sinks Canyon in spring, returning to the sky as evaporated water, and then falling as winter snow in the Wind River Mountains.

At the same time I was reliving that experience, I was also aware that I was in the cave with the queen and the others, smelling the tang of damp limestone and hearing the lap of ancient Lake Gosiute on the granite shelf shore, pure water over ten thousand years old. Was I to draw this to fill swimming pools, irrigate almond groves, and grow alfalfa to feed cattle destined for the slaughterhouse? Perhaps, in part. But even more so, I was drawing this pure water for the indigenous people in the Southwest who conserved this life-giving resource. Native people who protected precious water just as the elk did, saving it for the future because Earth would always need it.

I held my eyes shut, again becoming that molecule of two hydrogen atoms and one oxygen, imagining myself as part of this *Aqua Antiqua*, ancient water. And then I raised it up in my mind, the synchronicity of water, the fluidity of its flow, pulling my fellow molecules along. I became one with the water.

Countless droplets merge within me to form a stream, and we flow up the shelf like a reverse waterfall to enter the tunnel Kya's efforts produced. We forge forward, swirling through the tunnel to the Green River which joins the Colorado, eventually draining into the Sea of Cortez on the west coast.

Pushing headlong into the banks of the Green River, the fierce flow of water poured into the sunlight above ground for the first time in over ten thousand years. The rush of fresh air built up explosive bubbles when we joined the Green, my fellow molecules laughing and singing a chorus of ecstatic synchronicity as we moved with our cousins in joyous unity. We invaded the Green and dispersed quickly in the forceful flow of the pure mountain waters racing toward the sea.

Just when I became concerned about how much water I was withdrawing, a loud rumble reverberated through the ground and the tunnel collapsed, trapping some water inside as the flow faltered and halted. The tunnel was open no more.

That's all the water we'll draw today, I thought, willing myself to return to my body in the cave. I'd transported water to the surface, making an expensive withdrawal from a lake worth more than gold. I'd removed water that wouldn't be replaced for centuries.

I rushed to Kya. She leaned against the cave wall where the tunnel opening had been moments before. Already, the water receded to the lake. I sat next to her, the cave floor wet and cold beneath me.

"It collapsed," Kya said, her shoulders slumping. "I'm sorry." Her sapphire eyes implored me for forgiveness.

"It's just as well," I said. "We withdrew enough water for now, and I was about to stop the process." I put my arm around her slender shoulders. "You did a fine job. I couldn't have done this without you."

She sighed and leaned against me, holding the kyanite necklace in her hand. "This helped me remain strong. But you helped also, Diana."

Indigo fluttered close and perched on Kya's other shoulder. Soft feathers touched my hand as Indigo rubbed her head against Kya's face.

"You performed well, young goddess." The queen stood next to us.

"Thank you," Kya said. "I lost control at the end, but it worked long enough to draw water."

"Your work here is done for now," the queen said, turning to me. "You alone have the power to draw water from this lake. Return only when it's absolutely necessary."

I stood to face the queen, feeling Kya come to her feet next to me. "I am grateful for your help," I said, thinking that was not enough to say to this grand being. "I won't return unless it's necessary."

She nodded and stood back. "Follow the path to the surface. I'll stay here to monitor the lake for a while." She lowered her head next to mine.

I reached up to stroke her soft muzzle, and my elk teeth warmed my neck under my shirt. "I will see you again," I said. Somehow, I knew that would happen.

We turned and walked up the path, climbing into the chariot for the flight home.

"Don't forget the Blue Forest," Indigo said, fluttering to the front.

"Okay," I said. "You direct us there."

A short time later, she chirped brightly. "There. Down there."

Looking over the edge of the chariot, I saw nothing but sagebrush, red sand, and rocks. Disappointed, I turned to Indigo. "There's nothing there. Where is the forest of blue trees?"

"Remember?" she said. "Marty told me most of the blue petrified wood is underground. People have been coming out here and digging it up."

After we disembarked, Kya ran forward and kneeled, placing her palm on the pebbly sand, bowing her head as if communicating with the earth, blessing the rocks. She raised her face, looking at me with serious, dark sapphire eyes. "This forest is a merger of my brother and me," she said. "Wood turned to stone." Her blue gaze gleamed. "I found a piece of blue wood on the surface." She held up an ordinary rock. But when she turned it over, I saw grey-blue tones.

"I'm connected to you and Spruce because I'm blue," Indigo peeped.

"Yes, you are," Kya said, touching a finger to Indigo's cerulean tail feathers. "I just don't know why we are connected." She studied Indigo intently.

"We'll figure it out," I said, even though I knew there was no guarantee.

***

We were quiet on the ride back to Squaretop, and I mused that the merger of once-green wood into blue stone was indeed a symbol of Kya and Spruce. I wondered what power this transformation contained. "Something very strong," I said out loud. "I think petrified wood from the Blue Forest could be very strong."

"I agree," Kya said.

"It's the power of blue," Indigo said. "The power of the courage in my heart."

"The power of water and the sky," I added. "We have it, and we can harness it. Remember last summer when you came to Grams' wedding with an entire flock of Mountain Bluebirds?"

Indigo nodded.

"Together, the three of us have the power of blue," I said, looking at my companions. "Just like last summer when you learned being blue on the outside didn't matter, Indigo, as long as you had inner blue, the courage symbolized by the color blue."

"We all have the courage of blue," Kya said.

I nodded. "Hopefully, this draw of *Aqua Antiqua* will provide enough water to buy us some time. If Poseidon can cover the glaciers with seaweed, slowing the ice melt, and keeping Earth's temperature in balance while we come up with other solutions, it might work. Then we can start saving more glaciers."

"Seaweed will save glaciers?" Indigo asked.

"Yes," I said. " After Poseidon told me that he's working with the merfolk to cover glaciers, I read an article where scientists have developed seaweed coverings for glaciers, just like Poseidon is doing."

I didn't even want to think about how to solve the problem of microplastics.

After flying for some time, I noticed a glint of light reflecting off water in the far distance. "That must be Picket Lake," I said mostly to myself.

"That's right," Indigo said. "Marty told me that's an important stopover for migratory birds, like geese, swans, and pelicans."

"Swans and pelicans?" I repeated. "Here in the desert?"

"Yes," Indo said, flying from her perch on the bench to join me at the helm. "On their way north and south in spring and fall, they stop here to rest and eat."

"Do you mean Trumpeter Swans?" I recalled earlier this summer when a Trumpeter Swan had flown above the chariot and dropped a white feather, which was safely tucked in a wooden box on the dresser in my bedroom at the bunkhouse. I still didn't know why the bird had given me the gift, but I sensed it was important.

"Yes. Marty told me they've been making a comeback since they were almost wiped out in the 1930s," she said. "He wasn't alive then, but magpies like to talk among themselves about the history of other birds in the area. He said his granddad told him that in the early days of his childhood, humans hunted as many Trumpeters as they could because they are bigger than a man from beak to webbed toes."

"Why Trumpeters?" I'd seen them once at Yellowstone Lake; we'd camped there when I was a kid. "They're magnificent birds."

"That's partly why they were hunted so much. They have strong, large hides and beautiful white feathers," Indigo said. "I'm glad I'm too small to be huntable by humans."

"But you're still valuable," Kya said, coming forward to join us in front.

By now, we were much closer to Picket Lake, a large body of water in the sagebrush desert, visible for miles from the air. As we approached, I could see cattle grazing on one end of the lake, small dots of black and deep red. "Those are red and black Angus." I pointed toward the animals. "I don't see any birds anywhere."

"It's only July, so few birds are migrating through," Indigo said. "Marty told me this is an ancient body of water that's been here for centuries."

"Let's land down there," I said, pointing again. "Glenda could use a drink of water." The mare whinnied as we flew through the air, agreeing with my assessment.

As Glenda landed smoothly and trotted in the grassy area above the shoreline, I pulled on the reins to stop her progress. She slowed to a walk and waited patiently while we unhitched the chariot so she could walk to the lake. I didn't want to risk getting the chariot wheels stuck in the sandy shoreline. We watched as she waded into the water and began to drink. Say's Phoebes darted around, waiting for us to resume our trip so they could once again provide cover.

I walked along the shoreline, moving away from the others. Keeping my eyes on the ground, I recalled Dad telling me that people used to hunt for arrowheads around here. He even knew a guy who said his grandpa dredged sand from the bottom of the lake, hauling out pans full of arrowheads. Natives had hunted birds here for thousands of years, as evidenced by the countless arrowheads people found. Now, it was illegal to pick up arrowheads and take them from the area, but I knew people still did it. However, the pickings were pretty lean.

I strolled along, listening to the calls of Say's Phoebes as they darted in and out of the sagebrush away from the shore. The dry desert wind ruffled my hair, and the sun warmed the back of my neck. I kept my eyes down, hoping to see an arrowhead. Just as I turned to head back to the others, I spotted a pointed black rock half-buried in the sand. Leaning down, I pulled it from its resting place near the lapping lake water. An arrowhead emerged as I tugged, and I washed it before bringing it closer for inspection.

Years ago, before I knew he was my real grandfather, Willy had told me that we should never keep an arrowhead. "You can hold and admire the craftsmanship of chipped stone, but don't take it."

"Why?" I'd wanted to know.

"The legend of my people is that each arrowhead contains the soul of the maker," he said. "It takes great patience and skill to chip stone with another stone, and my ancestors spent hours honing their stones into arrowheads. When you find the arrowhead, you can do one of two things. Either bury it under sagebrush so no one else can find it, or break the arrowhead in half, releasing the soul of the maker, setting them free."

Now, I looked down at the pointed, carefully shaped obsidian stone, remembering Willy's words. In my hand, the spirit of an ancient ancestor rested heavily against my palm. I didn't want to bury this arrowhead. Instead, I wanted to pocket my find and leave quickly, but I knew I'd regret it. Before I could change my mind, I gripped the arrowhead firmly between my hands, and, with sudden strength, broke it in half. A sigh escaped my lips, a sigh of relief and a sigh of freedom. My heart lifted and the wind stopped, catching my sigh and holding it above my head, until I realized it wasn't my sigh anymore, but the spirit of the long-dead maker of this arrowhead who'd spent hours chipping the black stone into a smooth and shiny surface to hunt food for his family.

The sound drifted above, and the wind resumed, carrying the sigh of relief. I heard nothing more, but an immense pressure lifted from my heart, replaced by a sense of freedom so glorious that I followed it on the wind, flying with the sigh toward Squaretop Mountain. My lighthearted feeling remained as I wondered about what I'd just experienced.

I turned to the others, expecting them to recognize the moment, but

Kya and Indigo didn't seem to notice as they sat in the chariot, chatting. I looked at the shallow lake and then up to the clear blue sky, feathered with long strings of light, high clouds. Mares' tails, Grams called them.

I smiled, knowing I had done the right thing by breaking open the arrowhead. Looking over the lake, I threw both halves as far as I could, watching them plop into the water. After I walked back to the others, I told them about the arrowhead while hitching Glenda to the chariot. The euphoric feeling remained with me as we flew back to see Bia on Squaretop.

When we landed there, I released Little Elk to find the ancient ancestor. By the time Kya, Indigo, and I finished eating some honey cakes, my copper elk returned.

The grey-haired woman looked different. Her hair and buckskin dress were the same, but her eyes lit up when she smiled warmly while walking toward us. After stopping right next to me, she reached out to touch my hands, clasping them in her own. "Diana, you released the spirit of my descendant. I felt it up here on the mountain, and I heard his voice on the wind. Thank you."

"You mean when I broke the arrowhead? Willy told me to do that to release the soul of the maker," I said, startled by the change in her demeanor.

"You give me hope for the future," she said. "I became a bitter old woman after watching the white man destroy my people and our culture. But maybe the old ways will return."

"We have buffalo on the Wind River Reservation now," Indigo peeped. "Marty is going to see them."

"That also gives me hope," Bia said, reaching out to Indigo where she perched on my shoulder. "The copper cups gave me great pleasure when I saw myself and the happy days of my youth. Now tell me what happened with the Red Desert elk. Did you find them?"

We sat and I relayed to Bia all that had transpired. When I finished, she nodded, her warm brown eyes direct. "I think you made the right decision for now," she said. "We'll find out if this infusion of fresh water helps the drought in the West. I'll tell Limni about this. She's checking Minor Glacier right now."

"Thank you, Bia, for all you have done," I said as we stood to leave. "I'll come back here next summer and let you know how things are going."

She gathered me in her arms, surprising me with the strength of her hug. "You bring hope for the future of our planet," she said, releasing me, but still holding my upper arms in her strong grip. "I'm returning your copper cups to you."

"You keep them as long as you need them," I said, in spite of the fact that I missed them.

Bia shook her head. "I've seen my childhood self in the copper cup, and that has restored my sense of hope for children of the future. And now, you've released the soul of my descendant. You've pulled forth water for the planet to gain time for the glaciers. I return these magical cups to you. They have restored my sense of hope and my childhood wonder at life. Finally, you gave up something personal to learn the secrets of the Red Desert. You deserve to keep your cups. Limni agreed and she returns hers to you as well." Bia reached into her pocket and pulled out the cups, holding them by the handles and extending them to me.

"I'll accept them," I said, realizing it felt good to feel the cool touch of copper in my hand.

Indigo fluttered to Bia's shoulder and rubbed her cheek, and Kya walked closer for a hug.

I stashed the cups in my pouch under the bench. Glenda trotted briskly along the flat, grassy surface and pulled us into the sky. "Goodbye," I yelled. A flock of magpies came up from below, and Indigo flew out to join them.

Kya came to the front. "That's great Bia returned the cups."

"I'm glad we have them back," I said. "Imagine when Grams and Willy see themselves. I didn't have time to show them before we left." I smiled at her.

As we flew over Green River Lakes, I glanced down to see a perfect mirror image of Squaretop Mountain glimmering in the water below. Then it was gone as we flew onward. I looked ahead, thinking about all that had transpired in the last two days, eager to tell Grams, Willy, and Persephone about my decision to draw ancient water. Indigo returned to her special perch under the rim of the chariot, and we all settled in for the ride back to the other side of the Continental Divide. Had I done the right thing? I wouldn't know right away, but I was glad to be going back to the comforting routine of the ranch.

CHAPTER NINETEEN
SPRUCE IN THE ROOTS

That evening, when we returned to the ranch, I told Grams, Willy, and Persephone all that we'd experienced on our trip.

Indigo was reunited with Rock, and she told me he agreed to go see the Birds of Dawn next summer. The entire family came to the deck and listened while I told our tale. The fledglings sat quietly while I talked, their bright black eyes darting everywhere, indicating they were paying attention, but not daring to peep after a warning look from their mother. Indigo definitely had learned how to be a good parent from her mom, I thought, watching my friend expertly manage her children. Rock sat on one end of the line of fledglings, keeping his eye on the kids, too.

Grams laughed several times and gasped at others, all the while lively and attentive. When I described meeting Bia and releasing the soul of her descendant, Willy told me I'd done the right thing, his quiet joy evident.

Persephone sat back, clearly pleased with Kya's part in the adventure.

***

One week later, we set off to pick up Spruce in Pando. Persephone told us she trusted Pando to take care of Spruce, so she had left him there after staying for only a few days. Kya and I rode with Persephone in her chariot, pulled by Hades' black horses. Indigo stayed home. She told me she wanted to spend time with her young brood and Rock.

The crisp morning breeze rubbed against my face as I sat in back, watching Persephone teach Kya how to drive. As we glided through the sky, protected by a flock of Western Meadowlarks, I marveled at how much Kya had matured in the last two months. She would remain forever young, just like her mother, but our adventures in the Red Desert had provided her with a new confidence, evidenced by the way she straightened her shoulders and eagerly took the reins.

We flew over the Continental Divide and veered southwest toward Utah. After several hours, we spotted the green expanse of Pando, and I looked over the edge as Kya handed the reins back to Persephone. Instead of landing immediately, Persephone directed the stallions to the center of the forest. I looked down at a small clearing next to a tall aspen which towered above the other trees. This had to be the original tree in Pando, the one that had created clones which grew into a one hundred and six-acre forest.

When we landed in the clearing, I noticed a small mound at the base of the large Quaking Aspen, so named for the way its leaves trembled in the breeze. The stallions brought the chariot to a halt, and Persephone immediately jumped out, running to the mound. As I approached with Kya, I inhaled sharply, whispering Spruce's name.

A sob from Kya echoed my fear.

Lying on the ground was Spruce. His arms rested at his side, his head pillowed on green grass. His face remained peaceful, but under his lids, his eyes moved back and forth, as if he were in a deep, dreaming sleep, so I knew he was alive. I gasped when I saw white fungal tendrils coming between blades of grass to his head, twining through his hair, attached to his scalp.

"Spruce," Persephone called sharply, "wake up,"

His eyes opened immediately, and I exhaled in relief, glad to see the clarity in his brown gaze. "Mom," he said in a raspy voice. He cleared his throat. "You're back."

"We're here," Kya said, moving to his side.

I hung back, hesitant to interfere. "Is he okay?" I touched Persephone's shoulder.

"He's fine," she said. "Right, Spruce?"

"I'm okay," he said. "How long have I been here? It seems like only minutes since you left." He attempted to raise his head, but the fungi tendrils held him to the ground.

"What's going on?" Kya said. She reached down to touch his arm, gently rubbing one finger along the surface.

Spruce's entire arm, from fingertips to shoulder, was covered in white bark, the same smooth bark on every tree in the grove. Only his neck and head were void of it, his brown skin a vivid contrast to the barky covering on his hands and arms.

"I'm okay," Spruce repeated. "Pando wanted to talk with me, so he used the same method he uses to communicate with other trees. Fungi. This network of small tubes connected to my head is what's underground, a convenient communication system for trees."

"But how does he talk to you?" I asked. Moving forward, I touched his arm. The bark was cool to the touch, but I could feel it was alive and flexible.

Spruce raised his hand to Kya's face in a loving gesture. I watched her profile as she closed her eyes, clearly holding back her tears. "I'm fine, Sis," he said, running one barky finger down her cheek.

"We'll get you out of here," Persephone said, her voice determined. "I know Pando means you no harm."

"Right, Mom," Spruce said. "He just didn't know any other way to tell me things. He told the fungal roots to cover my head so he could send chemical signals to my brain, the same way he communicates with other trees. He knows you're here and he said he'll let me go."

"Good," Persephone said.

"But I have to tell you everything I've learned from Pando," Spruce said.

"You know what?" Persephone said. "We want to hear what you've learned, but let's wait until we get you safely home, okay?"

Spruce relaxed, his head resting against the grassy pillow. "Okay." He seemed suddenly tired, and I realized Persephone was right.

She stood up and walked a few feet away, putting her palm on the smooth white surface of the largest Quaking Aspen, the *Arbor Antiqua,* the ancient tree in this dynamic forest. "Pando," she said in a confident voice, reminding me she was the daughter of Demeter, goddess of agriculture and growing things. "Release my son. His work here is done."

Nothing happened at first. Birds chattered in the trees and a breeze stirred the aspen leaves. I looked from Persephone back to Spruce. If anything, his face was paler and his breathing slowed. Wanting to help, I started toward Persephone, who turned to me and shook her head in warning. She leaned closer, whispering to the tree. Whatever she said worked because I heard snapping noises from behind and watched as the fungal growth binding Spruce to the ground popped apart vigorously, snapping like rubber bands stretched too far, before quickly retreating underground.

Persephone patted the tree with both hands, then bowed. "Thank you, *Arbor Antiqua,*" she said. "Thank you for teaching and releasing my son."

Suddenly, a great wind blew through the small clearing, bending the trees and blowing my hair. It stopped as quickly as it arose, the trembling leaves of the Quaking Aspen at the edge of the clearing the only evidence of its passing.

"Mom?" Spruce sat up, shaking his head weakly. "I'm free and Pando said goodbye." He attempted to stand but made it no further before Kya leaned down.

"Let me help you," she said, grabbing his barky arm. "Your hair is not even wet from that fungi."

"Nope," he said, rising to his feet and leaning against Kya. Persephone took his other arm. "That wind coming through helped dry me off."

Flanked by Kya and his mom, Spruce managed to get to the chariot.

"Let's get on board and go home," Persephone said. She looked at me over Spruce's head. "You drive and I'll sit in back with the twins."

As we trotted through the clearing and the stallions became airborne, I looked back to see Spruce leaning against Persephone while Kya held onto his hand on his other side. He'll be fine, I thought. After all, he is a god.

I called out a high note, seeking the cover of birds. Far in the distance, a blob of white headed our way. By the time we flew over the edge of the forest, the flock of birds covered our flight. "California Gulls," I said. "Raucous flyers. But that will do."

We flew northeast and I knew we'd reached my state's border when the gulls flew to the left and right, giving way to Western Meadowlarks, the Wyoming state bird.

"We'll be home soon," I said to my passengers.

When we landed at the ranch and I had a chance to really look at him, I noticed that Spruce's smooth, tanned face looked a bit older. Bark still covered his arms, and his sister leaned over to gently touch him as we all sat around the picnic table on the deck. Indigo and Rock returned to the deck railing, eyeing their fledglings as Spruce talked.

"Interesting," I said, reaching out to touch the smooth bark skin. "When did that start?"

"Soon after I arrived," he said. "I think it's because I spent so much time in direct contact with the trees that my arms became covered. It's smooth like the bark on an aspen tree."

"Will it keep growing and cover your body?" Kya asked, continuing to pet his barky arm.

"No," he said, looking down. "It's already started to recede a little bit. It seemed to stop growing when I left the grove. Mom said we'll ask Grandma about it." He looked at Persephone, who nodded calmly.

"Demeter should be able to explain it," Grams said.

Spruce smiled at her and turned to the others, brightly reporting on his adventures in the aspen grove, one of the oldest living beings on the planet. "Pando is an amazing creature," he said. "I really came to know him well in the past two weeks."

As he talked, I noted other changes in Spruce. His voice seemed deeper, and he was more confident. "You seem a little older," I said.

"We both had adventures that challenged us," Kya said.

"I feel like it," Spruce said, nodding. "Pando taught me a lot of amazing information about plants on our planet."

"Like what?" I looked at him with anticipation.

"Wait," Grams said. "How did he talk to you? Does he speak?"

"He sends signals through his root system. He told me to lie down on the ground and he sent root tendrils through the ground to my head. They literally adhered to my scalp, and my brain interpreted what he was saying. Plants communicate by sending chemical signals to one another, and I can interpret these."

"Did it hurt?" Grams asked.

"No. It kind of tickled when his roots caressed my head," Spruce said. "I spent a lot of time talking to him that way."

"I think that's why his arms began to grow bark," Persephone said. She smiled reassuringly at Spruce, but I could see he wasn't worried.

"I like it," Kya said.

"Me, too," Spruce said, looking down at his arm. "I'm kind of sad it's going away."

"I like how it's aspen bark," I said. "If you talked to a cactus, would you grow needles?" I meant it as a serious question, but the others laughed, even Spruce.

"I don't know," he said. "Someday we'll try that."

"We won't let you talk to plants for too long," Grams said. "You'll morph into one."

"We don't want some tree nymph falling in love with you," Willy said.

"We have to stop cutting down old growth trees because they hold more carbon than younger trees," Spruce said, tilting his head sideways while gesturing with his right hand. "We have to rethink our forestry policies."

"What do you mean?" I asked.

"Well, Demeter already told me that old trees are important, but Pando really made it clear when he talked about a place called Fairy Creek Forest on Vancouver Island in Canada."

"What happened there?" Kya said.

"Scientists have proven what Demeter and Pando told me. The oldest trees are bigger and can capture more carbon, which helps the planet," he said. "Fairy Creek Forest is one such place. Scientists have studied the trees in great detail by climbing into the highest branches and finding new surprises. Like that on the largest branches, the layers of debris decay and form soil, which sits there. During times of drought, the trees literally grow new roots near the branches and tap into the nutrients there. It's like they create a safety valve for dry times. When the ground soil doesn't have enough carbon, the tree can use the soil on its own branches because it contains more carbon."

"Even in a drought, the tree branch soil is moist?" I said.

"Because it's protected by the tree canopy, the soil on upper branches doesn't dry out as quickly as the ground soil does. Plus, it contains more carbon, which is food for trees and plants."

"That's cool," I said. "Does that happen around here?"

"Only the oldest and largest trees in old growth forests have this capability," he said. He turned to Persephone. "Can we go visit Fairy Creek?"

"We'll have to wait until next summer," she said. "This fall, we'll be so busy with harvesting that we won't have time. But next summer, we could go."

"Can we all go?" Kya said.

"Me, too?" Indigo chirped.

"Yes, we could all take the trip in Hades' large chariot."

"Maybe by then, I can fly with Daphne and Galene," I said. "Poseidon said they'll be big enough to carry a chariot then."

"It's kind of a long trip," Persephone said. "We'll see how they're doing next summer."

"Okay," I said. I hoped they'd be ready.

As Spruce and Kya talked excitedly about the trip to Fairy Creek Forest, I thought about the fact that Kya knew the potential of her powers with stone and rock, and Spruce knew his potential with plants. Both of them would help me a great deal.

CHAPTER TWENTY
BEAVERS IN THE SKY

My last task of the summer was moving beavers to the Green River Basin. It would be like a deposit in the Water Bank of the Future. Of course, this was a voluntary program, comprised of young beavers willing to go where there was space to make dams, creating a new riparian environment. They were descendants of Zosime, the beaver I met last summer in the Wind River Mountains.

Deer, elk, moose, birds, and insects would all come to the ponds created by the transplanted beavers.

On this trip, six beavers flew with me and Indigo in the chariot, curled up next to each other, sleeping. Willy told me that wildlife biologists learned transplanting an entire beaver family was more likely to be successful because they would stay in the area as they worked together to build a new dam. On board were two parents, two young kits born last spring, and two yearlings from the previous spring. I knew beavers learned how to build dams by staying with their parents for at least two years.

These beavers were going to build dams in rivers that flowed to the Colorado River and then the Pacific Ocean, not the Atlantic of their ancestors' days. With a little shove from Zosime, the family had chosen to head west over the Continental Divide. I provided the transportation.

"I hope it will work," Zosime had said that morning when I met her in the meadow to pick up the beavers. "You will be reclaiming and taming the waters of western-flowing rivers and streams," she said to the young recruits.

On the flight back to the area of Squaretop Mountain, they had chattered excitedly. But now they were asleep, their long rubbery tails wound close to their round furry bellies.

I faced the front, looking ahead for a meadow near Little Sandy Creek, a stream that eventually fed into the Big Sandy River, which flowed into the Green. The pond they would create by building a dam would slow the snowmelt next spring, holding back waters into the fall, preserving *Aqua Pura* for the future.

I thought about the positive effects of repatriating this keystone species, the beaver, who would restore the land and provide space and plants for countless animals and insects, from moose to blue mountain dragonflies, trout to eagles, and magpies to mule deer.

Looking at the Bridger Wilderness area below me, I guided the chariot over Sweetwater Gap, following the pass through the mountains. My goal was to land next to Little Sandy Creek so the beavers could start building in the area inside the wilderness area where they would be protected. Wheeled and motorized vehicles were not allowed in wilderness areas, and I was counting on swooping in undetected. My chariot had wheels, so I was in violation of that law but had no choice.

My plan was to drop off the beavers and let their instincts take over. Once the shorter days told them that fall was in the air, they would immediately find a space and begin cutting nearby trees with their enormous front teeth, intertwining the strong tree limbs with rocks, and, finally, layering mud at the bottom of the dam.

After the pond formed, the beavers would trowel out sections, creating fish habitats and deep-water protection for themselves. Instead of flowing into the Atlantic Ocean as their parents' pond water did on the other side of the Continental Divide, these new transplants would slow the progress of water toward the Pacific Ocean, thus helping to ease the drought.

We landed in a meadow next to Little Sandy Creek, and I put on my ring so I could communicate with the beavers. "What do you guys think?" I asked, placing them on the ground to waddle about, which they eagerly did, raising their noses to sniff the pine-scented air.

They continued to look around and inhale the scents of this new location, rising up on their back legs to see better.

"This feels like a good place," Zosime's son said. At least I thought it was a male because he was larger than the smaller beaver near his side. "And I hear water."

"We must go right now to the water," the smaller brown architect said, her orange-stained teeth protruding from under her upper lip. "Stay close to me, children." The smallest beavers complied, but the yearlings continued to look around eagerly.

"I understand," I said. Last year, Zosime told me that beavers were compelled by the sound of running water, an instinctive hereditary impulse to build. Water running over rocks meant they must build a dam.

"We're going to go look at the water," said Zosime's son. "Thank you for this opportunity to find a new building site. It was getting crowded on my mother's creek."

"You're welcome," I said. "Thanks for coming here to preserve *Aqua Pura.*"

With a nod, he dropped down on all fours and looked at his mate.

"Thank you, Diana," she said. "I'm honored to help repatriate our ancestral lands. Beavers once constructed great dams and created magnificent ponds on this side of the mountains. Now, we'll honor the memory of those long-ago slaughtered creatures by rebuilding in the areas where their happy laughter once floated over mountain streams."

"Well said." I bowed to the poetic female beaver. "Your work will help save the planet." I smiled down at her. I pictured the beavers lovingly grooming their young inside the beaver lodge throughout the winter and teaching them how to build dams during the first two years of their lives. They did seem to be happy creatures with a sense of purpose who cared deeply for their young.

I held out my hand, and she placed one powerful paw in the center of my palm. Her sharp black claws rested gingerly against my skin. Claws that could easily rip through my flesh gently touched the meaty part of my hand under my thumb. The brown, oily fur complemented my tan hand. I knew she used those paws to rub her belly and stimulate oil glands, and then she rubbed the oil all over her body, helping to keep her warm and water-tight in frigid water.

Her intelligent brown eyes looked up at me. "We'll do our job," she said. "We always do."

I followed them to the banks of Little Sandy Creek, and watched as the adults and their children entered the water, disappearing under the surface with a flap of their tails.

TWENTY-ONE
A BLUE GOODBYE

I walked from the bunkhouse to the barn, inhaling the scent of dew-covered grass. The cottonwoods provided shade down here, and I reveled in my privacy away from Grams and Willy. I loved being with them, but it was wonderful to have my own place on the ranch. Living in the bunkhouse provided the space I needed, and I'd miss that when I went back to school in two weeks. This would be my junior year of college, and I looked forward to challenging courses in forestry this year.

The horses neighed when I walked into the barn to brush them before putting them out in the horse pasture with the others. I brushed Golden first, giving the young ones time to nurse. Even though they were almost six months old now, they still nursed. Regular horses had to be separated from their mothers while weaning, but my magical flying horses would be allowed to nurse as long as they wanted to.

Demeter had told me that they needed to drink their mother's milk as long as possible to ensure strong wing development.

When their snorting and stomping told me the twins were ready to start their day outside, I turned to them. Absently running my hand along Daphne's shoulder, I stopped in surprise when my palm encountered a large lump just behind her right shoulder that was bigger than her normal wing bud.

"What's that, girl?" I looked closer, worried that something had burrowed under her skin. I gasped when I saw the wing bud was covered in almost transparent skin, about five inches in diameter. It would have been gruesome had I not seen the fine feathers under her skin, trapped into submission by a thin layer of hairless skin. "What's going on?" I looked at Golden. Even though I'd never talked to her with my ring on, I felt she understood my speech.

Golden bobbed her head, pawing the ground with her front right hoof. Then she lifted her wings slightly.

"Oh, my gosh, Golden," I said, "are the wings growing? I didn't think it would look like this."

I peered at the red-gold feathers under Daphne's skin. She didn't seem to mind when I gingerly touched the area. I pressed a bit harder and felt a large lump. I darted to Galene. Gently rubbing my hand on her shoulder, I looked at the transparent skin covering her feathers.

"Does this hurt?" I spoke more to myself than the filly, knowing she wouldn't reply. She did whicker softly, seeming to tell me that my hand on her hide didn't hurt. In fact, she pushed back against me.

"Does that feel good?" I rubbed, moving carefully across the hairless skin. She pressed harder against me, apparently enjoying it.

"I've got to get Willy. You guys wait here," I said.

I tore out of the barn and raced up to the house, anxious to tell Willy and Grams. I burst through the deck door and found them at the kitchen table with coffee and newspapers. Grams halted her cup mid-way to her mouth when I announced my news. "The fillies are growing wings! Come look!"

We rushed into the barn. Willy calmly patted Golden on the neck and turned to the fillies, who eagerly pressed close to him, as they always did. Grams and I watched as Willy smoothed his wrinkled brown hand over Galene's wing bump.

"Demeter told me they'd develop wing buds at around six months," Willy said, his deep voice comforting me.

"Isn't that amazing," Grams said, moving forward to see for herself.

"Look at those beautiful feathers under her skin," Grams said. Daphne turned her head to look at her own shoulder, gently nibbling on Grams' fingers with her lips.

"It's important they keep nursing and spend lots of time in the sun," Willy said. "We can't cover them up all the time with a blanket while the wings are growing. Demeter said it's kind of like the way deer grow antlers, pushing through the skin."

"I remember she told me that also," I said. "I just didn't think about how miraculous this would be. Let's cover the mares and send them out to the pasture. They all need some morning sun."

We made short work of the task and stood next to the corral, watching the four horses run across the pasture. "We'd better get some small blankets for the little ones. You know, just in case someone comes," I said as we turned back to the house. Willy nodded. We rarely had unannounced visitors out here on the ranch, but I wanted to be ready because it might happen.

***

The only visitors came the following week when Persephone and the twins landed at the ranch to say goodbye before I left for college. Kya bounded to the ground first, followed by Spruce, with Persephone trailing behind.

"Diana," Kya said, embracing me in a fierce hug. Stepping back, she held onto my shoulders. "We're going to Nebraska to see Grandma

Demeter. She asked us to help with the fall harvest."

"Wow," I said. "This will be your first time doing that." I gripped her shoulders with my hands, keeping her close while I gazed into her bright blue eyes. "I can't believe the summer is almost over."

Spruce walked up and put his arms around both of us, and we engaged in a group hug, the energy of his warm skin enveloping both of us. "I'm really excited to see how fall harvesting works," he said, breaking off our hug.

"I'm going because Dad is still busy combatting fracking in North Dakota," Kya said. "Isn't that where your dad is?"

"Yes," I said. "Ironic, isn't it? We're saving pure water on the planet, and he's helping to bring oil out of the ground."

"Will he stop doing that?" Kya said.

"We need the money, so I don't think he'll stop," I said. "But he's coming home next week to take me back to school."

Persephone joined us. "Let's go say goodbye to Helen and Willy."

I linked arms with Kya and Spruce as we followed her to the house. Grams and Willy sat on the deck with their morning coffee. Indigo, Rock, and their hatchlings had relocated to the mountain meadow where the main flock of bluebirds practiced flying as a flock in preparation for their migration south in September.

"I'm going to learn from Grandma Demeter exactly how to harvest corn and soybeans in the Midwest," Spruce said. "She's trying to convince farmers there to grow a variety of crops, but the large, corporate farms are difficult to work with because all they want to do is grow money-makers like that, instead of growing a variety of crops that will help the soil. We'll keep working on it, though"

"I'm going along to help," Kya said. "Later, I'll join Dad when he checks on the status of the Ogallala Aquifer."

"Demeter told me about that last summer," I said. "Humans are drawing way too much water from there, and now it's empty in some areas. Another challenge for us."

"We'll let you know how it looks," she said.

"Good," I said.

"Are you excited to go back to school?" Spruce said. "I'm interested in what you'll learn in your forestry classes this year."

"I *am* excited for school," I said. "I'll let you know about my classes."

"What about Galene and Daphne?" Kya said.

"Demeter said they could stay on the ranch all winter with the mares. Willy and Grams can take care of them. Plus, I plan to come home at least once a month to see them."

"You can keep track of their wings," Spruce said.

"Right. I'm coming home in September to say goodbye to Indigo before she migrates, so I'll see them soon anyhow," I said. "Lots of kids come home throughout the year. I can easily catch a ride."

We talked for a short while longer, and then Persephone stood. "Time to say goodbye, kids. We need to take off."

Persephone and the twins hugged Grams and Willy before turning to me. I embraced Persephone, and stood back, remembering when I'd first met her a year ago in June. Her beauty still glowed, from her emerald eyes to her poppy-red lips. Now that we were such good friends, I realized her true beauty came from the confident way she held her shoulders and the honesty in her green eyes. They deepened in color as we smiled at each other, and I realized she still clasped my hands with her strong brown fingers.

"You're closer to understanding your full powers, Diana of the Wind Rivers. You'll have my children to help you save pure water on the planet," she said.

"You'll always be my first companion," I said. "My true friend." I hugged her close again.

"You've helped me grow," Spruce said, wrapping me in his strong arms. The scent of pine drifted from his skin. "Next summer, we'll be back." He released me and we both turned to Kya.

"We're here for you," Kya said. "We'll keep learning together. More adventures are ahead of us." She pulled me close, and I inhaled the smell of granite and stone, taking me to high mountain cliffs where birds soared on the wind. "Hold out your hand," she said.

I did as she requested, surprised by the cool touch of stone in my hand. Looking down, I saw a piece of blue petrified wood resting in my palm. I looked up at her twinkling eyes.

"That's from the Blue Forest," she said. "Mom took us there so Spruce could see it for himself. Keep this with you. We don't know its magic yet, but wood turned to blue stone has special meaning for both Spruce and me. I think it's important, and it will bind us until we see you next summer."

"Thank you," I said softly, marveling at this unexpected gift. "I'll keep it with me." I pocketed the blue wood to admire later.

We walked to the pasture together, and I showed them the wing buds I'd discovered.

"This is normal," Persephone said. "The wings look very healthy." She touched the thin skin covering the fine feathers underneath, and it broke open.

I inhaled sharply. "What happened?"

"It's time for the wings to sprout out," she said. "These are healthy feathers. You'll be flying with these fillies by next summer."

I reached out to tentatively touch the now-revealed feathers.

"They're almost a red color," I said. "Like strawberry-blonde hair."

"That's amazing," Willy said. He brushed a finger against the split skin and it widened to reveal ever more feathers. "Do they need any kind of special care?" He looked at Persephone.

"No. I'll tell Demeter about this. Red feathers on flying horses are very special. Poseidon gave you a fine gift, indeed," she said. "These will be marvelous flying creatures."

Grams gasped when her fingers gingerly touched the titian wings.

Persephone looked at Daphne's other side. "This wing bud is ready to pop out soon, too. Let's check Galene." The moment she put her hand on the transparent spot on Galene's shoulder, it split open. Rubbing gently, she encouraged the feathers to come free of the skin covering. "This also looks healthy. Welcome to the world, little feathers."

We left the barn, and they climbed into the chariot. Waving goodbye as they flew into the sky, I heard Kya's voice from above. "Goodbye, Diana."

Standing with Grams and Willy, I tested my feelings. I wasn't sad, but I did feel a bit lonely without the lively voices of the twins bouncing around me. I looped my arm through Willy's, thinking about the way things change.

"Nothing stays the same," Grams said, as if sensing my thoughts. "It's good. Change is good." She put her arm around my waist. "Let's go back to the house."

I nodded and turned, walking with Grams and Willy, one on each side of me. Their love is something that never changes, I thought. That's a constant in my life.

***

Dad arrived just in time to take me back to Laramie on Labor Day weekend. I talked while he drove, our usual practice on this four-hour trip to the University of Wyoming.

As I told him about saving Caligo, he shook his head in disbelief. "I hope I can see a glacier nymph one day."

When I told him about meeting Limni and Bia, he gasped. "I always knew Squaretop was an important place."

Then, I revealed my power, my ability to move water. "That's a special gift, Diana," he said. "I hope I can see you do that one day. I think you made the right decision."

When I described the beaver drop, he nodded. "Restoring keystone species will be critical to preventing water from rushing out of the mountains too soon."

"What are we going to do about the fact that we're working against each other?" I said.

"What do you mean?" He kept his eyes on the road as we passed two large semis.

"You work in an oil field, and I'm trying to save pure water on the planet. You're contributing to pollution, while I'm trying to curb the devastating impact that has on pure water. Did you know they've found microplastics on the bottom of the ocean and at the top of the world on glaciers? You know plastic is made from oil, right? It's like we're working against each other." I could hear my voice rise in frustration.

"I know all of that, Diana," he said, turning his gaze to mine. "But we need the money. You know I don't have enough to pay for college."

"I have some scholarships and grants," I said. "I could get a job next summer."

"You can't. You've got to work with Persephone and the twins to keep saving pure water." He shook his head, his grip tightening on the wheel. " Maybe I can get a different job. Working in construction pays well. I could look into that."

"Okay," I said. "I know it's a hard problem. Maybe we could take out a loan for school."

"Well," he said slowly, "I hate to do that, but we could. Let's think about it this winter."

"Thanks, Dad," I said. "I don't know what to do, either."

We drove without talking for a while, and I decided to change the subject. "So, what do you think about my summer?"

"I still can't believe all of this is true," he said, turning his eyes briefly from the highway to hold mine. He focused on the front again and laughed, shaking his head. "You never cease to amaze me. Just give me some time to adjust," he concluded.

"Okay. I will." We fell silent again, and my thoughts roamed over my summer events.

I had accomplished some things to help save *Aqua Pura*. I'd helped Caligo so she could team up with Tixi to save the glaciers on Younts Peak, the source of the Yellowstone River. With the work of the beavers, we might hold back more water throughout the summer on the western side of the Wind River Mountains. Their ponds might prevent spring runoff from cascading out of the mountains too quickly. I vowed to check on my builder friends next summer, hoping they would establish a stronghold on that side of the divide. Then I'd transport more beavers.

I'd eased Bia's suffering by giving her the magical copper cups and releasing the soul of her descendant. In turn, she'd helped me by returning the cups. I was proud she approved of my withdrawal of water from ancient Lake Gosiute, recognizing it as proof that I worked to save the planet. Even more so, I was proud that she recognized I was willing to give up something personal for the planet. Her joy at my decision to break open the arrowhead and release the soul inspired me, and I was glad to give her hope for the future.

Finally, the decision to withdraw pure water in Lake Gosiute weighed heavily on my mind. Had I made the right decision? Would it buy us time to save more glaciers by covering them with seaweed? Poseidon needed all the help he could get. I still had no idea what to do about microplastics, but I hoped the seaweed coverings would keep the minute particles from polluting glaciers.

***

I returned to the ranch in mid-September. The time for Indigo and Rock to migrate south was nearing, and I wanted to wish them a safe journey. I knew they'd winter in New Mexico, returning here in the spring to prepare new nests in the boxes on the pasture fence.

Pedaling my bike up Sinks Canyon highway, I turned left into the visitor center parking lot and coasted down to the bike rack. After locking up, I hiked the brief climb to the overlook where I could see the cave entrance and the river as it cascaded over boulders on its way into the earth. I leaned against the metal railing, my eyes scanning the top of the cliff. Before I left for school, Indigo had told me that she and Rock would join the larger flock of Mountain Bluebirds in the high meadow above the canyon. Even though they'd separated from the others last spring to use the nesting boxes on the ranch, they still intended to migrate with the flock.

Just as I hoped, a small cloud of blue appeared over the cliff wall, descending toward the railing. One by one, the children of Indigo and Rock landed on the railing, their little black feet stabilizing their bodies as ten pairs of wings fluttered. A soft grey landing brought Indigo to the front of the line, and Rock's cerulean blue body gracefully glided to the end.

"You brought both batches of summer birds," I said.

Indigo and Rock had produced five perfect hatchlings in each batch this summer, and the ten young birds before me represented both parents. Two grey females with intelligent black eyes and cerulean-tipped wings and tails stood next to eight magnificently blue males.

"I wish you all a great journey on your migration," I said to the attentive bird line. Bookended by their parents, they sat proudly, facing the front as any good flock of young birds should do. Their blinking eyes and the way they cocked their little heads sideways, all to the left, informed me they were listening to every word. I supposed it made sense that Indigo's children could understand me, but would I understand them? I decided to test my theory. "Tip your beak if you know what I'm saying."

Ten young beaks tipped upward, remaining in place, as if awaiting my orders.

"Lower your beaks."

Ten beaks pointed down. Only quick blinking revealed the young birds' excitement.

I laughed out loud. I'd been so focused on myself this summer that I hadn't even thought about talking to the hatchlings. This was phenomenal. I felt like I had my own flock of birds.

"We could start our own circus act." I didn't realize I was talking out loud again until an angry chirp brought me back to the present.

"Hey, Aunt Diana, we're not a sideshow." The largest female, sitting at the front of the line next to Indigo, puffed up her chest and ruffled her wings, breaking rank with the others. Her piping voice was confident, as if she understood all the complexities of the world and knew how to resolve them.

Not wanting to insult the young bird, I stifled a second delighted laugh and spoke seriously. "I'm sorry. I didn't mean to be disrespectful. I'm just so excited you can understand me." I ran my finger from the top of her head to the tip of her cerulean tailfeathers.

She inhaled deeply and closed her eyes, clearly loving this as much as Indigo did. "That's fine," she said, opening her eyes and looking up. "Do that again."

I laughed and complied, looking over at Indigo, who nodded proudly. "I wish you a safe journey," I repeated, running my gaze over the blue line-up, while the pure waters of the Middle Fork of the Popo Agie flowed steadily over the boulders behind them.

"Thank you, Diana," Indigo said. She flew to my shoulder and caressed my cheek with her soft head, her little feet tickling my shoulders where they gripped. "We'll be back in the spring. And then we'll take Rock to meet the Birds of Dawn."

"We'll do it," I said, kissing the back of her grey head before she flew back to the railing, taking her place at the front.

"Goodbye." I waved at the entire line, twelve birds in all. My own flock.

"Take flight," Indigo commanded, and then she flew above my head, around my back, and circled my ankles. She flew straight up the front of my body, creating a breeze that caressed my face. At the same time, she trilled in my ears, spiraling around my neck to the back of my head. Simultaneously, I saw another bird at my ankles, the brave young female from the front of the line. Right behind her mother, she breezed past my face, her higher trill indicating her youth.

To my delight, every bird followed the same path, winding around my body, creating a breeze on my face and music in my ears, until the last one, Rock, fluttered in my face before taking off to follow the others above the cliff and into the sky, disappearing out of sight beyond the trees.

As the last bit of blue disappeared, Indigo's voice warbled on the wind. "I love you." The words drifted down to the river, meeting me where I stood.

I turned to walk back, wishing I could keep the blue goodbye breeze on my face forever. Reaching the rack, I unlocked my bike and pedaled back to the ranch where Grams and Willy waited. As I rolled along, I wondered what new adventures were waiting for me in my quest to save pure water on Earth.

About the Author

 Nona Schrader experienced the beauty of the Wind River Mountains while growing up in Lander, Wyoming. After completing her B.A. and M.A. in English at the University of Wyoming, Nona moved to Wisconsin to teach. She returned to Wyoming in retirement to write the *Aqua* novel series.

The Wind Rivers contain the headwaters of four major river basins in the western United States. The beauty of this pure mountain water inspired Nona to use her love of Greek mythology to convince others to protect water on our planet.

Waves of Sage is her second novel.

Follow Nona at:

www.nonaschrader.com

www.facebook.com/nonaschrader

https://www.instagram.com/nona_schrader